HOW TO

Leave

THE

House

HOW TO

Leave

THE

House

Nathan Newman

VIKING

VIKING
An imprint of Penguin Random House LLC
penguinrandomhouse.com

First published in hardcover in Great Britain by Abacus, an imprint of
Hachette UK Ltd., London, in 2024

First United States edition published by Viking, 2024

Illustrations by the author.

LIBRARY OF CONGRESS CATALOGING-IN-PUBLICATION DATA
Library of Congress Control Number: 2024938925

ISBN 9780593654903 (hardcover)
ISBN 9780593654910 (ebook)

Printed in the United States of America
1st Printing

HOW TO
Leave
THE
House

"...and..."
– G. W. F. Hegel,
The Phenomenology of Spirit

"...or..."
    – Søren Kierkegaard,
            Either/Or

One

Natwest Is the Hero of the Novel

D espite all evidence to the contrary, Natwest was alive. His body was slumped in the hallway of his mother's house. Limbs were splayed. Cowlicks were present. The carpet embossed an ominous pattern onto his cheek. But there was breathing. And gently, reluctantly, he awoke. It took him a moment to recollect: he'd waited in the hall overnight, hoping to catch the postman doing his rounds first thing in the morning. At some point he must have lost consciousness, because now it was nearly 11:00 a.m.

Natwest rose to his feet, simultaneously yawned and stretched, felt dizzy and returned to the floor. His second attempt was more successful. When he was upright and sensible, he regarded the detumescent bump of his falling erection with a good deal of scepticism.

The package.

He'd ordered it the day before, and it was essential the package ended up in his hands and no one else's – hence the overnight vigil in the hallway. To risk his mother opening it was to risk a calamity greater than any he'd previously experienced in his short life. He wouldn't leave town until it was securely concealed in his suitcase. The alternative – any alternative – was too distressing to consider, so when Natwest opened the front door he fully expected to see the package before him.

But there was nothing there. He closed the door, waited for half a minute and opened it again. Still no package. After a brief spell of nausea, he stepped outside and looked in the food-waste bin where the postman left the red notes that said, *Sorry we missed you* – an odd place to put them, he thought, because there was a perfectly reasonable letterbox. Inside the bin there were no red notes, only the trimmings of a root vegetable and the flotsam of some brown fruit that he chose not to identify. It was the first instance of the day in which his inflexible aesthetic principles, which privileged the ugly and the difficult over the pretty and the satisfying, failed to align with his sense of smell, for the odour of the rotting fruit was too much for Natwest's delicate nose and he shut the bin lid.

His fears had been realised, and he may or may not have punched the wall in frustration. He ran down the short list of possible explanations: a wrong address, a computer error, an untrained postman, an exploded Royal Mail van. No doubt the reason for the missing package would be described as a *force majeure*, or some other European excuse. He called it Royal Mail doing exactly what you expect, which is never what you want. Humiliation, which was lurking around the corner of his life at all times, was now very much on his doorstep.

Natwest tried to look for positives, and could only find the sun, miraculously present in the sky. There was some pleasure in the warmth on his face, and the way the light generated inter-esting shadows and odd Rorschach shapes across the surface of the road. His door was one of dozens that lined the street, here in this unexceptional Midlands town in which he'd spent the entirety of his short life – and which he now desired, more than anything else, to leave.

On the other side of the road, Natwest spotted an attractive woman waiting patiently while her slobbering German shepherd took a large dump on the pavement. Despite the breed of dog, and the heat of the morning sun, the woman had chosen to dress the animal in a rainbow sweater – and while Natwest expressed his disapproval by imperceptibly shaking his head, the dog expressed its Gay Pride by staring him in the eyes as it confidently emptied its bowels. He waited for her to do the honourable thing and remove the excrement from the footpath, and yet the moment the dog finished its business the woman turned up her collar and started off down the road. Natwest could have left it there, gone back inside and resented her for a little while before returning to his own problems, but he noticed something shiny and potentially expensive fall out of her pocket. His first instinct was to punish the woman for the offending turd, but after a few seconds his better nature prevailed and he crossed the road to retrieve the fallen object for her.

He was disappointed to discover that it was the shiny wrapper of a chocolate bar, and that the woman was too far away for him to complain. The front of the wrapper depicted a slender penguin, and Natwest's Art Brain immediately connected the image with van Eyck's *Arnolfini Portrait*, as the penguin's dark coat of feathers unquestionably resembled that of the eponymous Italian merchant in the revered fifteenth-century oil painting. Anyway, he thought it was an overrated work of art – the *Arnolfini Portrait* not the Penguin chocolate bar – and it was impossible to take it seriously because of the freakish canine at the bottom of the picture, apparently meant to symbolise loyalty.

'Oi! Clean up your dog shit! You can't leave it on the pavement like that!'

The man's voice had come from one of the houses in front him, and Natwest searched the windows for its source. 'Don't

3

just stand there! Clean it up, mate!' – and now the voice came from a different direction.

'I can't!' Natwest shouted into the ether. 'It wasn't my dog!'

'You're standing right by it! I don't see anyone else!'

'But it wasn't me!'

The voice laughed then, and replied in booming, mocking tones: 'I *hope* it wasn't you!'

'I mean it wasn't my dog! I don't even own a dog! This has nothing to do with me!' But there was more laughter, and soon Natwest found himself screaming at the houses. 'Why don't you come down here and clean it up yourself! How about that!'

This last comment appeared to silence the complaints, for there was the sound of a window closing, and then an eerie quiet. He glanced down at the turd on the pavement – only for a second – and returned inside without cleaning it up.

Back in the hallway, he checked the confirmation email from Royal Mail. He removed the phone from his pocket in a beautifully fluid motion, but the device was so thin – was it usually this thin? – that it slipped from his hand.

He always expected it to fall in slow motion. Instead it collided with the wall and bounced onto the floor, adding a sizeable crack to the centre of the screen. He cursed the slimness of his phone and the weakness of his grip, then swiftly pledged to buy a phone case later that day.

He opened the Mail app. Apparently the package had been delivered this morning, Friday 17 September, at 9:24 a.m. But it was 11:00 a.m., which meant someone was lying. In despair, he leant against the floral print in the hallway and his eyes followed the lilies that climbed the opposite wall towards the white, blank ceiling. He noticed it was the same lily design, repeated a hundred times over. For some reason he'd always thought each flower was unique – how odd to notice the opposite, today of all days.

This morning, the most important thing was to find out where his package had gone. His first thought was that someone had tampered with it – and here Natwest allowed himself a rare smile, for it had been several months since anyone had tampered with his package. It brought to mind Georgie's Falstaffian erection, with its glorious surplus of foreskin. His own penis stirred in unison with the image. Once the package was found, he thought, there would be time to hook up with someone before the day was through.

He was pacing back and forth in the hallway like an angry cartoon, and when he registered this he planted his feet firmly on the carpet and resolved not to move, because he was neither a fool nor a comedian. He was an intellectual. His mind operated at the highest efficiency. His discernment was unparalleled.

But why was he bleeding?

He watched the single red droplet run down his thumb where a tiny glass splinter from the cracked phone screen was embedded in his skin. He flicked the shard away, put the bloody thumb in his mouth and sucked at the wound.

'Natwest, what are you hanging around the door for?'

It was his mother, gliding down the stairs in her orange nighty. Leighton's *Flaming June*, he thought. Then he felt ashamed of himself and tried a casual remark. 'It's almost eleven. You're up late.'

Their hands lightly touched as she passed by. 'I took the day off work. Wanted to be here for your last hurrah.' Then she grinned and disappeared into the kitchen.

'Did you hear the postman this morning? I'm waiting for a package.'

'You're shouting, Natwest. I'm right here. And what's in the package anyway?'

He pretended not to hear the question. Apparently the wound had started bleeding again because his thumb had turned a different colour.

'Have you packed for tomorrow by the way?' She popped her head into the hallway. 'Because I'm not helping you.'

'Mum, don't infantilise me.' He put his thumb in his mouth and sucked at the wound.

Natwest was travelling up to Bradford tomorrow for his first year of undergraduate study. It was not his first choice of university, but it was the only place that had accepted him. He'd catastrophically failed his A levels at eighteen and watched his friends leave town without him. Now, after a four-year purgatory of retakes, pandemics, and coffee-shop employment, it was his turn – at the tender age of twenty-three.

Yet he'd thwarted his own exit by ordering the package the day before.

'What!' He couldn't hear his mother over the sound of the kettle. 'What are you saying?'

She raised her voice, and the trace of her mysterious Scouse accent returned. 'I said, why didn't you order it when you got there?'

In the kitchen, his mother pouring milk into a cup of tea distinctly resembled Vermeer's *Milkmaid*, except the liquid was semi-skimmed and his mother less dumpy. He was always doing this. While his friends were partying at university, he'd spent the last four years learning everything there was to know about the great artists of the world. He'd seen every work of fine art on the internet, and now his hyperlink mind found infinite ways to return them back to him in the real world.

'Why didn't you order it when you got to university?' she repeated.

'I know.'

His mother raised the mug to her lips. 'It's okay. I'll post it up.' She took a too-long sip, betraying her intentions to do the opposite. General human freedoms such as the right to privacy, or the right to own property, existed in a state of exception here in his mother's household.

Natwest shook his head. 'I'm going to the post office to see if they've got it.'

'But have you checked with Joan?' she asked, because of course he hadn't.

Joan was their neighbour. Sometimes they received her mail, and vice versa. She was a spiteful old woman who went out of her way to inconvenience Natwest. His evidence was based on an incident that occurred when he was sixteen, on Halloween night. He and Georgie – slightly intoxicated – had rung her doorbell to request some Rowntree's Randoms. Nobody answered, so he rang the bell three more times until finally the door opened, and without a word Joan threw a handful of popcorn in his face and slammed it shut. She was not a kindly old lady. Natwest demanded a certain degree of friendliness in people over the age of sixty; if they were not sufficiently congenial, they were nursing offensive thoughts. He wouldn't be surprised if Joan had stolen the package to spite him.

'You know she gets our post all the time.'

'I know,' Natwest sighed, irritated that he'd have to play nice with the old woman. 'I guess I'll go ask her.' He ducked into the hallway and grabbed his rucksack. On the way out he knocked twice on the lily wallpaper for luck – a childhood habit – producing two slightly different hollow sounds.

'Wait! Have you had breakfast?' his mother shouted after him. 'Do you want some toast? You need to pack!'

But he'd already opened the door and left the house.

Two

Coq au Vin

When she was a young girl, her husband said she was the only person in the world who enjoyed running to catch a bus. Now Joan was eighty, her husband was dead, and time had proven him wrong. There was no pleasure in motion anymore.

Yet still the world insisted on it.

In this case, Joan was thinking of the frozen chicken crawling slowly up the conveyor belt towards the young cashier, here in the queue of her local Asda. The chicken – shrink-wrapped and pink – travelled away from her, and with some bitterness she reflected that this dead animal was currently moving faster than she ever could.

She checked the time – ten minutes to ten. An hour to go.

Better get a move on, Joan.

The chicken continued on its way, followed shortly by a large onion, bacon slices and a single misshapen sprig of parsley. These were the principal ingredients of a difficult French dish known as coq au vin – the dish which Joan was determined to cook this morning. It was a particularly ambitious undertaking, because her diet consisted largely of canned soup and cheese on toast.

'Is that everything?' asked the young cashier, whose nose was punctured by an alarming number of piercings.

Joan nodded and opened her handbag to pay. It had been a long time since she'd been this nervous – perhaps *agitated* was the better word for it – and an unpleasant lightness accompanied the feeling. Would the meal be enough to impress him?

Seized by an urge to look at herself, Joan glanced in the dim glass of the card reader – only to discover that she looked much the same as she'd looked ten minutes before, and the ten minutes before that.

Her reflection was erased as the screen booted up and informed her of the cost: £19.66.

'That's uh. . . nineteen sixty-six please.'

She eyed the cashier's perforated nose with suspicion. 'How do you breathe?' she asked.

O utside the shop, her eighteen-year-old granddaughter, Samantha – or "Sam", as she unfortunately preferred to be called – was waiting around and fiddling with her mobile phone.

'Did you get everything, Nan?'

'They were out of the good garlic, as usual. Fortunately, I've got some at home.' Joan nudged her granddaughter. 'Sam. . . please can you take the chicken. . .'

'Oh yeah. Zen.' Sam took the shopping bag from her, and they started off down the road together. 'I bet you're excited for later,' Sam said.

'No. It's meant to rain today.' Although everything was set in motion, Joan still felt it necessary to complain. 'I really can't believe you've made me do this, Sam.'

Her granddaughter shrugged in that irritating, tomboyish way of hers. 'It's just a date.'

'But you never know who's on these websites. If *I* can put up a profile, *anyone* can.'

'Just trust me—'

'People aren't always who you think they are,' said Joan. 'I've read about this type of thing. Nasty criminals pose as old men, then they arrange a time when they know that defenceless old ladies like me will be home alone. Then they rob them!'

'It's not like that, Nan. You need to have faith in people.'

'The robbers are probably immigrants too,' Joan added, just for the hell of it. Provoking her granddaughter was one of the few sources of amusement she had left.

Sam, predictably, went quiet and stared at her phone.

Her granddaughter was the principal architect of this morning's plans. She'd created a profile for Joan on a senior dating website called ThereIsStillTime.com, introducing the idea as a purely educational exercise to teach her how to use the internet.

'So, are you monogamous or polyamorous?' Sam had asked while setting up the profile.

'Polyamorous? Is that the thing where you can write with both hands?'

There was a great fuss over the pictures. Joan said she didn't care how she appeared on the profile, because nobody was going to see it anyway – but then spent several hours in her spare bedroom going through countless boxes of photos to find the best ones. They were mostly of her late husband Gene, and their son, and their old friends. It was sad to think she could fit her whole life in one room. Going through them for the first time in years, Joan realised that she hadn't taken a photo since Gene died. She wasn't surprised.

Joan returned empty-handed, so her granddaughter perched her on the edge of the sofa and took new photos.

'Be sexier!' she cried.

Joan assumed a pose.

'Sexier!'

She tried something interesting with her leg, but Sam looked disturbed. 'No, no. Just smile.'

She smiled as much as she could without displaying any of her remaining teeth. One of the great regrets of her life was that she hadn't brushed her teeth until she was in her thirties. Her Chinese dentist said to her once, 'At least you *started* to brush. Some people never have the willpower to change,' which struck her as a characteristically wise thing for a Chinese dentist to say.

To her surprise, Joan had matched with hundreds of other profiles, but Sam informed her that they were all young people indulging in a "granny fetish". Joan wasn't sure what to make of that, except it confirmed her suspicion that all people below the age of thirty were monsters. Most of the other profiles in her age range lived in different towns and, as she could no longer travel, she ignored their messages. Her granddaughter called this "ghosting", which didn't make sense to Joan. She thought it was the opposite; the point about ghosts is that you can't get rid of them – they're always there when you don't want them to be.

After a few days Joan finally matched with somebody who lived nearby. His name was Michael, and he was seventy-eight. His first message said:

If you would like we could have brunch together.

Brunch! After going back and forth for a day – and with much encouragement from her granddaughter – she accepted the offer. It was agreed that Michael would pay her a visit at eleven this morning.

They rounded the corner onto the next street. There were only forty-five minutes left until Michael was due to arrive.

11

'It'll be fun,' her granddaughter assured her, swinging the chicken back and forth as if it were a toy, and not the key to Joan's future.

'Stop it!' She steadied Sam's swinging arm. 'You'll split the plastic.'

'It's fine, Nan.' Then her granddaughter raised the chicken to eye level. 'Though I still think it's insane to cook coq au vin for brunch.'

Joan tutted. 'I know what I'm doing, Sam.'

Except she didn't. Over the last few hours, Joan had grown increasingly anxious – a feeling she was quite unfamiliar with. She'd thought the dish would be a brilliant gambit, because in one of Michael's profile pictures he was sitting in front of a coq au vin in an expensive French restaurant. She thought she'd impress him by rustling up her own. Now faced with the responsibility of cooking the thing – and the prospect that Michael would disapprove of a coq for brunch – Joan was feeling overwhelmed.

A black Bentley drove past them, and she pointed it out to her granddaughter. 'Gene's brother once owned a Bentley,' she said, hoping to distract herself from her own anxiety.

Sam nodded and returned to her mobile phone.

'What exactly are you looking at?' asked Joan.

'My friend got a cat,' said Sam.

It was infuriating, how this phone had taken over her granddaughter's life. 'I don't understand you. What are you getting by peeking into everyone's lives like that?'

Sam lowered her phone, 'What's the problem? Isn't it good to uh. . . observe and, you know. . . imagine other people's lives?' When Joan shook her head, Sam added in a playful voice, 'That's like the definition of empathy, Nan.'

'A silly modern word. If you seriously think that jumping into people's lives like that – from Sam to John, from Sam to

Paul, from Sam to Janet – if you think that's a good thing, you're more naïve than you look.'

'Do you really think I have friends called Janet?' answered Sam flatly.

Joan shifted her handbag to the other shoulder. 'Well, if you're going to look at that thing, at least make yourself useful. Go on and show me Michael's photos again.'

Sam complied, and a moment later Joan was holding her granddaughter's cracked phone and looking at her date. He wasn't particularly handsome. Enormous bushy eyebrows, and too many moles for her liking. But the pictures were tasteful: Michael reading a book; Michael at the races; Michael in a French restaurant, coq au vin in front of him. He wore glasses and was Jewish – and apparently proud of it because it was right there in his description.

'Look. He might be the one, Nan.'

She'd said it because Gene had been Jewish too, and something about her granddaughter's assumption got on Joan's nerves. 'How do you know he's Jewish, Sam? This profile is probably a fake, anyway. You can never trust Jews to tell the truth.' Then when Sam looked as though she was going to throw a fit, Joan added, 'Gene's words, not mine!'

She chuckled at Sam's horrified expression, but the laughter stuck in her throat. All of a sudden the memory of her late husband's deception returned to her, and it was as if she had been slapped, for she found herself leaning against the bus shelter, trying to catch her breath.

'You okay, Nan?' Sam took her grandmother's arm in concern. 'We can get the bus if you'd like?'

'No, I...' Joan handed the mobile phone back to her. 'Listen, Sam...' She searched her granddaughter's face for some trace of evidence – as she'd done a hundred times before – but Sam looked away.

'Come on, Nan. You really don't want to be late to your own date. Not a good look.' Her granddaughter gently patted her on the back.

'Alright, alright. . .' Joan regained her composure by authoritatively kicking a small pebble into the road. 'I'm coming.'

Ten minutes later they were standing outside Joan's house.

'You sure you don't need a hand?' asked Sam.

'I'll be fine, thank you.'

'Okay. I'm meeting a friend in a bit so. . .' Sam offloaded the chicken to her grandmother. 'Good luck with the coq. I bet you'll have fun.'

Inside, she heaved the chicken onto the kitchen table and checked her watch. Twenty minutes to eleven.

She had timed this poorly.

She reread the instructions which Sam had printed out for her – an online recipe from somebody calling themselves "The Microwave Monarch". In the absence of a slow cooker, or any similar device, Joan had made the brave decision to cook this morning's coq au vin using only her microwave.

After defrosting it with a preliminary blast of the device, she diced and rolled the chicken in flour, adding bacon, mushrooms, garlic, parsley and red wine. She poured the entire mixture into a large Tupperware dish, put it in the microwave and set the timer for fifteen minutes.

She took a step back from the appliance, slightly in awe of her newfound ability to cook. She'd defeated the complicated dish with relative ease, and finally she had nothing left to do except wait for Michael.

After a few minutes of angst-free thumb twiddling, she was struck by another urge to look at herself.

'Go easy on me,' she mumbled, as she approached the mirror.

She never doubted her looks with Gene. She'd been eighteen when they met; he'd been twenty-six. In her mind she was young and attractive by default. No longer. The wrinkles in the reflection carved up her skin into discrete sections, and her face seemed like a mosaic made up of time itself. She traced the lines in her face, like the cracks in the glass of her granddaughter's phone screen, and watched her sad reflection do the same. She was not beautiful, exactly; no chance of that now. But perhaps like Michael, she was dignified. Was that the kind of woman he wanted?

Joan checked her watch – it was eleven – and glanced at the front door.

All of a sudden a dark figure appeared in the window above it.

Her first thought: would he knock or ring the doorbell? Sometimes people didn't see the button, so they hammered at the door – which usually irritated her. But for some reason she wanted Michael to knock.

Doorbell!

She took a deep breath to steady her nerves and opened the door.

It was a boy. No, a young man. Him from next door. Penny's son. What did he want?

'Yes?' said Joan.

The boy tried a sympathetic look. 'I'm from next door.'

'I know.' Joan looked past him to see if there was anybody else on the street. 'What is it?' There were only a few people about, but none of them was Michael.

'I was wondering if you'd had a package delivered to you by accident, because I'm waiting for one and I haven't got it.' The boy appeared to hop from one foot to another. What was his problem?

'No. I haven't received anything today.'

'Not a letter or anything? Like a little red slip?'

15

Joan wanted to shut the door in his face – which in all fairness was not unattractive. In fact, it reminded her of Gene as a young man: the same jaw, nose, brown eyes. In every face there were other faces. She had seen so many in her long life that each one referenced someone else she'd once known – and it occurred to her that there weren't even that many of them. Not really. Just billions of names and hairstyles, and maybe only a hundred faces in the whole world.

'Nothing's arrived. I'm sorry,' said Joan.

'I thought it would—'

'I hope you find it,' she lied, and shut the door.

People were so spoilt.

Just then, the air was pierced by the rude beeping of the microwave, and Joan rushed to the kitchen to fetch her coq au vin.

She opened the microwave door with a good deal of eagerness – but was met with a faceful of dirty smoke and a wretched smell. This was followed by a fierce bout of coughing and the sound of the smoke alarm, generally adding to the apocalyptic atmosphere in the kitchen.

It hadn't gone to plan.

She pulled out the dish and shoved it in the sink. Significant portions of the Tupperware were inseparable from the meal. The edges of the plastic container had catastrophically melted into the stew. The dish was now a gelatinous sludge.

Her coq was ruined.

Once she had cleared away the mess, Joan sank into a chair and began to sob quietly. Everything stank of garlic and melted plastic. She had flown too close to the sun and been punished for it. Worst of all, she'd failed Michael – who was now fifteen minutes late. People were disappointing.

'Doors are made for opening,' her husband used to say. And when she was young she believed him. She thought that a door was always the beginning of something. How many novels begin with a door opening? How many days begin when you leave the house? Now she believed that a door is more likely to mark the end of things. For instance, when a man rings the doorbell to notify you that your husband is in hospital after suffering an intracranial aneurysm. That was one ending. Another popular lie: that the ending of something is always the beginning of something else. The opposite is more credible. More often, an ending leads to the ending of other things; when one door closes, others close with it. If Joan were a philosopher she might say that life is measured in doors.

She shook her head and wiped her eyes with a handkerchief. That was the kind of thing Gene would think. Unlike him, Joan wasn't interested in philosophy.

But then she never really knew what he was interested in, did she?

She raised herself slowly from the chair. For the second time that day, the memory of that terrible morning, a few months after her husband's death, appeared before her.

It was the day they installed the memorial bench for him in the park. She'd spent a good portion of her pension organising the whole thing, and she'd had one of those bronze plaques inscribed and then fastened to the wood:

In memory of
Gene Shapiro
A loving father, grandfather and husband

It came out exactly as she'd hoped it would, and she was certain that Gene would be proud of her. When she returned home she decided to clean his study, which she had barely stepped

17

into since his death. As she tidied the room, she noticed the bottom drawer of his desk getting stuck on a loose nail. After some effort she managed to prise the nail out with a hammer, and, to her surprise, when she removed the drawer she spotted a brown envelope hidden in the space underneath. It was thick and heavy – more like a parcel – and as she drew it out, the contents spilled onto the floor.

She was surrounded by hundreds of photos, ranging from old Polaroids to computer printouts. All of them of young girls, between the ages of six and fourteen, most of whom were naked or partially naked. Some of them posed for the camera, some of them didn't. In several pictures, faceless men interacted with the girls, stroking their bodies, inserting themselves.

The first thing Joan thought of was her son – thank God there were no boys in the photos. And then she thought of her granddaughter. Wonderful, naïve Sam. She stared at the photos again, now picturing her lovely face, so much like the faces of these anonymous children. How many times had Sam been left alone with Gene as a child? Joan frantically sifted through the images, but her granddaughter's face was not among them. They contained nothing familiar; she recognised none of the children, nor the penises – all of which were grotesque in the way her husband's hadn't been.

Yet it was little comfort to Joan; she'd never since been able to shake the doubt that something happened to her granddaughter under her own roof. Even struggled to look Sam in the eyes without thinking of the photos. She would take the question to the grave, for how could she ask it?

Joan spent the remainder of that miserable day sitting in front of the door until the light faded out through the window, then she returned to the study and gathered up the photos. She placed them all into a metal fire pit at the bottom of the garden and, thinking only of her granddaughter, doused the pictures in alcohol and set them alight.

N ow it was twenty minutes past eleven, and nobody had arrived.

She stared at the computer in the corner of the living room, the one on which Sam had set up the dating account. She'd agreed to the meeting with Michael because of her granddaughter, because some part of Joan believed that a new man would erase the sins of the old one. Had Sam realised this when she'd suggested it? And then, thought Joan, how many photos had her husband found on that same computer? They'd owned the computer for years. He'd been looking at those photos and finding new ones right until the end. She'd spent her entire life loving someone she never knew. It was like an awful prank performed at her expense – and the punchline was that it was too late to start again. Her life was almost over.

And just then Joan noticed a shadow in the window above the front door. Somebody was outside, fumbling around for the doorbell.

He was here!

Joan suddenly caught a whiff of the wretched smell in the room – coq au vin and melted plastic – and she was seized by a desire to flee. Hide in the bedroom! Sneak out the back door! Escape! But her time had run out. She thought of Gene, and his lovely, disappointing face – and then of the failed brunch, unrecognisable in the kitchen bin.

Air freshener.

She grabbed a can and sprayed it behind her back, trailing deodorant all the way to the entrance, before chucking it behind a curtain. Then she smoothed down her outfit and practised a smile. A man was outside her house, and she would be presentable.

'Go easy on me,' she thought.

At last, there was a knock on the door.

Three

Natwest Makes a Plan

I t was the right weather to travel on foot. Almost European. The pavement sweated away the remnants of last night's rain, and the September sky was blank and blue like a swimming pool. Underneath it all: Natwest, soaking up the last gasps of summer and applauding his decision to leave the red Hyundai at home and walk into town instead. He was halfway to the post office and already feeling good about it.

A plan was of the utmost importance to Natwest. His days and nights were informed, at all times, by some sort of order. A good plan was a rhythm of convenience, the only way he could manage the infinite possibilities of a morning. The slightest interference could threaten a whole day. In fact, this year he'd spent countless days in bed simply because the morning (the weather, the shape of the world outside the window) had disagreed with the plan he'd constructed the night before. The way he saw it, there were good days and bad days – and the likelihood of a good one was proportional to how closely he stuck to his plan. So it was a pleasant surprise that, impelled by the necessity of finding the missing package, he'd managed to remake today's plan with relative ease. He took it as a sign of his growing maturity.

'Yo! Stop the ball!'

Natwest glanced in the direction of the voice. A group of

children were playing by the estate, and they were all gesticulating wildly at him. The aforementioned football rolled towards him, and he tried his best to stop it.

No luck.

It passed between his legs and rolled into the road, where it was knocked into the air by a passing car and landed, unreachable, behind a tall garden fence. He looked at the boys and flushed with shame.

They shook their heads in unison.

Natwest was humiliated. He felt suddenly old, unfit, emasculated. The boys' disappointed stares pierced him like the arrows in a St. Sebastian picture – in this case he was thinking of the Peter Paul Rubens work, and like that Sebastian, he felt naked before his attackers. He waved pathetically at the group and walked on.

To cheer himself up, he briefly indulged in a fantasy in which he was Rubens, showing his latest work to some king or another. All the members of the royal court applauded his talent. Cheers went up. The queen complimented his distinguished moustache. Several maidens offered to give him head in an adjoining antechamber. Natwest had the miraculous ability to imagine himself as the author of every book he'd ever read, the singer of every song he'd heard, the painter of every picture he'd admired. When he was feeling low, he would become somebody more celebrated for a little while.

The fantasy lifted his spirits, and he continued on towards the post office in a brighter mood. He would still attend Dr. Hung's exhibition in the town hall later that day. Apparently the dentist had taken up painting – which Natwest found very funny – and was due to exhibit his works in the town hall later this evening. Then he would gladly leave for university tomorrow. He might even have time to hook up with a stranger. As he went over the plan, it crystallised into narrative, which is to say inevitability, and with it the despair of the morning receded. There was no doubt in his mind: the package would soon be in his hands.

On the opposite side of the street, a somewhat menacing black Bentley crawled past him, its windows tinted so you couldn't see the driver's face.

Joan had been characteristically unhelpful about the package. Natwest looked forward to arriving at university, where he'd no longer have to think about Joan or anyone like her in this town. The idea that he could be a nuisance to people (other than when he chose to be) was impossible to think through to its conclusion – he was used to people liking him. He supposed it was due to his impressive knowledge of the world, because he could talk about anything, especially if it related to the arts. He liked to think of himself as a kaleidoscope given consciousness – a sentiment confirmed by his old English teacher, Mrs. Pandey.

'You're talented, Natwest,' she told him, after he'd submitted an extensive study of the blue-black sky in Geertgen's *Nativity at Night* instead of answering the hack question on Miss Havisham's overcooked dress in *Great Expectations*. 'But don't let it go to your head.'

Natwest had a soft spot for Mrs. Pandey (who was really Miss Pandey, but he never thought of her that way). She was the only person skilled enough to cut through the intellectual front he strived to present at all times – and thereby confirm he was as clever as he suspected he was. She was a dialectician. He still occasionally saw Mrs. Pandey around town, but their relationship had become an awkward affair after he'd failed to achieve the grades required for his place at university. A devastating day in the biography of Natwest, and one which left him reeling for years. When he bumped into Mrs. Pandey now, he was humiliated by her presence and felt as though he'd failed to become the talent she'd hoped for. By now he should be studying a master's degree, or a PhD, and thanking her in the acknowledgements of his first book. Instead he saw her on the high street, or at the supermarket, and they stumbled their way through polite conversation and false camaraderie.

Indeed, it would be quite unbearable to recall that email, so full of expectation, which Mrs. Pandey sent to him on the final afternoon of school before his exam results that summer. But unfortunately Natwest had committed it to memory.

Dear Natwest,

I know you will be very busy today, but I just wanted to wish you all the best for the summer, and your adventures at university and beyond. It has been a pleasure to see you grow through these last four years, and I can sincerely say that you are one of the most idiosyncratic and intelligent students I have had the good fortune to teach (even if your way of working is occasionally headache-inducing!). I can't wait to see what you will do in the future.

Go forth into it all! And good luck!

Best,

Miss P x

She was the only teacher he'd ever liked, and certainly the only one who took any interest in his future – unless you count Faith Fletcher, the poor school counsellor who was assigned to Natwest when he was fifteen. He'd had a brief depressive episode involving a box of matches and Mr. Claggert's *Collected P.G. Wodehouse*, and afterwards was forced to spend two afternoons a month with Faith discussing his emotions, etc.

The counsellor's conjecture was that he was acting this way because his father died before he was born, and now that he was becoming a man he was missing some essential father figure to guide him into adulthood. At least this is what Natwest presumed, based on the leading questions Faith would ask. The truth was, he didn't know how he felt about his dead dad – and he certainly wouldn't give this away to the counsellor. She had an irritating habit of listening intently while her hands did the opposite. She would constantly flex them, stretch her fingers, or else bring them together in her lap and form the shape of a house, her two thumbs facing towards her like a door. As he stared at her hands, he grew increasingly irritated, and instead of answering her questions would toy with her instead. He'd flip the script, ask his own invasive queries, and get her tangled up in knots of her own reasoning. Young Natwest knew Laing, Jung, some rudimentary Lacan. She did not, and he punished her for her ignorance. He wasn't interested in speaking to a millennial school counsellor. If he was going to be forced to talk to someone, he wanted hardcore Jungian psychoanalysis or nothing at all.

During their final session, Faith had become so exasperated by Natwest's avoidances and counter-questions that she angrily clasped her hands together – house-shape – and muttered, 'What exactly do you want me to ask you about, your sex drive? I'm a school counsellor, Natwest. You're fifteen.'

Which Natwest thought was precisely why she couldn't understand him. She was ill-equipped to deal with a generation raised on porn, who'd seen every possible combination of bodies and penetration before they'd even hit puberty. Of course he was obsessed with sex, and of course at the end he'd only find a shameful disappointment. A less-than-perfect partner, covered in his less-than-perfect semen, spurting from his less-than-perfect cock.

Faith asked the question again. 'What exactly do you want me to ask you about?'

'Well... I want you to be a proper therapist. Ask me about Individuation, Enantiodromia... uh...' Natwest tried his best to come up with other, preferably longer words, but could think of nothing else, '...and so on and so forth.'

Faith clenched her hands, frustrated, finally on the edge of cracking. 'You may not think much of me, Natwest. But I learnt this one phrase at university: negative transference. I think you're transferring your feelings of hostility towards your parents – perhaps your dead father, or your overbearing mother – onto me. How's that for school counselling?'

'That's Freud, Miss. No one reads Freud anymore,' he said dismissively.

Faith gasped in exasperation.

'You don't listen to anything!' Her hands collapsed in on themselves, and for the last time she snapped at him. 'One day you're going to realise that the reason you're so vulnerable is because you're so sure you're not.'

B y now the sun had done its work on the remaining puddles and the pavement was hard and dry. A young couple walked past Natwest on the other side of the road. They were not much older than him, the girl in an orange crop top and the boy in a colourful shirt – a repeated pattern of flowers, like the wallpaper in Natwest's house. Apparently the boy had said something funny because the girl couldn't stop laughing.

Natwest had very little patience for expressive shirts. He found eye-catching colours and psychedelic patterns obnoxious; it suggested a deficit of something in the wearer's personality. As they passed, he noted the couple's arrhythmic backsides bumping into each other, and the girl kissing the boy on his personality-deficient cheek. He briefly imagined what sex with both of them would be like.

Which reminded him: a colourful shirt could be useful for parties at university. He should text Georgie and ask him to return his old Hawaiian shirt before he left for Bradford tomorrow. Natwest had lent him the shirt because he'd needed it for some event at Oxford. Hopefully it hadn't gone missing.

Natwest reached for his phone.

It was gone!

No – it was in his other pocket. As usual, he was unnerved by the insane feeling of relief at finding his phone exactly where he'd left it. He reached for it a second time but fumbled, and the phone slipped from his pocket. He turned away from the impact with an impressively theatrical gesture – just in case someone had seen him drop it – and winced as the phone bounced twice on the pavement and lay still. He cautiously approached the phone, afraid to pick it up. From this angle it looked like a piece of roadkill, flattened by a passing car. He examined the damage: a fresh constellation of fractures in the bottom left corner of the screen, but otherwise not too bad.

When he unlocked the phone, he was surprised to see a message from Georgie.

How are you bro

Heard you're leaving for Bradford tomorrow?

The big city (!)

We should hang before you go

Would be nice to say a proper good bye ☺

Nando's?

27

Natwest reread the message, searching for passive aggression. Potentially the smiley face was a provocation, for it was unlike Georgie to emote. But then again he had been much changed since he returned from his master's degree in Conflict Resolution and Peace Studies.

Natwest sent a reply.

Hey friend!

Weird. I was just gonna text you

Yep I'm leaving for uni tomoz

The big city (!)

Nando's sounds perf.

I'm in town anyway so let's say late lunch
early dinner?

ALSO do you still have the hawaiian shirt that I lent
you a couple years ago? Can you pls give it back
when we meet up

Reckon I'll need it for uni things

Georgie was the ex-recipient of at least three of Natwest's bodily fluids. They'd had a vigorous sexual relationship throughout school, but once Georgie landed a spot at Oxford University their sometime partnership had come to a bitter end. He'd left Natwest behind. Add to that an irritating saviour complex Georgie had developed at university – he was always trying to get Natwest to read this or that article, apply for schemes and jobs, retake his A levels. Then there was the loftiness in his voice, that he'd gone where Natwest couldn't, studied at the place Natwest had always dreamed of.

After a moment's hesitation, he sent Georgie another message:

☺

On the high street, Natwest spotted Dr. Hung. There were only a few people out, and he recognised the lithe figure of the middle-aged dentist immediately. Dr. Hung was pottering in front of him, his little bald spot bobbing around like a fishing float. Natwest followed him up the street, leaving some distance between them; he had no interest in talking with his dentist, especially as he would be seeing Hung at the event later tonight, which according to Natwest's mother, he'd spent the whole summer organising. He wouldn't usually attend a dentist's amateur painting exhibition, but his mother was making him go because she worked as Dr. Hung's dental nurse and he did Natwest's teeth for free. She'd brought up the event a few weeks ago while Natwest was getting a cavity filled:

'I'm so excited to see these paintings, Richard,' said his mother. 'It's like this whole other side of you. I didn't know you were artistic.'

Natwest couldn't see her expression because he was staring up at the masked face of Dr. Hung, who was gently scraping a sharp tool against one of his molars.

'Well, we'll see how it goes.' Dr. Hung's mask shuddered as he spoke. 'I've been thinking about it for so long. And now that it's nearly time to do it, I'm terribly nervous.'

Natwest closed his eyes, and the bright light above turned the insides of his eyelids a golden colour. His mother's voice again: 'I'm sure Natwest would love to come to the exhibition. He loves all that.' Natwest – because the dentist had just injected a numbing agent into his gums – could no longer speak for himself, so his mother continued. 'He's studying History of Art at university, you know.'

'Yes, that's right.' Then Dr. Hung spoke directly to Natwest. 'I'd be honoured to have an expert there. But it's my first time, so don't be too critical!'

Natwest tried to emulate the dentist's laughter, but he choked on his spit.

He'd hoped the dentist would turn into one of the shops so he could pass by him without being recognised, but Dr. Hung walked like an NPC. His gait was so achingly slow that Natwest grew impatient and considered crossing the road to overtake him. Then it got worse: just as the post office came into view, Hung stopped dead in the middle of the pavement. He'd been accosted by teenagers, and now appeared to be involved in a leisurely discussion.

Natwest ducked into the nearest shop to avoid his field of vision, but banged his head on an extraordinarily low door frame. It was the local newsagent, and behind the counter a very short shopkeeper glared up at him.

'Just browsing,' Natwest mumbled, and pretended to look at some gizmos hanging from a revolving stand. He checked his socials, enjoyed a particularly amusing video of a cat refusing to enter a bathtub, and absentmindedly spun the stand around. He noticed a phone case hanging from one of the hooks that matched the model of his own. Might be a good idea to get one, he thought. But then he saw the time – 12:44 p.m. – and decided to get going.

When he looked through the door Hung had disappeared, and the street was empty.

Natwest walked to the post office feeling optimistic about the state of the world. The panic of the morning was hazy, like a dream that somebody else had relayed to him, and he felt like a citizen in a different, benevolent country. He heaved open the post office door and it made a little *trring!* as he stepped inside. There were only a few people queuing up at the desk, but they all turned to look at Natwest, and for some reason he gave them a wave in return. Then he recognised the man at the back of the queue: Dr. Hung, waving back.

Four

Erlöser Erupting

In June, Dr. Richard Hung had travelled to Italy with his girl-friend Ariyah to study the great mouths of the Renaissance. He'd dreamed of the trip for years, for in his spare time this dentist was also an amateur painter, and the subject of all his paintings was the human mouth. In his studio – a converted garage – you would find countless oil paintings on the walls, each depicting a human mouth in close-up. Occasionally there was a chin included, and rarer still a pair of nostrils, but the focus was the mouth, portrayed without exception in an open-wide position, plainly displaying the lips, the teeth, a tongue, and dimly, the back of the throat. This was his true calling.

So he and Ariyah travelled to Italy to study mouths, touring the country from Venice to Milan to Bologna. It was their first holiday together. Everything went splendidly – that is, until the regrettable transgender interlude in Florence. Ariyah, who was trans, wished to pay her respects to notorious cocksucker Donatello by visiting his femboy statue of *David*. But Richard wasn't interested in homoerotic interpretations of the great works, and so there followed a furious argument in front of Botticelli's *Venus* – 'Not everything has to have trans conno-tations!' said Richard. To which Ariyah replied, pointing at *Venus*: 'It's not her modesty she's hiding with that long lock of hair!' By the end of the day they found themselves on a train to Rome, exhausted after their first row. Richard, who was ambivalently straight, and flummoxed that the word 'queer' was now a good thing, looked forward to leaving Florence behind.

When they arrived in Rome the following morning, Richard was dizzy with excitement. He'd been to the city once before as a child, with his Catholic father to honour the religion which Richard rejected the moment he left Hong Kong. Now he was returning for his own pilgrimage: to see the sculptures of Bernini, whom he considered the greatest patron of the mouth in art history. At last he got his wish, and for hours he stood transfixed before the open, orgasmic mouth of *Saint Teresa in Ecstasy*. It was a depressing experience. Richard stumbled out of the church in a state of nausea, blindsided by the perfection of Bernini's craft. He would never create anything as magnificent, as intimate, as the mouth of *Teresa*. All the paintings he'd produced up to that point were insignificant in the presence of the Renaissance master.

For the rest of the day Richard followed Ariyah around the city, sulking quietly to himself. He was assaulted by his own inadequacy every time they passed a perfect work of art – which unfortunately was rather frequent in Rome – and by the evening he'd decided to give up painting. Ariyah tried her best to cheer him up by explaining the history of this or that culturally significant Basilica, but Richard largely ignored her until, finally, outside the Vatican, she told him to grow up and stop wallowing.

Richard looked up and sneered at his girlfriend, preparing to say something malicious – and just then realised he was standing in a huge piazza, among hundreds of tourists. He recognised the colonnades, the obelisk, the huge façade in front – but where were they exactly? Ariyah explained that they were in the square outside St. Peter's Basilica, and why hadn't he been

33

listening? Richard laughed piteously at his own misfortune, for this piazza had been designed by Bernini too. He couldn't escape the master.

Still, he had to admire the perfect curve of the structure, the two semicircular colonnades that enclosed them on either side with their even, teeth-like columns, the whole thing unified by the Egyptian obelisk at its centre. All of a sudden Richard saw the entire square from above, as in an aerial photograph on Google Maps, and he had an epiphany. It was obvious, wasn't it? The semicircular colonnades were gigantic lips, the columns like teeth; and the obelisk in the middle, a sharp tongue. He was standing in an enormous gaping mouth. Bernini's masterpiece.

After the epiphany in St Peter's Square that night in Rome, his feelings of inadequacy disappeared, and when he returned to England he immediately began work on a new painting, hoping to finish it in time for the exhibition that Ariyah had organised for him.

Three months later, on the morning of the exhibition, Richard woke up with an idea. It was the idea he'd been waiting on all week, which he'd been praying would arrive in time. And it did, at the eleventh hour, which was really Seven Thirty in the Morning.

'Hey, Siri!' he said, and the alarm on his iPhone responded with a compliant *bloop*, and there was silence. It had taken its time, this idea. He'd sat in front of the canvas every night, waiting to discover the final detail he knew was missing from the otherwise immaculate painting. A single feature that would transform the image into a masterpiece, like the looking glass in the back of the *Arnolfini Portrait*, or the pearl in *The Girl*'s ear. This morning, he finally knew what to do.

Richard slid out of bed, impatient to get the idea on the

canvas before it slipped away. First there was his reflection in the mirror, the thinning hair now dashed with grey, and the bags under his eyes, landmarks unto themselves. Then there was the unsightly cut across his forehead from the fight he'd had with Ariyah the previous evening. It had been rough. The details were hazy, but Richard must have said something wrong, trans-wise, because they argued for almost two hours. Voices were raised, clichés exchanged. 'I'm not your experiment!' she said. 'Every relationship is an experiment!' he replied. Then, at the height of the row, Richard had marched to the front door and told her to leave. 'Fine!' said Ariyah, and Richard yanked open the door as violently as he could – but unfortunately he was standing too close and slammed the door into the side of his own head. Now the wound was sensitive to the touch, and he marvelled at the way he could make pain *happen* by pressing down on it. It occurred to him that the idea of how to finish the painting had arrived with the argument, so he had Ariyah to thank for that – even as he pushed her to the back of his mind to focus on the work at hand.

He switched on his new Bluetooth toothbrush. It had six settings but Richard kept it on Daily Clean. He brushed methodically until the device played the first four notes of Beethoven's Fifth – thus indicating it had logged the details of his morning brush into the system. In the shower, he considered his salt-and-pepper pubes, his balls, which seemed to fall lower every day, and his penis. When he'd come to England as a fourteen year old, his father had given him the name Richard, which he'd rather liked – it seemed a particularly English name, and an artistic name – but on his first day of boarding school it was tragically shortened to "Dick", and for the duration of his time there he was known as Dick Hung. An Asian joke, Richard supposed, looking down at his not-inconsequential cock. Long years of disuse had endowed

35

it with moral attributes – qualities of patience and stoicism – and now in the presence of his girlfriend it could spring to life with extraordinary reserves of energy. In fact just the thought of her had made it grow in the shower, and he began to masturbate, recalling the first time they ever had sex. It was after a showing of *Parsifal* at the Royal Opera House, the night they met. She'd been the only other person in his row who'd come to the show alone, so they struck up a conversation. Richard had been mortally afraid of offending her, the first transgender person he had ever met – and yet he was fascinated by the sudden rupture in his sexuality which this blonde forty year old had inspired in him. She had the most indescribable mouth you've ever seen.

When they got back to her bedroom he was concerned that she'd have a larger penis than him, and he wasn't sure if that made him transphobic or not. But when he took off her clothes, he saw that he was bigger, and his confidence swelled. He lay Ariyah on her back and tenderly lifted her legs onto his shoulders, and then he entered her – and on the third thrust decided he was not, all things considered, a transphobe.

When he was dry, Richard strapped the smartwatch to his wrist – Eight Twenty-Four in the Morning – and stepped into his studio. The strip lighting of the garage provided a harsh, even light. In the centre of the room: the painting. He approached it, slightly overwhelmed that he was capable of creating such a vast object. It was an eight-foot-wide canvas propped up by three easels, and the image on the canvas was a gigantic depiction of Ariyah's mouth.

One of the reasons he fell in love with her: she never asked *why*. Why the mouth, of all things to paint? Why wasn't Richard interested in anything else? He'd spent his working life looking at mouths in the dental surgery, only to make them the subject of his art in private. It was the reason his painting had remained a secret, for he was frightened that his audience would misunderstand him, find it grotesque that he was a dentist who painted mouths. But Ariyah told him that wasn't the case, that she would love to have her teeth examined by a dentist who was as passionate about mouths as an artist is about his subject. She was his champion. Only Richard Hung understood the infinite gradations of white and yellow required to transform a tooth into a vessel of extraordinary feeling; and his discovery of the Escheresque quality of tongues, each one an impossible pattern, a unique cipher; or his demythologised lips, an encounter with the Real. Ariyah was educated in theories of art and philosophy, and he was often mystified by the words she praised him with. But then that was their relationship: she was the Warhol to his Basquiat, and in private he began to view himself as the great artist she thought he was. 'You've turned me into an advertisement for myself,' he once said, and she replied, 'It's called Self-Love.' She was always there with a quote to encourage him and had an enviable ability to relate her vast knowledge of art criticism to his work. He'd committed his favourites to memory:

> A man's work is nothing but the slow trek to rediscover, through the detours of art, those two or three great and simple images in whose presence his heart first opened.

> – Albert Camus

So: Lips, Teeth, Tongue. When he mixed the white and yellow paints required for his teeth, he'd recall another of her quotes, this one comparing the artist Lynette Yiadom-Boakye to Lucian Freud:

Everyone is born with a subject, but it is fully expressed only through a commitment to form, and Yiadom-Boakye is as committed to her kaleidoscope of browns as Lucian Freud was to the veiny blues and the bruised, sickly yellows that it was his life's work to reveal.

– Zadie Smith

So: Richard was the Lucian Freud of mouths. The teeth, his life's work. As a trainee dentist, Richard had – as they used to say – cut his teeth at the Centre for Aesthetic Restorative Dentistry, under the prodigious John T Furtwangler, DDS. His mentor taught him that Dentistry was an art like any other, and the masterpieces were the million smiling mouths, straightened teeth, and filled cavities of all the patients who sat in your chair in a lifetime. Richard's works sat comfortably alongside those of the other great mouth-artists, an artistic tradition he'd been obsessed with since he was eighteen, when he was drawn to photography and the infinite possibilities of the mouth therein. The mouth as instrument: the album covers of Elvis Presley and Little Richard; the mouth as politics: Arbus' *Germaine Greer*, Scargill at Jubilee Gardens; the mouth as absence: Dorothea Lange's *Migrant Cotton Picker*, Mapplethorpe's *Croland* Polaroids; and the mouth as perfection: Avedon's *Monroe* portraits. Eventually he graduated to sculpture and painting. He wasn't interested in *Mona Lisa*'s boring, invisible lips; he desired open mouths, the gaping jaws of Caravaggio's *Medusa*, or the allusive tongue of the *Boy Bitten by a Lizard*. He was riveted by Frans Hals' cackling *Laughing Boy* and *Yonker Ramp*. And he'd never forget the moment he opened a book on Raphael only to be greeted by the horrific maw of *St Margaret and the Dragon*, surely the greatest study of the throat ever committed to canvas. Then of course there was Bernini. Every mouth was not a mouth alone, but an echo of another. He hoped that tonight's exhibition would be his formal entry into this great tradition.

He pulled a chair up to the canvas and leant into Ariyah's giant mouth.

Everything was as it should be, the lips and the tongue, the cavernous throat, the skin along the edge of the canvas – all exactly as he'd envisioned it. Everything but the teeth. They'd been puzzling him the whole week, even though to anyone else's eyes they were a perfect depiction of the teeth in Ariyah's lovely, large mouth. It was only this morning, as he recalled the explosive argument with his girlfriend the night before, that he'd grasped the essential detail which the painting required.

'Alexa, play *My Painting Playlist.*'

'Playing *My Painting Playlist,*' replied Alexa. It was a fearfully long collation of his favourite recordings of Wagner's operas, and today the music of *Parsifal* sounded throughout the studio. How right that it should be this piece which Alexa opted to play this morning. The strings of the *Prelude* rose about him, and he reflected that he'd taught himself everything – the history of art, music, painting – without ever attending a class. He was the Lucian Freud of mouths. It was his vision alone that would complete the painting.

So how to fix the teeth? On the furthest back-left molar of the lower jaw, he would add a hint of decay, the spectre of a cavity, a touch of black on the brilliant white tooth.

Wagner's horns kicked in, and Richard felt the rush of creation. 'Alexa, volume up!' He touched his brush to the canvas and a glorious energy raced from his hands to the fine hairs at its tip. An ecstasy was upon him. 'Louder, Alexa!' he cried. 'Louder!' And like that, he finished the painting.

*

39

R ichard did his best not to trample the dandelions which sprouted from the cracks in the pavement as walked to the high street, but he crushed a few. The sun was out, and the landscape was transformed by the music in his earphones. The sun became The Sun, the road, The Road, and the people he passed on the street, Noble, Beautiful, Tragic. An elderly gentleman, one of his patients, stopped in the middle of the pavement and waved in his direction. Irritated, Richard removed one of the earphones and shook the old man's hand.

'Dr. Hung, nice to see you!' He peered over his thin, wire-frame glasses. 'I imagine you're rather nervous for the opening tonight.'

'Yes I...' His voice was drowned out by the Wagner, suddenly immense in his right ear. He paused the music. 'I've set everything up in the town hall yesterday so I'm not too worried about it. I just need to drive the last painting up there.'

'I must say, I'm really looking forward to it, Doctor. I can't remember the last time we had an art exhibition here – I've been telling everyone in town about it.'

Richard resented the elderly gentleman, despite spending most of the summer encouraging his patients to spread the word. The resentment was a symptom of his greatest fear; either nobody would turn up, or everyone would – and find his work repulsive. Fortunately Ariyah had laid on mountains of strategically free wine to make the event a little more palatable.

'Well, I hope you're not disappointed,' said Richard, searching for the man's name and drawing a blank.

'Oh no. It's something to do, isn't it?' The elderly gentleman cocked his head to the side and tutted at the dentist. 'That looks nasty.' He pointed at the cut on Richard's forehead.

'Oh, it's nothing. Doesn't hurt.'

'Vinegar,' he said, with some force, and there followed a brief silence. 'Listen... I heard a joke the other day and I thought of you.' He cleared his throat. 'What did the dentist get at the award ceremony?'

'A little plaque?' replied Richard.

'Oh, you've heard it before.' The elderly gentleman's disappointment was crushing, and Richard apologised profusely. 'No, you don't need to say sorry, Doctor. It's not irritating at all.' The old man winked. 'A good dentist never gets on your nerves!'

Richard laughed out of kindness at the old pun, but the truth was that he'd always been wary of jokes. He could never tell them successfully himself, so he disliked hearing them from other people – especially gags of the dental variety, of which there are fewer than you'd think. He had a hundred birthday cards sitting in a drawer, all warning him that he was getting long in the tooth.

And let's not forget the most famous dental joke, the one he hears at least once a month, which no dental professional can escape: *when's the best time to go to the dentist?*

Tooth Hurty!

At boarding school, he was often told a racist variation of the joke with a mock Chinese accent. *What time da Chinese dentist opern?* And this was before he ever wanted to be one.

He thanked the elderly gentleman, who patted him on the shoulder and waved him on his way.

'Anyway, chin up, Doctor. Good luck!'

The high street was the most attractive part of town, lined by white Victorian facades with Juliet balconies and hung windows. He strolled past it all, listening keenly to the final scene of the opera playing through his earphones, and emitting quiet, gentle farts in time with the music. If the town were a stage, right now Parsifal would be lifting his Holy Spear aloft in a perfect climax of redemption.

Richard was on his way to the post office, having missed the postman during the ecstasy of painting. He reached into his pocket and removed the red slip that had been posted through his door instead.

'Chiu-Yin!' a girl called out.

Richard flinched, recognising the voice. Ella crossed the road with one of her friends trailing behind. She was Ariyah's daughter, eighteen years old, and nothing like her. 'Hello, Ella,' said Richard. 'How are you?'

'Good thanks Chiu-Yin; this is Sam. Sam, Chiu-Yin.' Ella pointed between Richard and her friend. He regretted telling her his Chinese name, after she'd asked him with an obnoxiously sincere tone one evening at Ariyah's house. She hadn't called him Richard since. 'What did you do to Mum?' Ella said, cheerfully. 'She's pissed at you.'

'It was just an argument, Ella.'

'Mhm. Hint: you should really go over there and sort it out.'

Richard rubbed the wound on his forehead, thinking of the night before. After Ariyah had left the house, Richard had felt rotten, and so he'd devised a plan to ask her forgiveness.

'I'm going round to your mum's after this to apologise,' said Richard. 'Uh. . . I've got. . .' He debated for a moment. 'I bought Ariyah some earrings last night. Really nice diamond ones which. . . just really expensive ones.'

'Earrings?'

Ella's tone sent Richard into a panic. He had searched the web for the most overpriced jewellery that could be delivered to his house by the following day. In the end, it was the single most expensive thing he'd bought that wasn't a house. What more could he do than that?

'Yeah I'm. . . I'm just picking them up from the post office now.' He raised the red postal slip in the air. 'I'm going to give them to her today? Right after this? What do you think?'

She laughed. 'Worth a try.' What the hell did that mean? But he couldn't ask her because Ella had already shrugged and walked off with her friend. She shouted back at him over her shoulder. 'I'm rooting for you, Chiu-Yin! Good luck!'

'Thanks,' he mumbled, disturbed by the whole interaction. He pushed open the heavy door of the post office and stepped inside.

T he electric bell screeched again, and Penny's son, Natwest, entered the post office behind him. Neither party had any choice but to start a conversation.

'Did you miss the postman as well?' asked Richard, and Natwest nodded. 'What were you expecting?'

'Just a package,' said Natwest, looking down the length of the queue. 'Like a book or whatever.' The boy was completely different from his mother, Penny, who'd been his dental nurse for almost ten years. She was useless at her job, but she was one of the few friends he'd ever made at the surgery. She had an enviable way of making small talk with the patients, getting them to laugh and relax. The opposite of Natwest, whose presence usually set Richard on edge.

'Oh, by the way I'm coming to your painting thing with my mum tonight,' said Natwest.

'Thanks. Are you. . .'

'Yeah, yeah, I'm looking forward to it.'

Very soon he would be studying the History of Art at university, and Richard felt a pang of jealousy towards this young man who still had so much life ahead of him.

'What should I expect?' asked Natwest.

'Well, I don't want to spoil it. What are *you* expecting, as the local Art Historian in training?'

'I'm sure they'll be great paintings,' said Natwest.

43

Richard couldn't resist asking. 'No, I mean, what sort of subjects do you think I paint?'

Natwest looked impatiently at the front desk. 'Uh. . . dunno, teeth?' He laughed at his own joke, and Richard smiled back thinly.

'Yes. . .'

'Landscapes maybe? You seem like a landscape guy.' Richard took this for an insult, although he did in fact love landscapes.

He approached his next question with caution. 'It would be funny, wouldn't it, if I painted teeth?'

Natwest laughed. 'I guess, yeah. It would be weird because you're a dentist, right?'

It was the answer Richard had feared, and feeling defensive, he tried one of Ariyah's comments. 'But wouldn't you feel more comfortable. . . Wouldn't you rather have your teeth looked at by a dentist who was as passionate about teeth as an artist is about his subject?'

'Never crossed my mind before,' said Natwest, smirking now. 'It would feel odd though, because it's like this hypothetical dentist is *really passionate about teeth.*'

Richard thought: what's wrong with that? Why does this country treat you with suspicion if you become passionate about something?

'And you know,' continued Natwest, 'that's fine in theory but. . . I mean it's also a question of morality as much as art. Who? And why? What do we really think of a dentist who paints teeth? What's the agenda of the consciousness behind the canvas – or the dental mask, if you will?'

Richard felt personally attacked by the young man and his zoomerish ethics. 'I think that's a question your generation is overly concerned with.'

'My generation? Don't insult me.' For a moment Natwest seemed genuinely offended, but then he laughed. 'I'm joking.

But the point I wanted to make is really quite complex. It's like—'

'No, Natwest... All I mean is... isn't it a good thing for a dentist to paint teeth?'

'A good thing?'

'The dentistry would be better, and the art would be better,' said Richard.

Natwest dismissed the point. 'No. The important question is: *how* would they be good teeth? Are they conventional or not? Are they unexpected? Profound? I'm not interested in comfortable dentition.' And here he grinned. 'We need to be challenged. The greatest teeth will never be the beautiful ones; the greatest teeth are more likely to be inconvenient, maybe even ugly, painful, unexpected. Shane MacGowan.'

Richard wasn't sure about that. Couldn't conventional teeth, depicted accurately, with care and precision, be profound? Weren't his teeth profound? And what about his dentistry? He gave his patients exactly what they wanted. Wasn't there art in that?

'So you think that great art means not getting what you want?' said Richard.

'It's not that simple – but there's no challenge in a happy set of smiling, pretty teeth. The greatest artworks are all challenges to the audience's sense of—'

'If the art moves you, it moves you,' Richard cut in. 'You can't argue with that.'

'Yes you can!'

Like most young people, Natwest confused variances of taste with failures of intellect. His point was a stupid one.

'Natwest, aren't you describing the same thing as me? It just depends on who you are, no? Either way you're getting what you want, depending on what it is *you* want. Expectations are still being met. If you want the happy ending, or the easy route, or the convenient image – the kind of "weak" art I think you're talking about, you'll get what you want and you'll be moved.'

'Exactly,' said Natwest.

'But if your idea of great art is something that's challenging and unexpected – ugly, difficult art, an unhappy ending, a hard time, Shane MacGowan, whatever it is that you mean – then you're *still* getting what you want when you encounter a work of art that gives you that. So it's just a matter of taste, in the end. Or am I misunderstanding you?'

Natwest opened his mouth to reply, but was interrupted by the clerk at the front desk. 'Are you two together?'

'Uh yes... no...' Natwest's speech faltered. 'You go first, Doctor.'

'No, no, it's okay. After you.'

'I was expecting a package this morning, at 9:24 a.m.,' said Natwest. 'But it didn't arrive. However I received an email that said otherwise...'

Richard tuned out while Natwest told the clerk a long, involved story about his missing package. He wanted to speak to Ariyah as soon as possible. The conversation with Natwest had unnerved him, and he desperately sought her encouragement and forgiveness.

'I'll have a look in the back,' said the clerk. 'And you, Sir?' he was pointing at the red slip in Richard's hand. 'I'll get your package while I'm back there.'

The clerk disappeared through a back door, leaving Richard and Natwest alone again.

'You're going to university soon, aren't you?'

'Tomorrow, actually.'

'I hope you've packed your toothbrush,' said Richard, then regretted it immediately. He never made anyone laugh.

'Uh... I still need to pack.'

The door at the back opened, and Richard caught a glimpse of a vast room full of parcels, then the clerk appeared carrying two packages. He handed one to Richard.

'I'll see you later then,' Richard said, and Natwest, who appeared unreasonably happy at the sight of the clerk holding the other one, nodded at the dentist. 'Yeah, yeah. Good luck.'

Richard left him there and headed for Ariyah's house. It was nearly Two in the Afternoon. Soon, his redemption.

H e carried the package under his arm and walked up the long gravel driveway which led to Ariyah's large house. On the doorstep, he noticed a single yellow leaf, prematurely fallen from a tree. It was the yellow of a rotten tooth, and Richard mused that it was no accident that dentists call the first set of teeth you lose when you grow up 'the deciduous teeth'. He lamented how few second chances you're given in life, then he stepped over the dead leaf and rang the buzzer.

As he waited impatiently, he checked his watch: Two Thirty.

Tooth Hurty in the Afternoon.

The front door swung open, and Ariyah – lovely in a white shirt and black jeans – turned around in the same motion and disappeared back into the hallway. He entered the house and found her in the kitchen, where she was boiling a kettle. 'You want a cup of tea?'

'No, thank you,' he said, and placed the package on the kitchen table. 'I completed the painting.'

'My big mouth?'

'Yeah, it just came to me. It was quite easy in the end.'

She didn't say anything, just kept on looking at him, her lips slightly pouted, like she was finishing a sentence.

'You have to see it, Ariyah. It's the best thing I've done.'

She poured herself a cup of tea, then pointed at the package and asked what was inside. 'It's a gift,' said Richard, putting on a weak, defeated smile. 'For you. To apologise for last night and everything that happened.'

She raised a catastrophic eyebrow. 'You think that's the right call? Buy me a present so I forget about it?'

'I just wanted to say sorry.' And in the uncomfortable silence that followed, Richard felt a trap door opening beneath him. He pushed the package towards her. 'So... I'm really sorry, Ariyah.'

It wasn't clear what she wanted, so he opted for a look of confusion. It didn't work, because Ariyah obliterated the dentist, called him an idiot, said he never paid attention to her. If he thought he was special because he painted pictures, he wasn't. He was like every other man: he didn't listen to women.

'That's unfair!'

'It's true, Richard.'

'No it's not!'

'So what did we argue about last night, then?'

She said it rhetorically, but when Richard tried to recall the night before, he couldn't actually remember what he'd done wrong. 'It was about... I said something that offended you.'

'You said something unforgivable.'

'Did I?'

'That's just it, isn't it?'

He tried to focus on her mouth and the words coming out of it, but it was a losing battle. Why were women so confusing? Why did she always speak in riddles!

'Look, Ariyah... I can't remember because... because I hit my head!' He said it triumphantly, but it didn't help his case – in fact it was a disaster. He had dug himself into a hole, one with a huge sign above it that said: 'You are a Man who ignores Women' (and underneath that sign there was an addendum: 'and Trans Women are Women!'). They went back and forth, and with every question he failed to answer correctly, he dug himself deeper, and added more signs: 'transphobe', 'misogynist', 'narcissist', 'cunt'.

His only plausible way out was the earrings, so he pointed in desperation at the package and begged his girlfriend to open it. 'Please! It's a really expensive gift!'

'What kind of person do you think I am?'

'But you haven't seen what it is!'

'You're an idiot, Richard.'

'Okay! That's fine! You're smarter than me! But I'm not going to stand here while you insult me – that's not my idea of listening to you. The exhibition is in...' He looked at his watch. '...three hours. We need to get my new painting to the town hall ASAP.'

'I really don't care about the painting, Richard.'

He had nothing to say in response, because he loved her, and he didn't believe her.

'I said, I don't care about the painting.'

'You're just saying that to hurt me,' he replied.

Ariyah's lovely face fell into something pained and sad. He was naked before her, and everything he said was wrong.

'Ariyah...' He couldn't get any words out.

'I'm waiting for you to say something.'

'I think... we should...' But he sighed and gave up, because he didn't know what she wanted.

In the silence that followed, Ariyah gestured at the package. 'What is it... a ring? Jewellery? You going to propose to me?' Her mouth had looked exquisite when she'd said *jewellery*. 'If you ever listened to me, Richard, you'd know I wouldn't want anything like that.'

'But...'

But it was over. When he lifted his head, Ariyah was eyeing him sadly, like a piece of bad art, made in earnest.

'I'm sorry, Ariyah.'

She picked up the package and ripped off the tape. Richard looked away, sunk into his shame and unable to bear the sight of his failure. And just then Ariyah made a noise – not of delight, nor of anger – but one of surprise. He glanced up, and she pulled out a long plastic tube from the box and turned it around to face him. It was a huge, pale dildo.

He didn't understand. The garish red lettering on the tube described it as a King Cock Ultra Hung Girthy Suction Cup Dildo, 9.5 Inch.

Richard jumped out of his seat and tried to snatch the giant dildo – the King Cock – away from her, as if he could erase her memory by taking it back.

'That's not – That's not what I ordered – I didn't –' Then all the possible meanings of the giant cock fixed into one meaning, and Richard recoiled in horror at what he'd done. Ariyah would think he was mocking her with an objectionable, cruel joke. Whatever she'd thought of him before, now there was no disputing his status as a hateful transphobe.

But he wasn't! He wasn't! 'I don't know what's happened, Ariyah, I'm so sorry—'

She wouldn't allow him to take it back. Instead, she tore the massive dick from its packaging and with a bewildered look gave it a hard squeeze. Her perfect mouth turned huge with an infectious, ridiculous grin, and she burst out laughing. Laughing! She began waving the dildo in the air like a flag, and Richard was struck dumb.

She held out the cock, and he cautiously took it in his hands. His eyes followed the engorged rubber veins running along its length towards the smooth, featureless glans, and all of a sudden he realised what had happened. He chuckled, because somewhere in town, right at this moment, Natwest was carrying a parcel of expensive earrings.

Richard held the King Cock aloft, like some sort of spear,

and in a shaky voice announced, 'I'm like... *Parsifal!*' His laughter went back to Ariyah, and they fell into hysterics. It went all the way down their throats, and if they tried to speak the laugh got there first.

When they were finished there was a divine stillness in the kitchen, and with some reverence they returned the dildo to its box and re-taped the package shut. Richard pulled Ariyah towards him and kissed her on the mouth.

'Is it sore?' She lightly touched the cut on his head.

'A little,' he said. 'It comes and goes.'

Ariyah gave him a kiss on the forehead. 'It's getting late, and we have to get your new painting to the exhibition.'

'Alright.' But he pulled her back into an embrace. 'Just one more minute.'

'Okay, Richard.' Ariyah closed her eyes and rested her head on his shoulder. 'But then I want you to show me the painting.' Her voice, barely a whisper. 'Show me my giant mouth.'

Five

Natwest's Annunciation

The high street flowed with shoppers, and Natwest walked among them, full of a renewed gratitude for the universe. Immense joy that he existed in the world with these people, in this old town where he'd lived for so long. It was capricious, joy, and he considered how it was contingent on the smallest convenience, as simple as getting what he wanted.

Finally, he had the package.

It was smaller than expected, and weighed less, but he'd ceased to care about the product inside and was simply relieved that it was safe in his rucksack. Everything was turning out as planned. He walked amiably past Short Cuts, the barbershop where he'd been getting his hair cut since he was a child. The owner, Rob, was sweeping up hair. He was a stocky, balding man, but a lovely one, and he waved at Natwest through the glass. Natwest returned the gesture. He felt like the prince of this small town – something he would miss once he left for the city. There he'd only be a small fish – albeit a preternaturally talented one – in a frighteningly large bowl.

As was its habit, his joy was swiftly displaced by a bog-standard melancholy. His brain was a machine that he couldn't turn off, and joy was a trick that he would think himself out of.

Dr. Hung was an idiot.

This was Natwest's main conclusion as he headed for the park. The dentist had no discernment when it came to the arts and should probably stick to doing people's teeth. If there were a ledger, with all the idealised and harmonious and pretty artworks on one side and all the difficult, painful, realistic works on the other, Hung, who believed they were equal, would by that very fact come down on the side of the former. Natwest had no illusions about the real world. He'd grown up with it, witnessed more terrible things in his short life than a fifty-something dentist ever could.

e.g. Top Five atrocities he'd seen before the age of fourteen:

1. 12/07/07 Baghdad airstrike
2. Execution of Saddam Hussein
3. Beheading of a US citizen by Jama'at Jihadists
4. 2 Girls, 1 Cup
5. Cadbury's Gorilla advert

Fourteen was also the age Natwest had been when he last cried. It was a typical childhood story: he'd been in class and accidentally called Mr. Claggert 'Dad'. His unpleasant peers had burst out laughing, and Natwest had fled, teary-eyed, to the bathroom. He'd decided that afternoon to never let anything get on top of him again. True to his word – and onion dicing aside – he'd not shed a tear in nine years.

He walked past the town hall, where Dr. Hung's exhibition would be taking place later that evening, and headed for a nearby park. There were benches along the park's edge, and before sitting down on one he made sure to read the bronze memorial plate fastened to it.

HOW PERFECT IS THIS,
HOW LUCKY AM I.
Andrew Orchard
1966–2005

Natwest had an obsessive compulsion regarding park benches. It was very important that he read the inscription before sitting down – in fact it was psychologically impossible for him to ignore a memorial plate. He wanted to believe it was his soul forcing him to honour the dead, as he himself would wish to be honoured. But really it was just his habit-addicted brain, denying him the privilege of bench-related autonomy.

Honouring the dead.

It was a favourite pastime of Natwest's, imagining his own funeral. The long line of colleagues and contemporaries, fellow art critics shuffling their papers and preparing to deliver their respective memorial lectures – Jerry Saltz gave a particularly moving eulogy that involved the prized phrases, 'gone too soon', 'the world is poorer', 'too well loved to ever be forgotten'. Hundreds of wreaths were hand-delivered by influential people, including three heads of state, the remaining Beatles, an emotional Geoff Dyer, Banksy so disconsolate he had to reveal his true identity... The fantasy could only go so far once he pictured his mother weeping at the grave and threatening to throw herself in after him. The pleasure instantly drained from the daydream. His imaginary funerals always resembled scenes from movies, because in truth he'd never actually been to one – unless you counted his in-utero attendance at his father's funeral, which like the man himself was an event he didn't believe in, so he'd never counted it.

5PM?

That good?

He read the text from Georgie. Now that the package was safely in his hands, Natwest had a clear day ahead.

Sounds good

See you later

He unzipped his rucksack and looked around to ensure he was alone before opening the package. He wasn't.

It was Mrs. Pandey, crossing the park.

Eye contact; and now she was walking towards him, a slight Indian woman in her thirties with thick black glasses, wider than her face, and behind them big saucer eyes which could turn you inside out if they wanted to. He stuffed the package into the bag and returned Mrs. Pandey's wave.

'This is a nice surprise,' she said.

'Hi, Miss...' They exchanged pleasantries, and she asked if he'd travelled abroad over the summer holidays.

'No. But uh... I got a lot of reading done, so...' Once again, and despite himself, Natwest was trying to impress his old teacher.

Mrs. Pandey grinned. 'Always reading. I remember the first day I taught your class. You had a copy of *Ulysses* on your desk. You were... Year Ten? Even I hadn't read it yet.'

'To be honest, Miss, I used to carry it around with the cover facing outwards, so everyone would see it and be impressed.' As always happened in her presence, Natwest surprised himself by speaking candidly. 'I didn't actually understand much of it at the time. I was just showing off.'

'And now you're going to university.'

He rolled his shoulders back. This had been the principal microaggression of Natwest's summer, and now his old teacher had joined the long list of offending parties. Yes, he was *finally* going. He recalled the email she'd sent him on the last day of school. *I can't wait to see what you will do in the future.* Turns out she'd had to wait a long time.

'I'm leaving tomorrow,' he said.

'That's great. No doubt it'll do you good to get out of here.'

He squeezed the phone in his right hand. 'Yeah, I suppose... I'll be back home at Christmas, though.' He looked away, embarrassed by the small talk they were engaged in. On the opposite side of the street, there was the local nail salon, 'Nail Again. Nail Better.' Beside its garish blue sign, there was a close-up picture of the hands from Michelangelo's *Creation of Adam*, an exact reproduction, except the nails on the hands of God and Adam were painted with glitzy pink nail polish.

'Look at that,' said Natwest, pointing at the nail salon, hoping to fill the silence. 'Such a stupid image.'

Mrs. Pandey looked at the sign and smirked. 'It's not that bad. Quite clever, really.'

He raised a critical eyebrow in reply. 'Clever? I have to disagree with you there, Miss. It's like... everything that's wrong with our culture.' He felt the pleasure of debate stirring within him. 'It's a debasement. A totally vapid, meaningless joke. A forfeit to—'

'Natwest, you're looking at it wrong,' she interrupted. 'I think you've made a judgement about the work of art—'

'Work of art!' he cried, throwing up his hands in protest.

'—yes, the work of art, without fully considering the image before you.'

He glanced at the nail salon, then waved a dismissive hand in her direction. 'No, I think you're missing the point. I'm saying the picture's a symptom of a culture which—'

She grinned at him, and he knew that he'd fallen into a trap. 'No, Natwest, I think it's *you* who's missing the point. You're not generous enough. Or perhaps—' and here she patted him on the shoulder '—not mature enough.'

56

He blushed violently and kept his mouth shut. She was the only person who had this power over him. 'Try thinking about it this way,' she continued. 'What would happen if you treated every work of art as *perfect*, and then worked backwards? If you presumed that every "blemish" or "failing" or "irregularity" in tone or pacing or structure or payoff was intended by the artist? Or author. Or director. Or whatever. That these faulty elements were by design, to communicate a significant idea?' She gestured at the *Creation of Adam* behind her, carried away with her point. 'If your *starting point* is that the image above the nail salon is a perfect artwork, what *then* can you say about it? Well... the world opens up.' Natwest opened his mouth, but Mrs. Pandey wasn't finished. 'For instance, the picture might reveal itself as a work of extraordinary Pop Art – except unlike so many gallery fake-outs, one that really exists in the world. It's Pop Art returned to its source. This is Warhol's soup cans, restored to the Asda aisle. Transported back to the public arena...'

She spoke with such authority, and Natwest was impressed by her argument. What if this image above the nail salon really were a masterpiece?

'And Natwest, it's a work of camp, too,' she continued. 'Of drag, of queerness. A revisionist Michelangelo that taps into the artist's probable homosexuality. An intentional tackiness designed to draw attention to the lie of commercial beauty – which to be fair, is a pretty bold way to advertise a nail salon...' She carried on, bandying about a dozen theories: it was Žižekian, an admission that anti-capitalism is widely disseminated within capitalism; it was Jungian, a radical surfacing of *Anima* and *Animus*; it was metamodern...

Mrs. Pandey had been transformed by the act of speaking, and he saw a glimpse of the teacher's former brilliance – it turned out she still had things to teach him. *Imagine every work of art as perfect.* How curious an idea, and one so alien to Natwest's critical mind. Still, he tried his best, and a few moments later joined in with her breathless flow of ideas.

'And Miss, it's also a political artwork,' he said. 'An indictment of the hollowness and hypocrisies of institutionalised religion. An institution obsessed with itself, obsessed with its own orders and images, with its own prettification.'

'Yes, yes,' Mrs. Pandey took over excitedly. 'Because there's no such thing as simple faith anymore. People have to be lured in by the promise of beauty, by the grandeur of cathedrals and ceremonies and basilicas. The nail salon comments on the essential vapidity of the church. Even God has to wear nail polish. The contemporary individual is forced— Ah!'

She grabbed her side and winced.

Natwest stood up in alarm. 'You okay, Miss?' He felt suddenly and surprisingly protective of her.

'Yes. I'm fine.' Mrs. Pandey waved him back onto the bench and went quiet. In the gap she looked – for a moment – as if they could be the same age. But then she pushed her huge glasses up the bridge of her nose, and her face returned to that of the exhausted millennial pedagogue he'd remembered from school. There was a stillness out on the street, and they were both embarrassed by how easily they'd gotten carried away. Natwest was unsure what to say next.

'Uh...' He had been repeatedly turning his phone over in his hand, and when he broke the silence – 'So when does school...' – he dropped the device on the floor.

'Fuck-sake,' he said, and quickly added, 'Sorry, Miss.'

A tight smile from Mrs. Pandey. She bent down and picked up the phone. 'You ought to buy a phone case,' she said, examining the cracks across the screen.

'No, don't worry, it was already like that.'

For a beat they were back in the classroom, and Natwest had spoken out of turn.

'So uh… when does school go back?' he asked again.

'We went back two weeks ago.'

'Oh, so aren't you—'

'I called in sick,' she said. It was Mrs. Pandey's turn to look embarrassed, and she raised a finger to her lips and made a playful *shh* gesture, but it came off awkwardly. 'We have a new head of department, he joined this year…' As she spoke, the image of Fra Angelico's *Annunciation of Cortona* came to mind. Natwest pictured himself as the seated Virgin Mary, and Mrs. Pandey the angel Gabriel standing over her. The angel was telling Mary, *I can't wait to see what you will do in the future.* No pressure. Imagine if Mary went through this scene and the baby Jesus never arrived. All that expectation – that potential – just to be abandoned to a life of penury with Joseph and his stupid furniture start-up.

Mrs. Pandey had finished talking and was waiting for an answer.

'Yeah, yeah,' said Natwest, hoping it wasn't a question he'd been asked.

There was a cataclysmic silence. It was clear he hadn't been listening, and his old teacher looked away in obvious disappointment. 'Good luck with university, Natwest. I think you'll really like it.'

'Uh-huh.'

They both stared sadly at the nail salon, then Mrs. Pandey shook her head and left him on the bench, making her way slowly towards the high street. The encounter had emptied him out, and all of a sudden Natwest felt small, like a baby abandoned at the door of an empty house.

H e went to open the package again but was delayed by a babbling elderly couple sitting on the bench alongside his. While he waited for them to leave, he completed the *Times* crossword on his phone in blinding speed, attempted two unsuccessful Sudoku puzzles, and watched thirty to forty TikToks – until at last the old couple moved on. When he was alone, he ripped off the tape and the package fell open – but the shape inside was decidedly less phallic than he'd expected. Instead there was another box, wrapped in gilt paper. He ripped that one open and discovered a layer of bubble wrap underneath, concealing an even smaller box. Either he'd been seriously short-changed on the rubber cock, or a disaster was imminent. It was like a nightmarish round of pass the parcel, and after opening several nested packages he was finally holding a blue velvet box no bigger than a Rubik's cube.

Inside were two heart-shaped diamond earrings. His first thought was: 'This is a perfect artwork.' His second wasn't a thought, but rather a terrible sequence of feelings: nausea/panic/ fear/trembling – He was sprinting as fast as he could, winding his way through the afternoon shoppers. They exclaimed as his rucksack swung around and hit them or their children – but he could only shout 'Sorry!' over his shoulder and continue valiantly up the high street. The sun had emerged from its cloud cover, projecting a desert heat onto Natwest's back. He broke into a sweat. Thighs ached. Air was gasped. There was a collision with a woman outside the estate agent. 'Sorry!' He did a double take – it was Mrs. Pandey he'd crashed into – but he decided it was best to ignore her.

When he arrived at the post office, he imagined the missing package as a simple box, in a corner somewhere, in the anonymous warehouse in the back – that would be the best option. The others were too hideous to contemplate. As he heaved open the heavy door, he was interrupted by the phone vibrating in his pocket. A message from his mother:

> Doctor hung texted me and said that he has your package and you have his one. Come and see me im with my friend at your coffee shop! x

Dr. Hung! He rapidly connected the dots. The incompetent post office clerk must have mixed up the packages, and now the terrible object was in the dentist's hands. All of his fears had been realised.

The image of Dr. Hung, grinning foolishly as he unwittingly handed the package to Natwest's mother now appeared before him. It was an image worse than death itself. Under no circumstances could she be allowed to get her hands on it. It wasn't just that he would be exposed as someone who liked dick, it was that he'd be exposed as someone who liked nine and a half inches of it. What would his mother think?

Then his phone vibrated again.

> I've got the package now x

Six

Imam at the Movies

Mishaal was a man split in two. There was the first half of his life: the filmmaking degree, the women, the cinema; and the second half: his wife, his glorious appointment as the local Imam, the great bonfire of DVDs in the firepit in his garden. As you'd expect, it was a woman who changed him. She sold homemade candles for Islamic Aid, and Mishaal, twenty-seven and mysteriously drawn to her, purchased a candle, then returned every day until his flat was full of them and she agreed to go on a date. They were soon married, and she gave birth to his son; all the while he followed her back to the religion of his childhood, disposed of the parts of himself that were disallowed, and for the last sixteen years had lived faithfully as a committed husband – and now, a leader of prayer.

But it wasn't that simple. Sometimes it felt as though two hooks – one halal, one haram – were pulling Mishaal in separate directions. The pleasures of his past life continued to haunt him, and he would catch himself staring at a movie poster on the side of a bus for too long, or lingering on certain memories of his youthful encounters with the female sex. So it was that on this Friday morning, Mishaal received a text message from another woman, and taking stock of his unsatisfied life, he decided to be unfaithful to his wife.

Salima laid out a small bowl of porridge and yoghurt, and with characteristic chastisement told him to watch his weight and to please cut down on the chocolate bars because there were none left for their son.

'Look.' She held up the empty packet.

'Okay. If you insist.' Mishaal spooned the flavourless oats into his mouth and thought that his wife should take her own advice.

She paced around the kitchen trying to look busier than she actually was. 'What are you doing after your sermon?'

'I'm going to hang around the mosque and sort some things out,' he lied. And his wife, apparently convinced, nodded her approval.

'Stories of the Prophets?'

'Yes, exactly.' He continued to eat in silence, contemplating the text he'd received from Caroline, less than an hour ago, requesting his presence.

'Maybe you could ask about my plans for the day, Mishaal.'

'I was going to, dear wife,' he said sarcastically. 'What are you up to?'

Salima explained her plans, which involved various chores that were meant to benefit him. The blame for his forthcoming misdeeds would be on her head as much as his, because Salima had changed too. For one, she'd lost her sense of humour – one of the things which made him fall in love with her in the first place. And her perfect faith, once an ideal to strive towards, now felt like a competition she dragged her husband into to make him feel unworthy of her love – and he was the Imam of the town! It was shameful.

His sixteen-year-old son, Tariq, entered the kitchen without ceremony. He greeted his mother with a kiss on the cheek, ignored his father, poured himself a bowl of cereal and carried it out the room.

'Where are you going with that?' Mishaal asked, and his son stopped at the door, rolled his eyes and carried on out the room. 'Tariq! Get back here and eat breakfast! We're a family!' His explosion caught the boy off guard, and Tariq returned to the table without a word.

'Don't shout at him, Mishaal,' his wife said, resting a tender hand on Tariq's shoulder. This relationship between them – it wasn't fair. He wanted nothing more than to be his son's best friend and teacher. He'd helped raise the boy, changed his nappies, taught him to swim, dealt with his smart-aleck questions as a child – '*Green Eggs and Ham*, but isn't that haram?' – yet the teenaged Tariq ignored him, spoke in monosyllables, and expressed an obvious distaste for his father's entire existence. Meanwhile, his wife lavished attention on the boy, appeared to reward his insolence, and made his father a stranger in his own house.

'Dad? What's your problem?'

He'd been staring with obvious annoyance at the sugary cereal the boy was shovelling into his mouth. 'My problem? That's no way to speak to your father,' he said, and taking one look at his wife – who was judging her husband's limited consumption of oatmeal – Mishaal pushed his bowl away and left the kitchen. 'I'm going!'

He retrieved the digital projector from his study and made for the door. 'I haven't given you your packed lunch!' Salima shouted from the kitchen, but the Imam left the house without a word to emphasise his point – whatever that was.

After a minute of fumbling behind the pew, the plug slid into place. 'You can switch it on now, Caroline!'

Standing at the back of the church, the Reverend Caroline Hancock pressed the wrong button.

'Not that one!'

Caroline snatched her hand away, but the damage was done, and the projector made a high whirring sound that echoed around the nave of the church. Mishaal marched over to the projector – mounted on an improvised pedestal of *Songs of Praise* hymn books – and indicated a green button on the side. 'You press *here*.' On the pull-down screen at the opposite end of the church, a blue projection appeared.

'Huzzah! It works!' She gleefully punched his shoulder, and they stood in silence for a moment, watching the screen. As the projector warmed up, the shade and quality of the standby blue deepened, became richer and more indulgent. Famous blues flooded Mishaal's mind: Dorothy's dress, *The Sound of Music*'s sky, Derek Jarman's *Blue*. He was being drawn back in, and felt the anger of the morning dissipate.

'I'll get the DVD, hold on,' said Caroline.

She disappeared into a room at the back of the church. The Reverend was a decade older than him, in her fifties, and unmarried. They'd met at a dreadful Interfaith Dialogue at the town hall last year. Amid the platitudes and promises of the event she'd made a joke about Orson Welles, and Mishaal was the only one who'd laughed. Following a rush of recognition, the pleasures of his previous life came back to him and a friendship of sorts bloomed. He liked Keaton, she liked Chaplin. He liked Hawks, she liked Ford. He liked Grant, she liked Stewart. Mishaal felt an immoderate affection towards her. How could he say no when she'd requested his presence this morning? The Reverend wanted to borrow his home projector for her Christian film club, and had asked if Mishaal would like to watch the film with her beforehand.

Caroline re-entered, carrying a battered DVD case.

'What's it going to be?'

'Have a look,' she said, passing him the case. It was the 1948

Victor Fleming version of *Joan of Arc*, and Mishaal frowned, disappointed in the Reverend's choice. 'Why this one?' he asked. 'It's not very good.' He flipped over the case and looked at the pictures on the back. 'And your religion has many classics. *Passion of the Christ, The Ten Commandments, Jesus Christ Superstar...*'

'I've seen those a million times,' she said, dropping her voice to a whisper. 'You know the film club's just an excuse to catch up on the classic films I've missed.'

He shook his head. 'There are old movies, and then there are *classics*. This is just an old movie. It's very stagey, Caroline, very stagey. Although...' He stared at the picture of Ingrid Bergman on the cover and noticed his heartbeat increase, just slightly.

'I'm trying to watch more Victor Fleming,' announced Caroline, 'if only to honour the fact that he made *Wizard of Oz* and *Gone with the Wind* in the same year. A bloody miracle.'

Mishaal sometimes wondered if the Reverend really believed in God, for how could she embrace both of these things, the worldly and the spiritual, with the same language? Yet another part of him, the same part he was indulging this afternoon, thought: it's true, how *could* Fleming make those two films in the same year? It wasn't a miracle, but it was close.

'I'll make sure it's all working okay,' he said, cracking open the DVD case. The sound was immensely satisfying, like a smell that sends you running back to your adolescence. He pictured every DVD and VHS he'd ever opened. Remembered a late night showing of Hitchcock's *Spellbound* when he was a teenager, and Ingrid Bergman's eyes, massive on the cinema screen. He'd never realised a face could contain a whole world until he saw one in black and white.

He handed the disc to Caroline, and as she bent over to insert the DVD into the player, Mishaal considered her posterior. He wasn't interested. Caroline Hancock wasn't a woman. Or at least, not a "Woman". He'd tried to explain this to his wife when she questioned why he was spending so much time with her – this woman who was not, after all, a Muslim. 'But that's one of the reasons she's not a woman!' Mishaal replied. This was how he justified his infidelity. He would never be unfaithful in body, only in spirit.

Cinema was technically haram, so Salima – the strictest of Muslims – explained to him before they married. Too much background music, sexuality, killing. 'But that's not why you watch it!' he'd protested. 'You watch it for Bette Davis, John Wayne, Ingrid Bergman!'

'Ingrid Bergman is haram,' she replied in a flat voice. And so he gave it up for her, as was appropriate for a leader of prayer.

Caroline cursed under her breath. 'Sorry, Mishaal. What time is Asr prayer, again?'

He checked his watch. It was two:thirty p.m. 'I've got about three hours, so we should get started soon. I'm running another "Stories of the Prophets" workshop after.'

'Perfect.' The Reverend took a certain pride in displaying her knowledge of Islam. She claimed to know much of the Qur'an by heart, which at the beginning of their friendship Mishaal found endearing. Today it irritated him.

The DVD menu for *Joan of Arc* appeared on-screen but the text was stretched out of proportion, probably because the aspect ratio on the DVD player was set to 16:9, widescreen, and the film was meant to be projected in 4:3, Academy ratio. She handed over the remote and asked Mishaal to fix it.

'You know, the director fell madly in love with Ingrid during the filming of this,' said Caroline, pointing at the screen. 'You heard about that? It was unrequited. Really sad stuff.'

Mishaal searched for the aspect ratio setting on the remote. 'Everyone fell for Ingrid. Spencer Tracy. Gregory Peck. Um. . .' He looked up at the vaulted ceiling, searching for another name.

'Rossellini,' Caroline suggested.

'Rossellini.'

She tutted. 'You're getting slow in your old age.'

The Imam laughed. It didn't make sense; why did he enjoy it when this older, Anglican woman teased him and yet hated it when his wife did the same? Perhaps it was because he could make Caroline laugh in return.

None of the buttons were doing what they said they did, and he made his displeasure known by grunting loudly at the remote.

'What are you looking for?'

'I'm looking for... 1.37:1... Or, 4:3.'

'Let me think,' she said, 'Psalms 137:1. By the rivers of Babylon, there we sat down, yea, we wept, when we remembered Zion... Now that doesn't sound like your sort of thing, Mishaal!'

'That's very funny, Caroline.'

'Qur'an?' she continued. 'That would be... An-Nisa 4:3, right? Marry the other women that please you, two or three or four. But if you fear that you will not be just, then marry only one...'

'I'm not looking for holy verses. I'm trying to find the aspect ratio setting. The button will say 1.37:1 or 4:3.'

'Ah!' She pointed to a button at the top of the remote, 'Is that it?' The image squared itself and the DVD menu became legible. 'Perfect! Let's get to it,' she said. 'What do the kids say? "Victor Fleming and Chill", is that right?'

Mishaal laughed. 'You got any popcorn, Caroline?'

'Sweet or salted?'

'Chaplin or Keaton?' he countered – but his words echoed around the empty spaces of the church, and there was a charged silence between them.

He was really going to do this.

The mention of popcorn reminded Mishaal of his hunger, and he recalled his wife and the packed lunch he'd rejected this morning. He considered the possibility that his rumbling stomach was the voice of God, warning him to stop what he was about to do.

'Actually, Caroline, I think I'm going to get something to eat—'

But Caroline had already pressed play, and the titles appeared huge against a velvety aquamarine background. He turned to leave before he was tempted further, when all of a sudden the Reverend flicked a switch and the church went dark. Mishaal's eyes followed the light of the projector to the screen, where the image was delicious, bright and massive. He sank into the nearest pew, helpless. 'I'll stay until the first close-up,' he whispered.

And there she was. Ingrid Bergman, kneeling before the broken altar of a desolate church. The walls crumbled, and the light through the ruined windows formed a spotlight around her. Bergman's hair was covered by white cloth, her hands clasped together in supplication. It would be an outrageous contradiction – 'Ingrid Bergman', 'supplication' – if it wasn't so convincing in that moment. One perfect performance can make a bad film worthwhile. Sometimes one perfect gesture was enough.

The first close-up came and went, and for thirty minutes Mishaal experienced Ingrid's pleading, holy face on the screen. It was simultaneously a titillation, a taunt, and an indictment of his own lack of religiosity. Ingrid seemed to be saying, 'Look how holy *I am* – only a performance – and how holy *you aren't* – a real life Imam. You are condemning yourself, and if you think you can come back from this egregious infidelity, you are mistaken. . .' He couldn't stand it any longer.

He jumped out of the pew in anguish. 'Stop it! I've got to go! Caroline, I've got to— Where are the lights!'

Caroline flicked the switch. 'Are you okay?'

'Yes, yes...' Mishaal was shaking, his shame exposed in the even light of the church. He checked his watch – three:thirty p.m. 'It's just I've got... things to do. Enjoy the rest of the film, Caroline.'

She looked hurt by the remark. 'Okay. Well... thank you for setting everything up. If you're free tonight you can always come back and watch the rest.'

'Maybe.' He made his way towards the exit.

Caroline pointed at a heavy wooden object in the corner. 'Mishaal, make sure you take the lectern with you.'

He'd forgotten about the lectern. She had needed one for an important sermon from a distinguished guest, and as the golden eagle was being refurbished he'd lent her a spare from the mosque.

'Yes, of course, the lectern...' Apparently the film had weakened him physically, as well as spiritually, because when he heaved it onto his shoulder he almost buckled under its weight. He managed to manoeuvre it out into the car park. 'Enjoy the film club, Caroline.'

'Thanks for everything,' she said. 'Don't be a stranger.'

'Okay.' Mishaal couldn't see her because of the lectern across his shoulder, so he spoke into the wood. 'Peace be upon you.'

The Imam marched blindly across the car park, hoping Caroline had returned inside without noticing that he'd forgotten his car and had arrived at the church on foot.

His return journey was something of an event, if only for those observing the curious sight of an Imam with a lectern over his shoulder, struggling up the pavement. God willing, somebody would assist him.

And yet after ten minutes nobody had offered their help.

Mishaal lowered the lectern to the ground and expressed his frustration – and his fatigue, and his hunger – with an impressive groan. Still nobody stopped.

Mishaal noticed a young man pacing towards him. It was a boy he didn't see much of anymore, who used to attend the mosque as a fifteen year old. He liked to be called – absurdly – Natwest. He'd gone through a religious phase after reaching the sensible conclusion that his secular upbringing would bring him only despair. His response was to trial all the religions around town, and for a brief two-month spell Natwest was quite the Muslim convert. The first day they met, Natwest quizzed the Imam, and Mishaal won him over when the boy asked: 'What are your views on homosexuality?' And the Imam, recalling his past life, answered, 'Nobody's perfect.' A very inquisitive teenager. But his Islamic phase had not lasted, and perhaps as a result of this when Mishaal saw him around town now he thought him quite unhappy.

Natwest stepped onto the road and purposely avoided the Imam. Very disappointing. However, Mishaal needed all the help he could get. 'Hello! Natwest! Hi!' Natwest looked back, feigning surprise. 'Come here, brother!'

Natwest nodded at him. 'Hey, Imam. Salaam.'

'You don't have a minute do you?' Mishaal indicated the lectern. 'I need some assistance.'

Natwest glanced up the street. 'I'm in a rush, I've got to—'

'Where are you going?'

'Uh... You know Higher Grounds? The coffee shop? I'm meeting my mum there.'

'Perfect! We're going the same way. Help me get this down to the mosque? I promise it'll take no time at all.'

Natwest checked his phone rather rudely, then made a gesture with his right hand that suggested plainly to Mishaal both his reluctance and his acquiescence in the matter.

Weight halved, they progressed down the street quite easily, but the boy was clearly agitated and barely spoke to the Imam. There was a little of Tariq in Natwest's demeanour, and just like his son, there was something adolescent and artificial in the boy's morose stance towards the world. The Imam was certain that Natwest, with whom he'd enjoyed numerous joyful deliberations on subjects as diverse as theology, silent cinema, music and Michelangelo, was neither as sad nor as serious as he wished himself to be.

Mishaal's twin instincts, as a father and as an Imam, compelled him to ask a question he'd never actually asked his own son. 'What's troubling you, Natwest?'

'Huh?' His knuckles were white and he switched the position of his hands to find a better grip. 'It's nothing. I don't want to be late.'

A woman stepped aside so they could pass by with the object. Mishaal nodded his thanks. 'Natwest, you can't carry the world on your shoulders. There are other ways to deal with it.'

The boy didn't reply, and the Imam searched for an appropriate verse that could better demonstrate his point. But Natwest was a non-believer now. In fact, he was never a believer, he only believed in the style of things. That was Natwest's problem. For a time, he'd believed in the style of Islam, as he had done with Christianity before it, and Transcendental Meditation, and Buddhism, and no doubt many other systems of thought and faith. Mishaal would not convince him of anything unless it was framed in terms the boy already believed in.

'Natwest, how can I say it? There are two types of people in the world. Charlie Chaplins and Buster Keatons. These are the two basic categories – not men and women, or adults and children – Chaplins and Keatons.

'I can tell that you desperately want to be a Keaton person. But I think you need to be more like Chaplin, because I know that's who you really are, underneath. It would be much better for you if you accept that. Will make you feel better too.'

Natwest laughed. 'I think you might be simplifying things a bit there, Imam.'

'Simplifying, yes. But simplicity is a door to more complex things.'

'So what, life is a comic phenomenon either way?'

He would usually emphasise a point with his hands when he spoke, but as they were currently wrapped around the base of the lectern, he had to make do with pointed movements of his head. 'No, no, if it's not Chaplin or Keaton, it's Spielberg or Scorsese. If it's not Spielberg or Scorsese, it's Truffaut or Godard...'

Natwest frowned. 'You can't divide everyone into two filmmakers.'

'So you're Hegel, not Kierkegaard; McCartney, not Lennon – but that's okay!'

'No!' Natwest broke in, agitated now. 'Lennon is real. He's singing about real shit, *screaming* about it. McCartney is off in some happy farmcore land. And Imam, the world isn't a happy farm.'

'I believe that a happy ending is at least as realistic as an unhappy one.'

'There's no way McCartney is better!'

'It's not a question of value, Natwest. For instance, McCartney is responsible for the brilliant medley at the end of *Abbey Road*, with all those disparate song fragments coming together to form one cohesive whole. Perhaps it's an illusion of unity, but it's still brilliant, isn't it? If Lennon had arranged it, it would be completely different – probably unsatisfying, jarring, definitely less joyous – but you can't say it would be better or worse. Simply different. Lennon could never have made McCartney's version, and vice versa. It would be a rubbish album if they'd tried. Don't try and be someone you're not, Natwest, or it'll tear you in half.'

'Why can't you be both? That was the whole point of the Beatles.'

'They only lasted seven years.'

Natwest shook his head in bemusement. 'So tell me, Mishaal... *My belle*... which are you?'

The mosque came into view at the end of the street. It was a small white building, only two-hundred capacity, but it was topped by a beautiful jade-coloured dome. All of a sudden Mishaal thought of the vast difference between domes and spires.

'That's not for me to say.'

A black Bentley with tinted windows passed by them. 'Look, I think you'll cease to feel like the world is on your shoulders when you stop trying to act like it is. You're not a teenager any-more. It's against your nature, all this, and that's going to cause you real pain, brother. Embrace your inner Chaplin.'

'Spare the khutbah.'

'As it is written in the Qur'an: "It may be that you dislike a thing that is good for you and that you like a thing that is bad for you." I see it all the time during prayer at the mosque. People ask me, "Imam, how should I pray?" and I tell them a story: imagine you were standing on the banks of a lake and you spotted a man in the middle of the water rowing a boat; if you had no conception of physics or how the world works, it may look as though he was using his oars to pull the shore closer to the boat – but in reality it's the other way around, he's pulling *himself* closer to the shore. This is the great mistake people make: they think they are pulling the world – or God, or whatever you believe in – closer to them when they pray – as if *they* could change it. This is all wrong. When you pray you should think of it as pulling *yourself* closer to God.'

Natwest coughed loudly, clearly impatient.

'Do you understand me, Natwest? If you're acting like

74

Keaton, and your true nature is Chaplin—' But he didn't get to finish his point because they'd reached the mosque and Natwest had lowered his end of the lectern to the pavement.

'Is this okay?'

Mishaal patted him on the shoulder. 'That's great. Thank you, Natwest. Peace be upon you.'

Natwest turned away from the lectern and started up the street, appearing no less anxious than before. In a moment of inspiration, and feeling a paternal love towards the boy, Mishaal shouted after him: 'Remember! What is to come will be better than what has gone by! Chaplin!'

Several people stared at the Imam in bewilderment, including his wife Salima, who was standing at the door of the mosque and scowling at him.

'What was that all about?' asked Salima.

'He uh...' Mishaal lay down his burden. 'He was just helping me with this.'

'Where are you bringing it back from?'

Mishaal attempted a nonchalant lean against the lectern. 'I was just... I went over to Reverend Hancock's church.' Salima raised her eyebrows a fraction, and the gesture was a cataclysmic indictment.

'Salima... I... listen...' All at once, Mishaal confessed to his infidelity, described how he'd set up the projector for Caroline, and had stayed to watch the first half hour of *Joan of Arc*. '...but then I left, Salima. I stood up and left.'

When he was finished, his wife put her hands on her hips and sighed.

It was over, thought Mishaal. There would be a row in front of the mosque, he'd be humiliated, lose the respect of his community. Lose his precious wife.

But Salima did no such thing. Instead she held up a plastic bag.

'Here. I knew you wouldn't have time to get dinner.' Mishaal looked inside: Tupperware, a knife and fork, and at the bottom, a chocolate bar. 'And I can tell you're starving. Eat something before prayer – I left a Penguin in there.'

Not for the last time, he marvelled at his wife's extraordinary capacity for forgiveness. Truly a holy woman.

'Thank you, Salima.' He squeezed her hand and removed the Penguin chocolate bar. 'My favourite.' He lifted the fold of the wrapper to find the novelty pun printed on the back of every packet, and read the joke before eating the chocolate.

'Don't leave the Tupperware in the microwave for more than five minutes,' she said.

'Uh-huh.'

'And don't bin the plastic bag, that's the one I use for shopping.'

'Mm.'

'I'm going to pick up Tariq from school.'

'Ah.'

'Are you going to be home late tonight?'

He thought for a moment. 'No. I'll be home right after the workshop.' This seemed to please his wife, and she said her goodbyes amicably and walked away – but not before Mishaal swallowed the remainder of the chocolate and called after her.

'Salima!' She turned around. 'What did the dentist see in Antarctica?'

'Sorry?' His wife leant forward.

'What did the dentist see in Antarctica?'

She paused for a second, then shook her head, 'I'll see you at home.'

He watched her disappear around the corner.

*

M ishaal began to pray. As he went down on his knees he
noticed a single loose thread in the blue carpet. It curled
up and out in a helix, and when he touched his forehead to the
ground it was still in the corner of his eye, taunting him. It was
a reminder that even when worldly things are forbidden, as in
prayer, the world always found a way.

He closed his eyes and in the blackness all around him felt as a
child before God. When it came to reciting a verse of the Qur'an
there was only one in his mind, and silently his mouth made
the shapes that formed the words of An-Nisa 4:3. "...*marry the
women that please you, two or three or four. But if you fear that you
will not be just, then marry only one...*" The blackness around him
muddied, turned brown, then slowly formed the broken walls of
a ruined church. He was seized by a holy vision.

It was the opening of *Joan of Arc*, except Mishaal was standing in a dark corner at the edge of the screen. Water dripped
from the gaps in the roof, and shards of broken glass scattered
at his feet. A figure knelt before the altar, her hair covered by
black cloth, her hands clasped together in supplication.

He called out to her. 'Ingrid! Ingrid!' But she didn't turn
around. Mishaal took another step forward and tried again:
'Ms. Bergman! Ms. Bergman!'

She lowered her hands and slowly rose to her feet; but
when she looked at the Imam, the face wasn't Bergman's, but
his wife's.

'Mishaal,' she said. 'Pray with me.'

As in a film, the image faded out and he returned to the
world. The blackness was ruptured by the variations in brightness through his eyelids as he stood and knelt and prostrated
and stood and knelt and prostrated again. Life was a losing
argument with God, he concluded. His fate was inevitable,
for he could no longer worship more than one thing. He pictured Salima leaving him with a bag of food at the door of the

mosque, and he wished that the people in his life could change, and not he. Why is there only one way to be together, while there are infinite ways to alone? The meaning of the verse he'd been repeating – those words which today had brought together the worldly and the spiritual for a brief moment, only to throw them both back in his face – crystallised in Mishaal's mind. Nothing comes together without loss, and if he were to move forward he had to cut himself in half. Wholeness is an illusion. Synthesis isn't a gain, but a privation.

At least that's what our Imam thought. The choice he'd been debating for sixteen years – really, his whole life – presented itself before him. Caroline or Salima; films or faith – how to be *as* one, and kill off the part of himself he loved the most. God willing, he'd have the courage.

Then it was over and he was kneeling on the carpet, his head bowed. He looked first to the right, then to the left. Opened his eyes. Light.

Seven

Natwest in the Lap

The day had turned cold, and the sky was scattered with low clouds. Those foolish people dressed for the sun looked up, expecting the worst, and Natwest weaved swiftly through them, irritated by the delay. His mother had either opened the package or she hadn't. He felt like the face on the back of a coin being tossed in the air. It could go either way, but the whole thing had a bitter taste of destiny to it, as if the coin had already landed and everybody else knew the result.

Higher Grounds was on the other side of town, and Natwest, an expert at pacing anxiously through the streets, was over halfway there. His detour with Imam Mishaal had been regrettable – principally because the Imam was so keen to imprint an unconvincing worldview on him. It was one of the reasons his Islamic phase had been so brief. For a time, Natwest believed in religion, but not in God. The aesthetics of it, the seriousness of it. But it didn't make him feel any better, and he grew bored of it. Now he believed in art, and not in religion. Had replaced his heavenly idols with more talented ones, like Picasso and Caravaggio.

And really, who did the Imam think he was? Chaplin? Life isn't a cheerful place. Joy is the exception, not the rule. Natwest thought of an example to prove his point: Carracci vs

Caravaggio in the 1600s. There was a reason Carracci, who was a commercial superstar back then – basically McCartney in the 1970s – has been discarded in favour of Caravaggio. Nobody wants to look at an ideal image of life anymore. Consider the Madonna and Child they each painted in Rome in 1605. There's Caravaggio's staggering *Madonna di Loreto*, with its ugly muddied pilgrims kneeling before an ordinary woman – a streetwise Virgin carrying a fat Christ in her arms. Then there's Carracci's *Translation of the Holy House*, an Ideal Mary floating in the clouds with a sweet baby Jesus in her lap – a gentle vision of the world, and an insistence on the *rightness* of life. Today we ignore the Carracci because it's false, thought Natwest, a saccharine invention that has nothing to do with living in the twenty-first century.

The proof is in the online pudding: *Translation of the Holy House* doesn't even have a Wikipedia page.

'Hey, what's up?' The voice came from a familiar figure emerging from Asda with a bag of groceries. A person of – let's say – inconclusive gender. They had long red hair, the colour of cherries. 'It's Natwest, right?'

Natwest had almost collided with them as he walked past, and so had no choice but to respond. 'Yeah, that's me.' He remembered the person's name: Kai, a twenty-year-old non-binary individual with whom he'd partaken in a threesome a few years ago – the two of them sucking off a middle-aged electrician, a lovely man who wrote YA werewolf erotica on the side. 'Listen, uh... I'm just in a bit of a rush. I'm meeting my mum at Higher Grounds, and I don't want to be late, so...'

'Oh cool, my ends. I'm going the same way,' said Kai, now walking alongside him. 'Been a minute, huh?'

'Yeah.' Natwest glanced into Kai's Asda bag and noticed several cartons of eggs.

'Just eggs...' Kai chuckled awkwardly, and blew a lock of hair out of their eyes. 'It's for this dumb event. Basically my older brother's wife is like five months pregnant, and she's absolutely insisted on having this, like, baby-shower-slash-gender-reveal party.' Kai gestured sarcastically at their body. 'Which is very considerate of her.'

'How are they going to reveal the gender?' asked Natwest.

Kai's eyes never appeared to look at anything for longer than a second, which made the conversation feel like it was running incredibly fast. 'So the fucking doctor contacts a bakery and tells them the gender *confidentially*, and then they bake a cake for the expectant mother. Then when she cuts the cake at some big event—'

'The filling is either blue or pink.'

'Exactly,' said Kai. 'And everyone goes, *It's a boy!* or whatever.' Natwest made consolatory noises, as he thought appropriate. In turn, Kai sighed wearily. 'Man, the millennials really failed us. They came up with this shit. It wasn't some ancient custom they brought back into fashion. They *invented* it.'

'Yep. They capitulated,' agreed Natwest. 'Then they became yuppies. Or scuba diving instructors.'

'Google employees...'

'Google employees who scuba on the side.'

Kai grinned, exposing a canyon-sized gap in their front teeth. 'By the way, what gender are you on at the moment?'

'He/Him,' said Natwest, somewhat apologetically. Although he wasn't even sure of that. The truth was, he hated identifying as any one thing – for no identity adequately described the extent of his erudition, his exquisite contradictions, his genius. There was only *one* word that described him fully, and that was: 'Natwest'.

'I identify as Natwest,' he wanted to shout. 'Natwest is my gender! Natwest is my race! Natwest is my sexuality!'

Kai pointed down a side street as the two of them reached

81

a junction. 'You wanna take a shortcut? I'm gonna head down there, it's way quicker.'

Natwest checked the time – which was running out. 'Okay, if it's faster.'

He followed Kai down an alley, where they emerged behind a row of terraced houses.

'My house is just up here. If you cut through my back garden, you'll end up opposite Higher Grounds.'

'Perfect.'

Kai picked up a stick and dragged it along the back of the tall garden fences as they walked by. The panels of the wood were covered in graffiti, and Natwest was unnerved by one insolent tag that said: *the detail of the pattern is amusement*. Equally disconcerting was the drone of the stick as it crawled across the fence. Fortunately, when the two of them finally arrived outside the house, Kai launched the stick into a nearby bush.

'This is my door.' Kai opened the gate and stepped into the back garden, gesturing at Natwest to follow them through.

In the garden, they were not alone. The place was overflowing with people – some kind of event, apparently, because there were dozens of thirty-somethings dressed in white. Balloons were present. *Kings of Leon* was playing. Flower crowns were abundant. In the centre of the garden there was a huge cake laid out on the table.

He realised he was standing in the middle of a gender reveal party, the same one mentioned earlier. He looked over at Kai, seeking some explanation, but they were handing out cartons of eggs to three other ambiguously gendered kids.

'Hi there!'

Natwest turned around. He'd been accosted by a drunk woman.

'I love your style,' she said. 'What do you call that?'

'Call what?'

The drunk woman gestured at the entirety of Natwest.

'Excuse me,' he replied. 'I need to go. . .'

Kai was on the other side of the garden. Natwest made his way over, but before he could say a word a middle-aged woman appeared and grabbed Kai's shoulder. 'Kyle? This is a surprise. . . I hope you've come to support your brother and sister-in-law?'

Kai removed her hand. 'I'm really sorry, Mum.'

'What is it?'

'Hey Kai,' said Natwest, interrupting. 'How do I get to Higher Grounds. . .'

But Kai ignored him and mounted a nearby table. After a significant throat clearing, they made a loud announcement to the collected millennials. 'Hello, everyone! Hello!' The crowd turned to face the table. 'I hereby declare this gender reveal party to be over! Please desist and make an orderly exit out the back door! Continued engagement in this deranged practice will be considered a provocation against me and other members of my community! You should all be ashamed of yourselves! However, you may keep your goodie bags. . .'

'Kyle!' A pregnant woman, presumably the sister-in-law, emerged from the crowd. 'Get down!'

'Sorry, Rosie. Please everyone, the exits are here and here!'

Natwest glanced around the garden. Everyone had stayed put.

'I repeat, the exits are here and here. . .'

Not wishing to be mistaken as an accomplice to Kai's absurd proclamation, Natwest took a step back into the crowd.

'Kyle, for God's sake!' Kai's mother tried to pull them off the table, but she couldn't reach. Rosie turned to her beleaguered husband – a quietly bearded man, who had otherwise remained silent. 'Your fucking brother! Get him down.'

'Last chance, everyone!' said Kai.

Nobody moved, and Natwest wondered how exactly he'd walked into this situation.

Kai sighed loudly, and with much ceremony. 'I'm afraid you've all given me no choice...' They reached into the Asda bag and produced a carton of eggs, then gestured at their three young friends to do the same.

'Kyle...' A look of horror descended upon Rosie's face. 'What are you—'

But Kai ignored her and with a great arching arm, threw the first egg directly at the huge cake in the middle of the garden. It hit the top layer, cracked open, and a perfectly golden yolk ran down the side.

'Kyle!' Rosie screamed.

All at once, the other kids followed suit and began pelting the cake with their own eggs, covering it in goop. Inevitably several missed their target and struck the people in the crowd.

Pandemonium ensued.

Kai's mother climbed onto the table. People were screaming and running for cover, or else trying to wrestle the egg-throwers to the ground. A few egg-splattered people tried to get their own back by catapulting hors d'oeuvres at their assailants. All the while *LMFAO* played over the garden speakers.

'What gender are these babies!' said one of the egg-throwers, launching a perfectly round egg into the stomach of Rosie's bewildered husband.

Natwest dodged several sausage rolls and made for the exit.

'Wait! Natwest, help!' Kai chucked a carton of eggs his way, but Natwest let it fall to the ground, pushing his way through the crowd and fleeing out the back door. The mother caught hold of Kai and began slapping them wildly. Rosie sat dazed in the corner of the garden. Among them all, the drunk woman who'd accosted him earlier was rolling on the grass, laughing hysterically.

Just before Natwest left the garden, he looked back and watched someone grab a handful of the egg-splattered cake and launch it into the throng. Naturally, it landed on Rosie's lap. She looked down at the blue filling streaked across her white dress, and someone shouted:

'It's a boy!'

N atwest finally emerged opposite Higher Grounds. He'd been angry at Kai for dragging him into their family drama, and some part of Natwest felt sorry for Rosie, sat crying in the middle of her ruined party – but now that he'd reached the coffee shop, he grinned at the outrageousness of Kai's actions. He respected the ambition of the assailants, even if eggs were a bit on the nose, aesthetically speaking.

His phone vibrated. As he removed it from his pocket he almost dropped the device – but in a spectacular motion he caught it in mid-air. It was another text from his mother.

Wherer you? Are you coming

It was 3:52 p.m.

I'm on my way. I'll be there in a second.

Her eagerness did not bode well. In all likelihood the package was lying open on the coffee-shop table, and his old colleagues were pointing and laughing. Privacy wasn't a consideration for his mother. It was another language, one that existed for other people. She wanted to know everything about her son, was constantly asking questions like, Where did you go last night? What did you do all day? Is she your girlfriend? When are you going to pack? He was the subject of a twenty-three-year inter-rogation. Worst of all, their relationship was a one-way system. Natwest had his own questions, but he was afraid of asking them. Questions like, What's the deal with Dad? But his mum never volunteered anything, only that his name was Jacob, and he was dead. You didn't have to be an award-winning detective to deduce that what little information she'd told him about the man didn't add up.

For instance:

When Natwest was fourteen he made discoveries. His mother had been out late, and he'd felt an urgent need to make use of her absence. He searched through her bedside cabinet and wasn't disappointed by what he found: a long blue velvet pouch; and inside, a purple dildo, about seven inches in length. He debated for a minute, then capitulated and sniffed its tip. A smell of silicone. Relieved – and a little disappointed – he returned the dildo to the cabinet.

There was another item in the drawer, an unsealed envelope containing a dozen old photographs. They were all of his father having sex with his mother. She was sprawled in various positions, sometimes on her front, her face in the pillow, or on her back with her legs splayed over his father's shoulders. Two close-ups: his mother taking his dad into her mouth, and her breasts covered in his ejaculate – exactly the same kind that carried Natwest when he was only a precocious spermlet.

He flicked through the photos, feeling hot and heavy with guilt, until he reached the final one, a picture of his father, now clothed. He was gazing down into his lap at a fat baby. Natwest knew it was a picture of himself. His mother always said that his father died before he was born, yet here was his dad – face obscured by dark, floppy hair – holding the baby Natwest.

After the discovery, he was at a loss over what to do for the rest of the night. Eventually he put his distress down to adolescent horniness, and so retrieved the velvet pouch from the bedside cabinet, lay down in the bathtub, and using a pot of face moisturiser as lubricant, eased his mother's secret dildo into his arse. However, the photos did raise troubling questions that weren't going to be answered. There was no chance of calling his mother a liar since that would mean admitting to the discovery of the illicit pictures. Once he'd vigorously paced the house, he decided he'd rather live the rest of his life in ignorance, than face the monumental embarrassment of revealing he'd found his mother's nudes. The biography of Natwest would only include a footnote on his father, and that was fine by him, because he considered the man irrelevant to his story.

He crossed the street and approached Higher Grounds. It was busy in the café, which was perfect because he didn't want to talk to any of his old colleagues. He'd quit at the beginning of the summer, the day he'd received his offer from university, after working there part-time for four years. During his tenure, he'd seen so many people his age pass through – coming back or going to university – he didn't have enough fingers to count them. He was always the oldest.

The building had large floor-to-ceiling windows that allowed you to see inside from the pavement, and he spotted his mother at the back wearing her hair down and sitting opposite a bald guy – presumably a date. This meant there would be small talk, mention of his university plans, his mother calling him a *late bloomer*. It would be humiliating.

Before stepping inside, Natwest checked for messages on his phone – and naturally the device fell to the ground, adding a range of new and interesting patterns to the cracked screen. He cursed his ill luck and stamped angrily at the useless pavement, noticing a small piece of eggshell on the toe of his shoe. You would think there was a plot against him. In despair, he glanced up at the sky, still low, still threatening rain, and wondered if there was anyone up there of interest – Islamic or otherwise – and if they even cared about his crisis.

Eight

Give Lilies with Full Hands

T he fact was, Penny wanted a dog. It had come on gradually, this desire. For her whole life she'd lived canine-free, had never considered the possibility of owning one, had even stored up a certain resentment for the mothers her age who'd replaced their children with the creatures. Yet the day her son secured a place at university, at the beginning of summer, the cravings started. She needed something else to pour her extraordinary energy into, and this morning – like thousands of middle-class mothers before her – she realised that the answer was a dog. It was a disappointment. From her impoverished childhood on the outskirts of Liverpool – the violent estate, the absent mother, the sexually abusive stepfather, etcetera etcetera – to a small-to-medium-sized designer dog. She had become one of them. Even the growing puddle of drool on her pillow attested to it, because to her sleep-deprived eyes its shape undoubtedly resembled a dachshund on its hind legs, leaping out of her mouth.

She wiped the pool dry with the back of her hand.

Good morning, Penny.

She rolled out of bed and breezed past the mirror, then doubled back to admire the view.

Looking good.

Hair impeccably dyed, eyes cosmetically desagged, teeth

present and correct. The angles of her body had changed, but she looked damn good for her age. As she descended the stairs in her orange nighty, she debated which breed of dog would appropriately match her indomitable spirit. In the hallway at the bottom, her son was pacing back and forth. She took a moment to admire his pretty face against the lily wallpaper – and was quickly defeated by the urge to preserve him. She lifted her iPhone and snapped a discreet photo.

'Natwest, what are you hanging around the door for?' she said, lowering the device.

'It's almost eleven. You're up late.'

It was true – she'd had a lie in. She'd asked for the day off work because it was her son's final day in town, and she wanted to spend it with him. She had the whole thing planned: they would memorialise his departure by rescuing a dog together.

'Wanted to be here for your last hurrah,' she said.

While she made herself a cup of tea, Natwest explained something about a missing package.

'Why didn't you order it when you got to university?'

'I know,' he said, oddly forceful. Penny's curiosity was piqued. So what exactly was in this package?

'It's okay. I'll post it up,' she said.

Natwest shook his head. 'I'm going to the post office to see if they've got it.'

'But have you checked with Joan?'

She took great pleasure in watching her son follow her instructions, for in the next minute he was gone. 'Have you had breakfast?' she called after him. 'Do you want some toast? You need to pack!' As the door slammed in the hall, she nursed her mug of tea and rehearsed the words she'd say to him on his return:

'That was quick.'

'She had the package right there.'

'So I was thinking. . . how about we go to the rescue centre?'

'What?'

'We can pick up a dog together!'

'Mum. . .'

'It will be fun.'

He would make some comment about being replaced, and she would take it with commendable good humour – 'Nothing could ever replace you, Natwest. . . except maybe a dachshund!' Then he'd laugh, 'I suppose it would be fun. . .' Yes, they would get ready for the afternoon together, pick up a dog, have lunch, attend Richard's exhibition in the evening. It would be a perfect final day.

She rose and placed four slices of bread in the toaster – two for her, and two for her son. Yet when the toast had popped up, he still hadn't returned. Even after she'd buttered the toast, even after the toast had gone hard and cold and she'd scraped the slices into the bin, he still hadn't returned. Then it dawned on her that he was never going to come back home, that Natwest's plan for his final day had nothing to do with her. Why had she been so foolish as to think it would? It was devastating. She settled into the empty sofa in the living room feeling like the butt of a cruel joke. She had never been able to fully consider the implications of her son's departure for university, had been pushing it off in her mind for months. But the future had arrived at last, and her son was gone – and now the rest of her life appeared radically foreshortened in his absence. She was finally alone.

Brring!

She grabbed her phone and stared at the incoming call.

A video call. From Facebook messenger.

It was Clive.

He was an old flame from the miserable, impoverished past which she'd put to bed when she turned up in this Midlands town twenty-three years ago, heavily pregnant with her son. They'd been together five years, from the ages of seventeen to twenty-two, a relationship which ended with her unexpected pregnancy. Now he was calling her, despite them having no contact with each other for twenty years – except the occasional Facebook like and a single (black?) thumbs-up emoji on her birthday three years ago.

What could Clive possibly want?

After a pause, she accepted the video request.

The first thing she saw was his chin, in dreadful close-up. Then the video signal cracked, froze, and flicked aggressively up the left nostril of the man she'd once loved.

'Penny?'

'Clive? What are you—'

'I'm driving, sorry – fuck! – sorry, prick cut me off...' The image on-screen shook violently with the motion of the vehicle, making Penny feel a little motion sick. 'Listen, Penny,' he continued, 'I'm in town for the day. On a business trip. What are you...' Clive began to break up, and his words came through in pauses and splutters. 'What... doing later?... want to meet... something to talk to you about... old times' sake?' The screen froze on a scrambled image. 'What do you think?' the disembodied voice said. 'You free today?'

'Clive, I—' But there was a horrible clicking sound and the signal died completely.

The call hung up. She put the phone down.

What the hell to make of that?

Penny's life was constructed of a series of delicate, contradictory desires. She'd always wanted to be middle-class – ever since she was a girl – to be seen as having *something* rather than nothing. But when she got it, she realised she could never go back – and so began to loathe the other middle-class women her age, and the dreadful dinner parties they hosted, and the endless talk of travel they indulged in. She'd worked tremendously hard to leave her past behind, and yet whenever she socialised with her posh friends, she found herself desperate to explain her background, to demonstrate how different she was from them (yet she always held her tongue, wanting to fit in at all times). It was impossible, this push and pull. And the worst of all these contradictions was that she loved her son more than life itself, only ever wanted the best for him – but she despised what the best had made him into: a pretentious, spoilt, ungrateful brat. Now, after the cruel rejection from Natwest this morning, she'd been offered an opportunity out of the Facebook blue to reconnect with her past – the same past she'd worked so hard to erase any trace of from herself and, above all else, from her ungrateful son.

So what to do?

She paced several laps around the house, then messaged Clive and accepted the invitation.

A few hours later, Clive pulled up in his van. The most prominent feature of the vehicle was an unsightly logo emblazoned on its side and large red letters that said, mysteriously: RE:HEAT. Clive was having trouble parallel parking – he would reverse a few inches, then pull forward, then attempt the whole operation again. She watched him fail from across the street, this old friend who expressed emotion through the time-honoured method of punching the steering wheel.

'Ah, Penny... Hi,' he said, rolling down the window as she approached the van.

She finally got to see his face in person. There was still the famous scar curling around his earlobe – though fainter now, more like a wrinkle – and where he'd once cut his hair short, he was now unfortunately bald.

'Don't worry about parking, Clive. I'll hop in and we can drive to the rescue centre.'

'Rescue centre? I thought we were getting a coffee.'

Penny climbed into the passenger seat. 'I was planning on rescuing a dog today. I'd already made the arrangements when I got your call, sorry.'

Poor Clive looked bewildered. 'Relax, we can chat on the way,' she said.

Clive scratched his head and squinted at her. 'Alright, I suppose.' Reluctantly he put the van into gear and they set off.

'It's nice to see you, Pen,' he said.

Pen. It had been many years since she'd been called that. Taken by surprise, she stumbled over her next words.

'It's – it's been a while, hasn't it?'

'Yeah.' He paused a moment, apparently at a loss for what to say. 'And you've got a son?'

She nodded.

'I'll be honest Pen, I never thought you'd have the kid with—'

'He's twenty-three now. He's going to university tomorrow.'

'Oh... Congratulations.' Clive sort of furrowed his brow. 'You didn't want to spend the day with him?'

'We're going to an event later, so... I...' She was seized by an urge to sneeze.

Don't do it, Penny.

Don't—

She sneezed three times, each one louder than the last.

'Bless you.'

She wiped her nose and glanced at Clive, who was staring, unblinking, at the road ahead. 'Is this your van, Clive?'

'Yeah. Well, company van. I should probably—'

Fuck.

She sneezed again, and attempted to hide her besnotted appearance by covering her face with both hands.

'You don't have hay fever do you?'

'Only in summer,' she mumbled.

'Right. . . I should probably explain, we purchased this van from a florist, and no matter how much we clean it. . .' – she sneezed again – '. . .we can't get rid of the pollen. So basically it's permanently summer in this van. Sorry about that.' He clicked open the glove compartment in front of her. Inside were a dozen boxes of tissues.

'Thank you.' She blew her nose.

Clive looked out the corner of his eye. 'So go on then Pen, how you been? Over twenty years, isn't it?'

'Something like that.'

'Mad. Feels like yesterday, though.'

She shook her head. Not for her. 'Clive, what did you want to talk to me about?'

He shifted in his seat, glanced in the rear-view mirror. 'Maybe we should sit down somewhere.'

'We are sitting down.' She pointed at a turn in the road, 'Left here.'

'Alright, well. . .' He cleared his throat. 'I've got a little business proposition for you. . .'

'Business proposition?'

'That's right.'

He turned towards her, suddenly very serious. 'Pen, tell me what you do with your leftover food?'

'Excuse me?'

'What do you do with your leftovers?'

'Is this the set-up of a joke?'

'No. It's—'

'Stop. Hold it.' She pointed at a convenient parking spot opposite the rescue centre. 'I see a space – that one there.'

*

Clive helped her out of the van and surprised her with a pat on the arse as she closed the door.

'Clive!'

'Oh. . . we're not doing that now, are we?'

'We're not kids anymore. Fortunately for you I'm going to turn the other cheek.' And she wiggled her bum at him. She was pleased to discover that her once legendary posterior was still an effective tool, because as they crossed the street and walked towards the entrance, Clive repeated his question in a newly breathless voice.

'What do you do with your leftover food?' he asked.

'Hold on.' She raised a finger and sneezed again. 'Sorry, continue.'

'What do you do with your leftover food?'

'Depends. . .'

'Let me guess. You put it in Tupperware – or whatever your food storage brand of choice is – right?'

He waited eagerly for her response. So it wasn't a joke. He'd really got in touch to make a sales pitch.

'Sometimes I use Tupperware, Clive, yeah,' she replied.

'And what's the main issue with your food storage?'

'My issue is usually the food inside,' she quipped.

The response caused him to falter. 'No. . . No. The main issue is that you can't put hot food into a Tupperware container. You have to let it go cold first – this means about twenty minutes of waiting for your food to cool down. Well, what would you say if I told you there was a new line of food storage products that could withstand any temperature – up to two hundred degrees?'

She shrugged.

'A whole world opens up, Pen. It means food straight out the pan and into the container. Sizzling stir-fry? No problem. Hot soup? Pour it in. We've practically defeated heat.'

The automatic doors slid open and they entered the rescue centre. Penny went to the front desk and gave her name and details. She looked around the waiting room – it was packed with middle-aged mothers, similar in every outward aspect to her, all waiting to be called up by the centre's volunteers to choose a dog.

'Let me introduce a game-changing range of food storage containers,' Clive was saying. '"Reheat", spelt "re:heat" – that's important. Doesn't the name make you want to invest? Isn't it genius? This is what everyone's going to be talking about in a few years. Think about the internet. Nobody knew it was going to blow up, and now you can't get away from it. I bet you wish you'd invested in Google back then. Well, this is your second chance. This is the next internet – in food-storage terms – so if you want be part of the next big thing. . .'

Poor Clive. As a young man he'd had many registers of speech, but desperation wasn't one of them. Where was the confident boy who took her arm and led her proudly down Church Street, who punched Paddy McGill in the face when he called her a slag? It was wretched to hear him so eager for approval now. She easily conjured up images of Clive's life. The plastic kettle. The sealed-up cat flap. The chippy paper in the sink. The fat girlfriend he fucked on weekends. He'd been an attractive boy but had grown into a lonely and defeated man. It was evident in the way he glanced nervously at the other women in the waiting room, the way he pounced at the offer of free coffee when the volunteer offered it, the way he poured three sugars into the polystyrene cup.

Apparently re:heat wasn't even his business. But don't worry, he said, it was well into the 'concept stage'. They simply needed to get investors involved. He had already invested ten thousand pounds of his own money to be a part of it.

'It sounds like a Ponzi scheme, Clive.'

'The fuck you on about?' And here his famous temper flared

up for the first time that day. 'I'm not a ponce, and this isn't a poncy scheme. I'm proud to be a man who's invested in a cooking product. It's the bloody twenty-first century.'

'A *Ponzi* scheme. It's when. . .' She attempted to explain it, but found that she wasn't quite sure of the specifics herself – only that it always ended in catastrophe.

Still, he refused to listen. He said he'd met the inventor, seen the designs – 'they've got an office in London!'

How was it that they'd come from the same place, been raised on the same estate, gone to the same school, and yet turned out so different? He'd had so many wild ideas as a young man. He was going to change the world. Make it a more equitable place. Somehow get rich in the process. But the few times he'd managed to put one foot on the bottom rung of a white-collar ladder, he'd blown it. Because of his anger, and his inability to hide his contempt for the people working above him. Was it any wonder that she'd grown impatient with his outsized ambition and repeated failures – and eventually found herself in the bedroom of another man?

Clive burnt his tongue on the coffee and swore. 'Fuck. Sorry. Anyway, what do you say?'

'No, Clive. Not for me.'

'Really? What's five grand to you? You're in the money now.'

She narrowed her eyes a little, annoyed at the comment. 'Clive, I'm not interested. My son's just about to go to university, I'm not throwing away money I worked hard for.'

'You're not throwing anything away. I'm not joking here. This is a proper breakthrough, Tupperware-wise. . .'

'Even if it's not a Ponzi scheme, it's a stupid idea, Clive—'

'Plastic Tupperware can actually *melt* in the microwave. Our containers can withstand up to two hours—'

'Who would want to put something in the microwave for two hours?'

He closed his eyes in frustration and for a moment looked younger than he was.

'Okay, Penny... what if I say please?'

She said nothing, simply observed the vein that had begun bulging in his neck.

'No? Please, Pen?'

She shook her head again, and then Clive threw up his hands in anger – 'Fuck it.' – and stormed out of the rescue centre.

The waiting area was sterile and oppressive. It was dominated by a sad fish tank in the corner, somewhat inconsistent with the project of a rescue centre. The blue of the walls was broken up by numerous framed photographs of dogs and, less frequently, cats. The canine/feline ratio on the walls was perhaps 4:3, but this split wasn't accurately reflected in the number of mothers who emerged from behind a heavy red door, invariably carrying a dog in their arms.

Penny was disturbed by the interaction with Clive, not least because it made her think of her voice. She must sound completely different to him. The day she moved to this town she had put on an invisible regionally neutral voice, and it had stuck. Now if she tried to go back to her Scouse accent it sounded like a parody. She'd successfully erased herself and been rewarded by rising improbably up the social classes. She had wanted to impress this fact on him, to show how different she'd become. But now she was embarrassed by it, this new life of hers. To him, she was a traitor and a fool, and the business with the dog had only made it worse. She'd hoped the trip to the rescue centre would be a way of deflecting the awkwardness between them – but in fact it had unmasked her. Sitting in this room, she was just as hollow as these other middle-class mothers. She'd been so quick to cast Clive as the desperate wreck, but perhaps in his eyes it was the other way around.

A horrible thought.

She recognised a familiar face in the waiting room. A short, delicate girl with glasses and a blonde fringe – someone from Natwest's schoolyear, apparently making every effort to avoid Penny's impressive eye contact.

'Zoë? Zoë?'

Zoë smiled weakly. 'Hey, nice to see you.'

'Are you getting a dog too?'

'I'm picking up my mum. She's in there choosing one at the moment.'

Penny nodded sympathetically. 'So how have you been? What are you up to now? Have you seen Natwest recently? He's going to university tomorrow, did you know?'

Zoë appeared to shrink behind her fringe. 'Um... My master's starts next week—'

'Oh, I thought you'd finished?'

'My second master's,' said Zoë, before adding sheepishly, 'I know, I'm terrible.'

Penny nodded in agreement; she was terrible. At her age, Penny was working two jobs after leaving school at sixteen. She suppressed an overwhelming desire to tell Zoë about it.

'You know Natwest's still in town?' she said. 'What are you doing for the rest of the day?'

'Meeting my boyfriend for dinner,' replied Zoë tersely.

'Oh... that's a shame.'

Zoë's mother emerged from the red door carrying a little white dog. She smiled at Penny, and Penny tried her best to act enthused.

'Oh, I love a Bichon Frise!'

For a moment everything seemed to stop. She'd said something wrong, obviously, because Zoë's mother covered her mouth and let out a humiliating little laugh at Penny's expense.

'It's called a Bichon Frisé,' explained Zoë. 'Not a Bitch-on-Fries.'

'Oh – I – Yes—' She tried to laugh it off, but the damage was done. Zoë gave her a sympathetic nod, then took the dog in her arms, and she and her mother hastily said their goodbyes and walked off – effortlessly posh. Just poor scum to them, Penny thought, and heaved herself back into the waiting room chair, depressed.

Idiot.

She gently tore at her nails, nibbled the inside of her cheek until she tasted blood.

Oh, he was here again.

She looked up at Clive, re-entering the waiting room, car keys peeking out from behind a clenched fist.

'Look...' he took a seat next to her, 'I'm sorry about all that.' His right foot tapped the ground in the spaces between his sentences. 'I've had another idea—'

'Clive...'

'Listen. Don't worry about investing in re:heat, I've got a better proposition... How about you get involved in an, uh, administrative capacity. I think I can wangle it with the other investors. What do you think?'

This time she tried a more sympathetic tone. 'Even if it's not a Ponzi scheme, Clive, I'm not interested in anything like that. Sorry.'

'Pen, it could be—'

'No, I'm sorry. I'm sorry you had to come all the way down here to hear that.'

Her old friend looked despondent. 'Pen... it's not fair. I could never get a decent start.'

'Fair?'

101

'Yeah, it's not fair.'

'It was just as hard for me,' she replied bitterly.

Still not convincing enough for some.

'So don't try that pity shit here,' she added.

Clive opened his mouth to respond, but he had nothing. He hung his head. When he finally looked up again, he couldn't make eye contact, only stared past her at the tropical fish glitching in the fish tank.

He muttered something under his breath.

'What is it, Clive?'

'Look at that thing.' He pointed at one of the decorative objects in the fish tank – a tiny model house, made entirely of glass.

'What about it?'

'It's so small,' he said. 'But look at the little details. It's really well done.'

She watched a single yellow fish dart in, and then back out of the doorway of the tiny house. It made her think of her own childhood home, the flat supplied by the council, which she'd grown up in and which she'd left far behind. She wasn't interested in engaging in a misery Olympics where people shirked responsibility for their lack of willpower by blaming their present condition on the misfortunes of their past. And yet sitting here with Clive, staring at the little glass house, it was all coming back to her. The memories poured in as if from another body. There was her estate. The low ceiling of her childhood bedroom. The corridors of her school. Her mum sticking her head in the oven, trying to turn the gas knob with a free hand – and failing comically, just turning the light on and off, on and off. Then there was the communion bench – she was terrified of kneeling, afraid people would notice the holes in her shoes. Her memory was a needle skating across a record, emerging in scratches and pops, before finally slipping into a groove: the concrete walkways of her childhood home, the past, and the things that went on there.

'You okay?' asked Clive.

'Yeah. Just remembering. . .' She glanced again at the little glass house in the fish tank. 'You want it?' she said.

'What do you mean?'

But she'd already rolled up her sleeve, driven by some insane instinct to shock the other people in the room. She reached into the fish tank and removed the glass house, taking a great deal of pleasure in the mortified looks of the other mothers. They had been deceived by Penny's outward appearance. She was not one of them.

She handed the glass house to Clive. 'Here.'

He shook the water from the object, then grinned for the first time that day.

'Thanks, Pen.'

As he pocketed the little glass house, a volunteer appeared at the red door and waved them over.

'Penny? You can come in now.'

The room had the appearance of a playground. Kennels lined the walls – not the steel cages seen in films, but rather a series of containers painted in bright colours – and in each one stood a dog in one of many possible stages of unhappiness.

Penny was immediately drawn to a small dachshund crouched in the corner, missing an ear.

'He was found on the side of the road. Still a puppy,' the volunteer said.

She crouched to get a closer look. The dachshund responded by cautiously approaching her hand.

What a lovely little thing.

Natwest would love you.

She pictured herself introducing it to him – and imagined Natwest expressing sincere remorse that he'd missed the opportunity to pick up the dog himself.

'Hello there,' she said, and the dachshund began burying his tiny head in her hands.

Just then a jealous mastiff in an adjoining kennel barked ferociously at the two of them, and she jumped back, alarmed.

'It's okay,' said the volunteer, but the mastiff continued to roar at the small dog. The dachshund quietly retreated to its corner.

'Poor boy,' said Clive. 'What do you think, Pen? He's cute, no?'

'Yes...' But in fact the opposite thought had occurred to her. The little creature was repulsive. The way it cowered in the presence of the mastiff, its dismal expression, its pathetic whimpering. 'No. Not that one,' she said.

'Why?' Clive bent down and offered the dachshund a hand. 'Look... he likes me.' Once again the little dog approached the front of the kennel, but the mastiff resumed its fierce barking, then began shaking madly and launching itself at the bars between them.

'Oi!' Clive's temper flared up. 'Leave him alone!' he shouted at the mastiff.

The mastiff returned Clive's anger, now barking directly at him – and more generally at the world.

Clive kicked the kennel, 'Piss off.'

'Sir, can you—'

'Clive, it's okay. I think we should go.' Penny pulled him to his feet.

'You should do something about that one,' said Clive. 'It's not fair on the other dogs.'

The mastiff continued barking – and to make matters worse,

the canine apparently had some authority in the rescue centre, because several other dogs joined him.

Fuck.

They were all barking now.

The volunteer tried shouting over the din, 'Don't worry, this is normal! They'll calm down in a minute!' but his words were inadequate in the presence of sixty dogs howling in anger.

It was unbearable. 'Can you please get them to stop!' she shouted, breathless.

'It's all normal, don't worry yourself!'

'Bloody hell,' muttered Clive. 'You alright, Pen?' He touched her arm, and she realised she was shaking.

'Please. . . Can you make them. . .'

'It's all normal!'

'Please. . .' But she couldn't hear herself think; in fact she only noticed the hot tears spring to her eyes when Clive wiped them away – at which point she pushed him off and fled from the room.

You're an embarrassment, Penny.

She splashed cold water on her face and reprimanded herself in the bathroom mirror.

You've humiliated yourself again.

First in front of Zoë's mother, then in front of Clive. She was always stuck in-between two unwinnable situations – in-between two unwinnable classes – and she was either an imposter or a traitor. It wasn't fair.

With a shaky hand she reapplied her makeup, cursing every few seconds to herself. God knows what Clive thought of her now. In her pocket, her phone vibrated.

Hi Penny. I saw Natwest at the post office today and I believe we got our parcels mixed up. Silly me! I'll bring it to the exhibition later. You can tell him to pick it up then and he can give me mine. See you soon!

Poor Natwest. She pictured him now, walking around town, searching in vain for the package. The truth was she was glad when her son failed his exams and had to stay home for a few more years. She would still be glad if he never left. That was simply the kind of mother she was – and it was better than no mother. Under her shirt, she touched the long scar above her pubis where they'd performed the emergency C-section – naturally, Natwest's head had been too big for a natural birth. She considered how much of her body was really a history of her son. How every scar on it mapped a different trauma. Why didn't joy leave traces on skin? Why couldn't her body express what her son really meant to her?

It didn't matter anyway. He'd left her behind. Just as she'd left her past behind.

Penny took one last look in the mirror, then left the bathroom and returned back to Clive in the Higher Grounds café.

'Here we are.' A waiter placed the mugs down as she took a seat.

'Ta,' said Clive. He peered at the foam flower outlined in the steamed milk.

'Think this is yours, Pen.' He swapped the mugs around. 'You should be made up with that.'

She stared at the flower drawn in the latte, then picked up a sugar cube and dropped it in, defacing the image.

'So what are you planning—'

'Sorry Clive, give me a minute.'

An idea.

She had an idea to make up for the humiliation in the rescue centre. It was suddenly imperative that her old friend – the past – bear witness to her son, who was the only future that mattered.

She sent Natwest a text.

> Doctor hung texted me and said that he has a parcel and you have his one. Come and see me im with my friend at your coffee shop!

She looked up from her phone. Clive was smiling generously at her.

'Penny for your thoughts?' he said.

'My son. . .' She sent Natwest another message.

> I've got the package now x

A lie. But it would get him here as soon as possible. As for the dentist's package, she'd make up some excuse when Natwest arrived – it wasn't like he was doing anything useful today.

'My son might be popping over later.'

'You were saying he's an artist?'

'Studying art.'

'Right, course.' He smirked to himself. 'Of all the people, I didn't think you'd have a kid with *Jacob*. Though I suppose he was always so good with the ladies. . . All that la-di-da floppy hair business. As I discovered myself. . .' He squinted at her. 'His family is all grown up and everything now, you know? One of the kids is running to be a local councillor up in Liverpool.'

'I've heard.'

'You told your son about him?'

She shook her head.

'Don't blame you. Must be hard to tell a boy that he was just, uh. . . you know, the accident of an affair.'

Bastard.

Uttering the truth out loud.

It was terrible to hear so plainly, but he was right. How *could* she tell Natwest that he was the illegitimate child of an affair? It would be telling him that he wasn't intentional, that he was not significant to his father – or worse, that he was an inconvenience. All things that were in fact true. And what would he think of her? A slut? So she'd lied to her son, said that his father had died before he was born – it seemed like the kindest thing to do at the time. And now that Natwest was old enough to know better, she couldn't bring herself to tell him the truth. She had unwittingly continued her family's terrible legacy of secrets. From what her stepfather did to her behind closed doors from the age of six to fourteen, to this. She'd failed to break the cycle. Perhaps that was why she was so keen on finding out everything about Natwest – searching his room, opening his mail, glancing at his phone over his shoulder. She wanted there to be no secrets between them, but she wasn't brave enough to break her own silence.

A loud car alarm sounded outside the café.

They both turned to look: it was Clive's re:heat van, and the culprit was the car parked in front, a black Bentley with tinted windows that had just backed into his van as it turned out of the parking space.

'Shit!'

Clive jumped up to do something, but the offending vehicle had already disappeared up the road.

'It's bloody driven off.'

It was the funniest thing, his face as he shouted after the car – as if the driver could hear him from outside the café.

She pulled him back into his seat and laughed. He looked frustrated for a second, then grinned and pointed his car keys at the flashing van to stop the alarm. This tiny gesture was enough.

And she softened a little. 'I might not seem it, but I'm really glad you called me this morning, Clive.'

He laughed. 'Really? I've been waiting for you to say that all day.' He shook his head in amazement. 'Twenty-three years, Pen...'

'We were so young,' she said.

'We were.'

And like that he began to talk of the past, and she joined him – making sure to discuss only the pleasant memories they shared, and omitting anything that might cause the other harm. There was the famous episode in the bowling alley, when Clive won £50 for bowling ten strikes in a row, then spent it all on one delicious night with her. Or the time they fucked on a mini-golf course, but were discovered by the furious manager, and so ran half-naked, freezing, past the miniature windmills and fake volcanoes.

'I think my knickers are still buried under the bridge of the second hole...'

Clive chuckled. 'You know, Pen... me and you...' He ran a hand over his skull. 'I know I blew it when we were together. I know why you... did what you did with Jacob... and whoever else. But I still feel like we never got a fair shot at being together.'

'Fair shot?'

'Well, we were so young... I didn't know what I was doing.'

Don't say it, Clive.

Please.

She had a feeling she knew what was coming, and so she avoided his eyes and stared at the bottom of the empty coffee mug, where tiny grains of coffee had settled into the remains of the foam.

'Remember that first night—'

'Of course,' she said, embarrassed, trying to get him to move on. She checked the time – almost four o'clock – and sent another text to Natwest.

Wherer you? Are you coming

'It was good while it lasted, wasn't it?' he said, and placed a hand over hers.

She winced. 'It was.'

'It's been so many years, but it still feels like it was yesterday, you know?'

'You already said that.'

'Well, it's true,' he replied. 'Don't you think?'

No.

She didn't.

But was that. . . tears in his eyes?

This was new. When Clive was younger, he never would have cried. Now his eyes had moistened, like an old man's, and he suddenly appeared frail and small in the high-backed chairs of the coffee shop.

'Clive, the past is the past. It's not like. . .' – she couldn't resist – 'it's not like reheating something in Tupperware, you know? You can't bring it back to life.'

'You're so funny. . .' He sighed, then squeezed her hands.

'You don't have to—'

'Listen, I've been thinking about you for a while.' He leant forward, his lips wet. 'I really think we should—'

She pulled her hands away. 'Okay, I'll invest!' Anything to delay a confession of love. She'd felt his shaking hands, seen how absurd this whole situation was.

'Penny? You really mean that?' But he waved a dismissive hand at his own comment. 'I don't care about the Tupperware. We can have another shot at this. Just to see what happens, you know? I can stay in town all week, you hear me?'

He'd really said it. Out loud. This was the actual purpose of the trip; not a business proposition, but a romantic one. She felt herself flush red. Looked at Clive's hands, stretched out across the table, waiting for a response.

Then he arrived. At last. She couldn't explain it, but Penny felt his presence in the room, and she stood up before she'd even seen him. 'Natwest! Natwest!' She turned to explain: 'He likes to be called that.' Clive followed her gaze to the door, where her son had just appeared. 'Natwest!' She called out to him across the coffee shop.

And there he was.

She heard Clive grunting in the background, noticed him retracting his hands and hiding them in his pockets.

Good.

This was her son. The evidence of her success. Her future. He had sucked his thumb until he was ten. Gave up sleeping in her bed when he was eleven. Collapsed in her arms when he didn't make it to university (and she'd been so grateful, in that moment, that he didn't have to leave her). He came out through her belly. Almost killed her. Made sure there would never be another to follow him. He was *her* son. Her only chance at a second life. How can you love someone so completely that the very thought of them makes you desperately sad and deliriously happy, all at once? That was the real contradiction, and nothing compared. She certainly didn't need a dog to replace him. And she didn't need Clive either. Who needed anything of that sort when she had a son who'd come when she had called? Who'd returned to her one last time? And just then a funny thought popped into her head: having children is exactly like a Ponzi scheme. You invest everything you have, and it all comes crashing down in the end when they leave you. But in the moment none of that matters – because at its height, the world is in your hands.

Natwest walked over to her, and she reached out.

Nine

Natwest Gets Wet

His mother was crying, and as expected it was Natwest's fault. Presumably that was the point she was trying to make by wailing in public and generally making everyone feel uncomfortable. But in Natwest's mind it wasn't entirely his doing – or at least they both deserved a share of the blame for the spectacle that was currently unfolding in Higher Grounds.

First he'd turned away from his mother when she tried to embrace him, then he'd been rude to the bald guy, Clive, who was sitting with her. When she'd tried to get them to talk to one another – which by the way Clive did not seem particularly keen on – Natwest ignored her and asked where the package was. Turns out his mother had lied, and he became angry and swore at her. Then the crying began.

'I'm sorry, Mum. . .' Natwest prepared to calm her down with the principal weapon in his arsenal, a generous hug. 'Come here.'

But he was too late, because Clive had blocked him off and was already wrapping a lascivious arm around her. He tutted in Natwest's direction.

'You ought to be nicer to your mum. You've only got the one, you know.'

'Mum, please.' All around Higher Grounds, eyes scrutinised

his next move. The café's Spotify had an annoying habit of privileging living singers over dead ones, which meant the whole scene was drowned in a deluge of contemporary R&B exhorting his mother to be a strong and sexually active woman.

'It was an overreaction,' apologised Natwest. 'It's just a package. I'm sorry I exploded like that... but why say you had it when you didn't?'

'She already told you it was her bloody predictive text. Weren't you listening?'

His mother balled up her fists and pressed them to her face, like van Gogh's *Weeping Woman*. 'It was the predictive text,' she mumbled.

'Mum, I'm sorry.'

'I think it's best you go,' said Clive, and he took a moment to stroke her shoulder, clearly indicating his lecherous intentions. Natwest inwardly cursed the bald man. He was reminded of the photos of his father making love to his mother, now perversely mirrored by this stranger. He felt something like jealousy on behalf of his dad, this supposedly dead man he'd never met.

'I'll go when I want to,' he snapped at Clive.

'Natwest! Don't be rude,' said his mother through tears.

'I'm not, I...'

And like that, Natwest realised his good fortune. It was in fact a terrific thing that she'd lied about the package, because it confirmed that it wasn't in her possession. The possibility of his humiliation had diminished – if only for a little while – and he changed his tone.

'Okay, okay, you're right. I think I'm going to go. Sorry Clive. Sorry Mum.' By the till, his ex-colleagues nodded solemnly in his direction. 'I'll see you later, Mum, okay?'

'Okay,' she sniffed.

When he was out on the street he looked back into the café. Clive was embracing his mother, mouthing something into her ear, grinning to himself. Natwest thought of the other *Weeping Woman*, the oil painting by Picasso. You can see a mother crying from a hundred different angles in that piece. It demonstrated the nightmare of too much perspective.

T he rain came on suddenly. A few umbrellas emerged, but mostly people sheltered under the shopfront awnings or pretended not to notice they were getting wet. In the downpour, everyone looked foolish. A builder in a high-vis jacket shook his fist at the sky. A mother struggled to raise the hood on a pram. An empty pint glass filled up. A crate of books outside a charity shop soaked. Two Indian men argued ferociously by the fish and chip shop; above them a sign: ONLY COD FORGIVES.

It was so beautiful, all this foolishness. It seemed to say: 'Life goes on.' The unbearable weight of the package had lifted for a little while. There was an hour and a half until the exhibition and thirty spare minutes until his dinner with Georgie; for the first time today, he felt free. It was cinematic. All manner of unrealities had converged for this one moment, and the world responded with a boy in a passing car, who offered a thumbs up through the window. Natwest returned the thumb. The word that came to mind was: 'Heroic'. He was a hero in this town, if only for his extraordinary capacity to feel free on a day like this. He strolled through the rain, humming the Gene Kelly song.

Isn't it wonderful, joy?

But precious.

And probably the most brittle emotion.

The issue with joy is that it creates anxiety that the joy is going to diminish – which of course makes it diminish. His joy was a dead end, in practical terms. Already it was waning. Sometimes he thought his brain was playing a chess match against itself, joy and despair taking turns to steal a piece before either one could take a strong lead.

e.g. He was getting wet. It was freezing outside.

Advantage black.

There was some trepidation about seeing Georgie again. Their last meeting ended with a spectacular fight over a mutual friend, a bespectacled posho known as Zoë – with an umlaut.

Natwest had experimented with her.

Vigorously.

Because he enjoyed the company of women too, a fact which Georgie found troubling. 'I'm glad you can finally be happy. With a cunt,' he'd said. To which Natwest had replied:

'A: sex with a woman is much more convenient, position-wise. You should try it some time. You just dip in and out.'

'So what, she's like a fucking wheel of Camembert?'

'And B: women's bodies are objectively superior. And that's a nice change.'

Georgie screamed at him. Kept screaming until Natwest left the room.

As teenagers, they had confused an exhausting relationship with a passionate one. In their case, the highlights were all sexual – giving each other head in the school toilets, touching each other at the back of class while Mrs. Pandey droned on about Wilfred Owen, the first bareback fuck in his mother's bed when she was out shopping – while the lows were psychological; mainly Georgie's problems, of which there were many. His worst trait was that he was enormously insecure about his body. Like everyone else. And he wasn't even fat. He was Kate Moss, in Rubensian terms.

Yet the hatred of his body was linked to his sexuality in ways that were hard for Natwest to untangle. You would fuck him,

115

and then ten minutes later he'd want to hurt himself. At least once a week, Natwest waited outside a locked bathroom while Georgie cut up his legs with scissors. It was too much to handle.

And yet he had also given Natwest his name. It was a banking joke Georgie made one morning while passing their local branch on their way to school when they were thirteen. Natwest, so desperate – even at that young age – to mythologise himself, had adopted Georgie's invention as his chosen name because it was phonetically similar to the name he was given at birth. He was attracted to it because it was an ironic joke, an embodiment of the mundane, small-town high-street exist-ence he abhorred. And he wanted to be more than the bundle of unremarkable syllables he was assigned at birth; already, he had his sights on the famous writer he'd become and the name he'd be remembered by. It was his way of betting favourably on his own significance. From that morning, Natwest had insisted on his new name, and everyone who loved him had to adjust. Which they did. He'd forever be in Georgie's debt for that.

The apogee of their relationship was school prom, a ridic-ulous event which Natwest wanted nothing to do with. So instead the two of them ditched the party to drink whisky in the park and fuck on the memorial benches. Over the course of the night they became increasingly drunk and recklessly sentimental, and eventually he persuaded Georgie to suck him off on their favourite bench. The inscription said:

The Best Mum In The World
Gone Too Soon
Irene Wilson
1952–2018

Just before dawn, they'd written their names on each other's cocks with permanent marker as a pledge of allegiance. But it was an empty promise; when Results Day arrived, he was left behind while Georgie departed for exalted Oxford and lost his way without Natwest to guide him. (He switched to a PPE degree.) After that day, Georgie only returned home to make Natwest feel stupid – e.g. stuffing his new obsessions down his throat. Things Natwest couldn't stand, like politics, or '90s and noughties hip-hop. One time Georgie dragged him to Glasgow for an unbearable middle-aged rap gig, then spent the entire nine-hour train ride home asking, Do you get it? Do you get it?

This was four years ago.

T he enormous sound of aeroplanes echoed around the high street. Everyone stopped what they were doing and looked up at the sky. Four droning Spitfires flew overhead in the formation of a cross, and for ten seconds they were the most interesting thing in the whole town. Then they disappeared into the rain.

Natwest lowered his eyes. A fly-past, commemorating something or other. As he checked his socials, he noticed a text from his mother.

> Sorry bout earlir! you know what im like. Are you still coming to Doctor hung's exhibiton later?

It was 5:05 p.m. He texted back.

> Yes. See you later.

Opposite Nando's, he spotted Georgie. He was wearing Natwest's Hawaiian shirt – weird, especially as he was meant to give it back today. Georgie had forgotten his umbrella too, so he looked twice as ridiculous in the colourful shirt, like he'd wandered off the set of a movie.

Georgie waved and crossed the road. Much to Natwest's alarm, his ex-boyfriend held out his arms for a hug, and in the same moment Natwest dropped his phone.

'Fuck!' he shouted.

'It's always comforting to know nothing's changed.' Georgie picked it up. 'Still works, though. You should get a phone case.' He looked up at the rain. 'Water damage too.'

'Thanks,' said Natwest.

He tried to grab the phone but Georgie pulled it back and emphasised the point with his newly Oxford-chiselled voice. 'Seriously, get a phone case.'

'I will.'

'Heard that before.' He chucked it high in the air – and Natwest caught the phone with two hands.

'Cheeky cunt.'

Ten

Hawaiian Shirt

That was his body in the mirror. Pink. Flabby. Lacking in tone, or definition, or firmness, or thew. He was fat. To repeat: he was fat. You couldn't think of him in any other way. He was not a bear. He was not a bull. He was not an otter. He was not a twink. He was not a cub. He was not a wolf. He was not a gym rat. He was fat. On his dating profile he ticked the box, 'a few extra pounds'. The situation was irreversible. He'd inherited his father's body. Would continue to inherit it. Those were his shameful moobs in the reflection. His wide, disgusting areolas. The uneven, patchy spread of hair between his nipples. The unsightly acne below his left breast. The brown discoloration under his right. The long white crease across his stomach. The two coarse hairs that grew back in the same otherwise hairless spot. The port-wine stain in the weirdly accurate shape of Bosnia-Herzegovina. And below that, a pimple that never went away. There was the scar from the mole he'd cut off with scissors. (Here's a tip: if you cut off a mole, scrape out the wound with a toothpick, or it'll grow back.) And his belly button, deep enough that it created its own shadow. The long overhang of his belly was streaked with hair that was constantly growing in ugly patterns. From certain angles, his torso never ended. His belly fat gulped up his hips. His thick, short penis emerged like a weed. The razor burn at its base, the ugly papules along its shaft, the too-long foreskin like the end of a rotten sock. There was the shaving nick on his scrotum which turned purple and never went away. The large, low testicles – too low for his twenty-three years. Then the top of his bulking legs. Another mole. The faint scars running around the insides of his thighs. Eczema above his kneecaps. His hairless shins. He liked his shins.

Georgie buttoned up the Hawaiian shirt and his body disappeared.

Was that his dad's voice outside the bedroom window? He looked into the garden. His father was on his knees surrounded by drill bits, cursing to himself about the width of a screw. Poor Dad. It had been his goal all summer to lay the decking. Every weekend there was a new dispute with the instructional videos on his iPad, or a complex operation involving his new tools, like the Bush Hammer, the Dogleg Reamer, the Ball-End Glass Cutter. If Georgie were a heterosexual he'd make a joke about it.

While he worked, his father listened to *Moby Dick* on audiobook – Georgie's comic suggestion, accepted in earnest. Poor Dad.

'Georgie?' Dad shielded his eyes from the sun. 'Come down here a minute.'

'Okay. Coming.'

Stupid Zoë. Stupid, skinny Zoë. The text from Natwest brought it all back. He saw Zoë riding his cock. Her perfect round ass in his face. His pretty circumcised member in her tiny pretty mouth. There were two hours until his dinner with him – and Georgie had formulated a plan to get his revenge.

He performed a flamboyant spin in the mirror – there were always new angles to condemn himself from – then threw up an East Coast gang sign in the direction of Pun, Biggie, and Rick Ross pinned to the wall. He went downstairs.

In the garden, Dad pointed at a white paint can, handed over a Flagged Tip Brush, and instructed him to paint a portion of the completed decking. 'Mind you don't get paint on your fancy shirt. Speaking of...' Dad stripped off his *Jurassic Park* T-shirt and tossed it into the garden. He nodded at his son to do the same.

Georgie went back inside and changed into an old top. When he returned, Dad was bent over the touchscreen, attempting to convert inches to centimetres.

Captain iPad

Ahab.

Mercifully, Georgie's literary knowledge was on the wane. He'd wasted far too much of his life learning about people who didn't exist – Natwest's favourite hobby – and he lost nothing when he forgot the many pointless details of their fictitious lives.

He picked up the paint can and went to work. The white paint sailed smoothly across the planks. He ran the brush back and forth in a linear motion, keeping each stroke vertical and straight. This was the kind of thing he was good at: no poetry, just a methodical, precise operation.

'Fifteen and a half centimetres,' Dad murmured.

He relaxed into the motion of painting. In his mind, he ranked the albums of MF DOOM in ascending order. The sun pleasantly warmed the back of his neck. Dad muttered something about Americans. Benedict Cumberbatch lustily intoned the unabridged *Moby Dick*.

> But there were still other and more vital practical influences at work. Not even at the present day has the original prestige of the Sperm Whale, as fearfully distinguished from all other species of the leviathan, died out of the minds of the whalemen as a body. There are those this day among them, who...

There were little pencil markings at the end of one of the planks, and he wondered who'd made them and what they meant – but he didn't want to slip into an inappropriately poetic state of mind, so he covered over them over with a single stroke of his brush. It evoked a memory. When the tutor laid out the syllabus for Early Modern Drama during his first English seminar at Oxford, Georgie noticed a series of letters carved into his desk. He ran his fingers over the markings and read the message:

www.youtube.com/watch?v=fxATyB6t-QY

A video of Biggie Smalls, aged seventeen, freestyling on a Brooklyn street corner. It wasn't the lyrics, or the music, or the crowd that captivated Georgie. It was the confidence. He made being fat sexy.

If only Georgie could rap.

When he went home for the holidays, his ex-boyfriend said he didn't care to listen to homophobic '90s rap music. Poor Natwest. He didn't understand that rhythm had taken on new meaning, and Georgie desperately wanted to explain it to him. Couldn't he hear the muscularity of a boom bap drum loop? The complex politics in the East Coast sound? Or the over-whelming, thwarted desire for joy in the Atlanta scene? Didn't he understand that The South got something to say, too? And what about the words, Natwest? The words! The intricacies of schemes and flows and hidden melodies, poetry that *actually exists* in the world?

He realised he was no longer painting in straight lines, but drawing all sorts of shapes on the decking. Delighted, he drew a few more. Square! Circle! Triangle! He dipped his brush back into the paint. Tree! Flower! House!

'That's enough, son,' his father said.

It was almost 4:00PM. He wiped the dirt from his shorts. 'Alright, I'm off. See you later, Dad.' Inside, he changed back into Natwest's shirt, slipped on his new trainers – a recent interest cultivated by his love of hip-hop – and left the house. On his way out, he peeked into the garden. Dad was painting over the shapes, and Cumberbatch had reached the end of the chapter.

T he rain came on thick and fast. Acid rain. How anyone could continue walking around while rain was eroding everything remained a mystery. He had a vision of his body melting into the drainpipes, leaving only his new shoes in the middle of the road. But there was so much of him that it would take years for him to melt, like some sort of oversized church candle.

A man carried a rucksack over his head as if he could shield himself from the erosion. To be fair, Georgie himself probably looked strange wearing this shirt in the rain. It was the colour of mustard, and the design was classic Hawaiian export: a repeating pattern of white flowers on a sea of yellow. He'd had the idea that instead of returning Natwest's shirt, he'd wear it to the restaurant without bringing a spare set of clothes to change into. A little sartorial revenge. Very petty. Very Natwest.

Very Natwest: he was smart at school but he never tried. He had opinions about everything, but wouldn't listen to anyone else. When Georgie needed help, in those six months in which he took to hurting himself because his body was disgusting and deserved to be destroyed, Natwest didn't have the patience. Instead he said that Georgie's sadness wasn't real sadness because he was a show-off about it, and that rendered it superficial. Said his immature moods didn't align with certain aesthetic principles, so he'd grow out of it. If you spoke to Natwest you'd think he owned the concept of misery.

Yet there were positives: Natwest made every day a parade. Sometimes it seemed he orchestrated the world to ensure it was as memorable as possible. For instance, Georgie smoked as a teenager because he thought it would make him lose weight. Natwest used to turn every cigarette into an event, by writing tiny love letters to him on his rolling papers so that when he smoked one, he ingested Natwest's words. The other positive: he provided a space away from the ritual homophobia of school. But even then Georgie would feel worse about himself if he got into a fight with Natwest, than if someone called him a faggot. His best friend Zoë explained it this way: 'What's better: homophobia, or having a dick as a boyfriend?', which made it even more reprehensible when she'd fucked him.

Engines sounded overhead. Four aeroplanes – Spitfires – flew past. By the time Georgie looked up they'd disappeared into the clouds, leaving faint chemtrails that dissolved in the rain. There was a hush among the shoppers on the high street.

'What's that?' A toddler standing next to him pointed at the clouds, but his father scooped up the child and the high street continued flowing as if nothing had happened.

They were meant to read English Literature at university together, but thank God they hadn't. There were a thousand Natwests at Oxford. Every single one of them was a pseud, and the English department was the HQ of affectation. The only straight guy on the course ended up in Georgie's bed after very little persuasion – and Georgie was disgusted to find the *Gravity's Rainbow* equation tattooed on his prick. Ultimate pseud alert. Georgie changed his degree to PPE, leant into activism and politics – all the things Natwest looked down on for being gauche because he'd never experienced the joy of them. Never taken part in a truly communal event, such as the Night of the Long Knives, an after-hours orgy in the German department involving several well-endowed strippers shredding Georgie's prostate with their immense *schafts*.

A white Range Rover drove past. An enormous German shepherd in the boot stared out of the rear window. Georgie thought of Walter Benjamin's 'Angel of History' – all this useless literary knowledge that Natwest had forced on him – and he decided the angel was the dog in the back of the Range Rover, and he the catastrophe thrown at the angel's feet. Or paws.

He met the dog's eyes. Yes, Georgie was the catastrophe. And Natwest would be part of his wreckage. He felt a demented, apocalyptic confidence when he spotted Natwest on the other side of the street.

Georgie waved and crossed the road, choosing to assert himself with a large hug. On cue, Natwest dropped his phone. The wreckage had begun.

G eorgie relaxed in his chair and waited for a comment on the shirt.

'Nice shoes,' said Natwest. 'I remember you used to wear the same pair of Timberlands every day.'

'They were good boots. Must have lost them at uni.'

'*À la recherche du* Timbs *perdu*.' Natwest tapped twice on the countertop. 'I love your pants too. Bermuda shorts are goated.'

The restaurant was busy. Georgie's confidence had deflated. Tinny hip-hop was playing over the restaurant speakers – terrible mid-2000s pop tunes – and generally he was on the back foot. He pointed at his shirt, 'What do you think?'

'Nice,' said Natwest. 'Shirt looks decent on you. Good fit. It's weird how everyone's wearing flowery shirts today – unironically too.' He sighed. 'All good things come to a trend. . . Sorry I have to take it back, brother.'

Georgie didn't say anything.

When their food arrived, Natwest changed the subject to his dentist. Apparently there was an exhibition in the town hall later, as if Georgie cared. He picked at his salad and grew increasingly irritated with the boy sitting opposite, and with himself for failing to take the lead. Natwest's preferred medium was the monologue, and Georgie was once again an eighteen year old, nodding along like the dog in the advert. His problem was that he was spineless, while Natwest's was the opposite. Georgie had desperately wanted to attend their school prom, for example, but his boyfriend decided it was all phony, so they went to the park instead and had cold, damp sex on a bench. Natwest's life had the grammar of movies, and when he was taken with a scene he would pursue it relentlessly. Georgie wouldn't say no, had never in fact overruled him. Even now he couldn't interrupt the monologue.

When he finished his dinner, Natwest pushed the plate away. 'Georgie, you're not gonna get what you want.'

He pinched the fat around his wrist. 'And what do I want?'

'You wanna bring up Zoë again. But we had our fight about it, mate. We've moved on.'

'We never had a proper conversation.'

To his surprise, Natwest nodded and told him to say what was on his mind. Georgie seized the opportunity, and with some pleasure described his anger and hurt at finding out Zoë had slept with him. 'We dated for three years, and you think it's fair game to sleep with one of my closest friends? After all that time we invested? You've literally spoilt the memory of our relationship. It's like. . . that's three years I'm never getting back, you know?'

'Georgie, every three years is three years you're not getting back.'

A particularly svelte waitress removed their plates and asked if they'd enjoyed the meal. Natwest nodded and made an inappropriate amount of eye contact. He inquired about dessert – potentially a slight directed at Georgie – and the wait-ress responded by putting a single hand on her hip and saying in a playful voice, 'Well, what are you in the mood for?'

'Is that your waitress pose?'

'Uh-huh. It takes years to get this good. I go method.'

'I didn't realise I was talking to the *Daniel Day-Lewis* of the service industry. . .'

Georgie watched the two of them pass comments back and forth, feeling insulted and left out. When she had left with their plates he turned to Natwest, '"A pose is a pose is a pose". What the fuck does that mean?'

'Just a bit of fun, Georgie.'

'You were flirting! And she's almost thirty-five!'

Natwest sighed. 'I get it. You can't handle the fact I'm not a wall-to-wall homosexual like yourself. But that's your problem, mate, not mine.'

'No, that's not my problem. My problem is that you're homophobic.'

'Well. . . that's impossible, actually. But you're definitely *bi*-phobic.'

'If I'm bi-phobic then you're. . . empathy-phobic. How about that? You're decency-phobic. Considerate-phobic. Compassionate-phobic.' He leant forward. 'You're Georgie-phobic!'

'Okay.' Natwest nodded to himself as if he were conceding a great debate. 'About Zoë. . . I'm not sorry we slept together. But I'm sorry you got hurt. How's that?'

'And what about all the other stuff? Everything that happened?'

'It's been four years. Move on, Georgie. We all did a lot of shit back then; you had your body image shit, the gay shit, whatever. But mate, I had that stuff too.'

'I thought you were bi now.'

'What do you want me to say, I'm sorry? Okay. I'm sorry that once upon a time we were teenagers.'

When did Natwest, who'd been stuck in this town his whole life, get to be the grown up? Georgie knew *real* things about the world. He'd been to Oxford. He had degrees. He'd done things. Met people. Knew international acquaintances. Had friends who owned flats!

But Natwest was finished with the conversation.

'Let's get the bill.' He nodded at Georgie's shirt. 'I guess you can get changed in the toilets.'

'I would... but I didn't bring a spare top,' said Georgie. His moment had arrived. 'I'm sorry, I've got nothing to change into.' And he sat back, victorious.

'You're joking?'

'Nope.'

Natwest looked around in disbelief. 'So why did you bring it? To piss me off?' Then he shook his head and stood up to leave. 'I mean, keep the shirt if you like it so much. Just don't be a dick about it. I'll buy a new one, and you can pay the bill.'

It was not the reaction Georgie had hoped for. He was seized by a feeling of shame and self-loathing. He wanted to make an Event of himself, had to suppress a strong urge to go to the bathroom and open up old wounds.

Natwest turned to go.

'Wait!'

'What?'

'There's... Have you heard of the Zen Master story?' asked Georgie.

'Fuck off.'

'Just listen. I learnt it on my post-grad—'

'In Conflict Resolution and Peace Studies.'

'Please. Just listen, okay? So the story goes: there's a pupil who just wants to please his Zen Master. If he gets something wrong, he gets hit on the head as punishment. You understand?

128

But if he gets something right, he *still* gets hit on the head. You see? So how do you stop getting hurt?'

Natwest shrugged.

'You snatch the stick out of his hand,' said Georgie.

'And you stealing my shirt is snatching the stick?'

He said nothing in reply, and after a moment Natwest shook his head and walked out of the restaurant.

Georgie was fixed in place for several minutes. The same svelte waitress seated a middle-aged couple next to him, and the couple immediately started bickering because they wanted a table by the window. She tried and failed to apologise. Poor thing.

Natwest didn't deserve his pity. Wasn't it Georgie who'd suffered? And now that he's being honest with himself, yeah, it did bother him that Natwest was bisexual. It was like he got the easy way out of being gay. As many opportunities for happiness as there were people in the world – wasn't that what being bisexual was all about, opportunities? It was another thing he had over Georgie.

Other things Natwest possessed that Georgie didn't:

Charisma.
A healthy body weight.
Good looks.
A body without scars.

It was unfair that Natwest could exert power over him without trying, when all Georgie *did* was try. He attempted to make a list of things he had over Natwest, and could only come up with his superior knowledge of the Accra Comprehensive Peace Agreement. That was it. Everyone was indifferent to his pain. Nothing was fair. If he could draw up a list of every slight against him, every instance of suffering in his life, and give it to Natwest, would that make him feel better? Probably.

The couple were still pestering the waitress to move to the other side of the room, and she explained that the place was too busy. Eventually the couple sat down in a huff and began drafting a bad review on Google. Georgie made sympathetic eye contact with the waitress, and she smiled generously at him.

Then again.

Things Georgie possessed that Natwest didn't:

An Oxbridge education.
A father.
An exclusive attraction to men.
Hairless shins.
A profound love of hip-hop, which presented many avenues for joy.

He recognised the classic 50 Cent track playing over the restaurant speakers. It was the 'clean' version of a song he'd heard performed live once before, near the end of their friendship, when he'd convinced Natwest to accompany him to a concert in a field in Glasgow. 50 Cent didn't come on stage for two hours and the crowd of meaty white Scottish men grew rowdy, throwing drinks and starting fights. Everyone was sweating, and all around the field thirty and forty year olds stripped off their tops, exposing beer bellies and tattoos. Georgie was sweating too, but he chose to keep his shirt on. Even in this company he was embarrassed about his body. When 50 finally appeared he opened the set with his biggest hit, the one that uses the word 'faggot', and everyone went wild. Natwest held on for dear life, but Georgie pushed him off; this was his song. When 50 started rapping, the crowd knew every single word, and for the first time in his life Georgie had a spiritual experience. He belonged here, and a dazzling feeling of love and community washed over him. He'd never felt more included, more *seen* – without shame, without embarrassment – than in this field, rapping 'faggot' in unison with a thousand topless men.

Georgie opened his wallet and left the money on the table. He had decided.

He began unbuttoning his shirt, first opening the top and exposing his bare chest, then going down through each button methodically – just as he'd painted the decking this afternoon. When the shirt was undone, he stood up and took the whole thing off.

Everyone looked up from their meals.

There must have been a slight breeze in the restaurant, because he noticed the hairs on his chest bristling.

Here we go.

The svelte waitress rushed towards the table in a panic. All around him people were staring, or whispering to each other. Georgie looked over the whole restaurant, then balled up the shirt in his fist, threw up an East Coast gang sign and dashed out the door.

On the street, he ran past a granny who stared at his shirtless body.

Past a man leaving the barber's with a fresh cut

Past the kids on the wall smoking weed

Past the Reverend carrying a projector

Past a cyclist who yelled, 'Jesus!'

Past the lovers kissing in the bus shelter

He ran in the direction of the town hall. Kept running, kept shouting at the top of his lungs, 'Natwest! Natwest!', exhilarated, breathless, with the cold rain on his chest and the Hawaiian shirt waving behind him.

Eleven

Natwest Considers Pricks

At the exit, Natwest allowed himself a single, disappointed look back at his ex-boyfriend. Georgie was all despondent, like the last Rolo in a tube of Rolos. Considering the pettiness of the whole rotten ordeal and Natwest's general disdain for going back on himself, he decided that this moment marked the end of their acquaintance.

Once more unto the street, he thought.

It was chucking it down in biblical quantities. Nothing beautiful about the rain, stripped of joy, cold and wet, his clothes soaked through. He couldn't help feeling this was all Royal Mail's fault. And Dr. Hung's. And his mother's.

He could only walk so far in the rain before it depressed him, so he sheltered under the awnings of a Vodafone shop. His mind turned back to Georgie and his constant suffering. Why did he get the monopoly on self-consciousness? What about Natwest?

He was thinking, of course, about his cock. To describe it for a minute (which was easy – he knew it like the back of his hand, and often his hand was the thing he was looking at when he beat off), its appearance was marked by a profound lack. Namely, the absence of foreskin.

Nobody had explained his condition. As a boy, he had discovered he was different by observing everyone else's willies in the changing room and thinking, Huh, what's up with that thing? This soon morphed into, What's up with *my* thing? There was no obvious reason for his circumcision, and the thought of discussing it with his mother made his skin crawl – the closest they ever got was a poorly spellchecked text she'd sent about former Prime Minister Bris Johnson.

One option he'd considered: his father had been a Jew. His name *was* Jacob, and he looked as though he could be, and his mother had never said he *wasn't* Jewish. But then again, Jews, in Liverpool? Was that a thing? Liverpudlian Jews? It sounded like a rare species of swan. The most persuasive evidence for his father's ethnicity was the photos he'd found in his mother's cupboard, in which the circumcised phallus of the man was clearly visible, towering proudly above her. The narrative about his father contained many mysteries, and about the only thing that Natwest could say with any certainty was that he lacked foreskin.

Not that Natwest would mind being Jewish – he wasn't prejudiced, he just wouldn't want anyone to know. It was a hang-up from school. Everyone in England knows that if you're white and you're circumcised that equals Jew. It's not just that you're different, it's that the thing which most clearly defines your manhood, your *wang*, is an alien creature among the normal, honest, unsullied members of your compatriots. Who could forget the merciless bullying of the Benowitz kid, the only Jew in school, who unfortunately had circumcision implied in his name? Or the poor gentile sod who had an issue with his foreskin and had to get it removed at thirteen? Who'd he let *that* slip to? So Natwest hid it, with very crafty and non-obvious towel movements that allowed significant portions of his shaft to be visible (as in, Hey look! Nothing to hide here!) but which always ensured a casual placement of cloth over the offending bellend.

Natwest was far more terrified that his classmates would discover his lack of foreskin than he was of them discovering his sexuality. It was better to be thought of as perverted than to have a deformed penis. His cock was the enemy within. He spent sleepless nights scrolling through quack remedies on the internet which promised to regrow his foreskin in three weeks, or else browsing expensive cosmetic surgeries from award-winning cock-doctors based in Studio City, Los Angeles.

It was different in Circumcised America. Their penises were like their products – everything was 20 per cent off. He would have been just a regular schmo there, and he didn't even have to be Jewish. Yet unlike everything else that country produced, the practice was never exported. Think of all the terrible things American porn normalised in England – facials, choking, racial stereotypes, teens – and circumcision wasn't one of them! Even the rubber cock in the package was circumcised; but if you had a real one, you may as well be wearing a yarmulke for everyone to laugh at – which was ironic, because a yarmulke always struck Natwest as a kind of foreskin for your head.

The point is, by way of his cock, Natwest reluctantly conceded to his Jewishness. You didn't have to go to shul to be a Jew. e.g. We know Jesus was Jewish not because he practised the religion – but because he went into his father's business, lived at home until he was thirty, and his mother thought he was God. All this, *and* he was circumcised.

The rain lashed at the pavement, but under the awnings of the shop it was dry and safe, as if Natwest were standing behind a plane of glass. It was 6:16 p.m., the town hall was nearby, and there were fifteen minutes until the exhibition.

Two famous depictions of Christ's circumcision came to mind. One was by Rembrandt, the other by Parmigianino. The question hovering over both works is obvious: does the baby Jesus want it? It's the Carracci/Caravaggio thing again. In the Parmigianino,

Christ is bright and haloed and sure of himself, staring down the barrel of the lens like Norma Desmond. The baby's saying, yeah, this might hurt, but it's basically necessary and I fully consent. In Rembrandt's rendering, the scene is soaked in ambiguity, and the baby's face is a blur, appearing to the viewer as powerless and uncertain as, well, as a child's would. The Rembrandt is the truly beautiful piece of work; the Parmigianino a lie.

On the other side of the road, an old woman closed her umbrella and stepped into the butcher's.

The Latin root of the word was *circumcidere*, from *circum* (meaning, 'going around', 'about', 'in a circle'), and *caedere* ('to cut'). In poetic fashion, he imagined his entire day as an act of circumcision; him, the knife, travelling around town searching for the parcel, returning at the end of the day where he began. What part of himself would fall away when the day was through?

His opposite, cock-wise, was Georgie. He used to say that when he grew up he'd get his foreskin removed, which Natwest found deeply offensive. Nothing he said about Natwest's penis counted as praise, because he hated everything about his own. It occurred to Natwest that Georgie's paradox was that he was proud of what he was on the inside but hated who he was on the outside.

I suppose university teaches you that, Natwest thought.

Georgie had returned home soaked in political naiveté, out and proud and accepted by his parents and the wider community. The whole thing seemed ugly, aesthetically speaking. How can you be proud of something you're born with? Isn't that the definition of arrogance? It seemed to Natwest that you should only be proud of the things you *do*. And you're only allowed to be *ashamed* of the things you're born with.

But Georgie hung a rainbow flag outside his window like the rest of them because he'd been taught that celebrating his minority status was a good thing.

'Isn't it a bit... cringe?' said Natwest.

'When you go to university, you'll see.'

'Are you not embarrassed though?'

'But Natwest, *it's so much fun.*'

Hopefully, no such change would occur once he got to Bradford University. For him, 'coming out of the closet' was strictly an issue of aesthetics. It was just too *gauche* to pretend that he mattered simply because he had a certain sexual preference. He'd refused the terms society wished to label him with, and his sexuality would forever remain hidden. His minority knob would stay in his pants. Nobody would celebrate his identity.

But a small part of him wondered whether maybe university would change him after all. Wouldn't it be nice to feel special? Maybe he would finally accept his cock. In the Bradford prospectus they boasted that the university had a society for everything you could imagine. Was there a society for the circumcised? Would he have to join JewSoc? Would he go attention crazy like Georgie? Running around with dyed hair and whipping out his minority knob, screaming, Look! Accept me!

He hoped not.

The thought of his own penis had given him an erection. He swiftly opened the gay dating app on his phone and scrolled through the unread messages.

hey

hi

you accom?

up to anything this evening

looking?

Below each one was an attendant cock pic. uncut. uncut. uncut. uncut. cut. uncut. white. white. white. brown. white. black. black. white. hung. shaved. hairy. bent.

More messages came through. Every few seconds, another anonymous, unsolicited cock.

When he was fourteen, he lost his virginity to a thirty-six-year-old French guy who wore the same baseball cap in both his profile picture and real life. Natwest had travelled to London to meet his mother for dinner, and with two hours to kill before the meal, searched the app and agreed to meet a stranger at his place. Thirty minutes later there was a battered Vauxhall Corsa waiting for him outside Shepherd's Bush station. Once they pulled up outside the estate, the walk from the car to the flat was the most terrifying thirty seconds of his life – nobody knew where he was, or who he was with. As he lay down on the mattress pallet, the French guy's cap came off, revealing an entirely bald head. Natwest was penetrated, and when he finally ejaculated over himself, he threw an arm across his face so he didn't have to look at the head of the man above him. To this day, to his shame, it was still the best sex he'd ever had.

The messages continued to come.

Author's note: in this box there should be a photograph of a penis. A kind of unsolicited dick pic within the pages of the novel. The publishing industry is deeply conservative, and I have been ordered to remove it. So just imagine your favourite uncircumcised cock in its place.

#ReleaseTheUncutDick

How much would you pay?

Natwest clicked off the app.

Two university-aged guys crossed the road in the downpour and joined him under the awning. Natwest recognised them – they'd been a couple of years below him at school and were remarkably obnoxious. To make himself disappear, he reopened the app and lifted his phone in front of his face like the Magritte painting; except the Apple in this case was an iPhone.

'You're crazy, Ed. And I don't want to be that guy... but that's fucked.'

'A smart girl, I said a smart girl.'

'But like... regulatory economics?'

Ed, the one with the upturned, arrogant nose, rested an elbow on his smaller friend's shoulder. 'Lemme explain it. When you talk to a girl – especially in the industry I'm going into – you talk about this kind of stuff all the time. *All the time.* You got to have a strong ideological position, you get me? No pussyfooting around, no graphs, no Lib Dem bullshit. You have to take a strong Left stance. So what's the best way to turn a girl on? Talking about economic regulation. Works every time.'

Natwest scrolled through the profiles, looking for someone more attractive than him.

Ed continued. 'Why? Because economic regulation is all about control. It's about rules, holding stuff back, enforcing limits, controlling the economy. And this quietly taps into a girl's sexual desire, something raw and almost shameful, their desire to be *dominated* in the bedroom. Restricted and ruled, just like economic reg.'

'I think that. . . you know, there are better ways to turn a girl on. Like, er. . . making a joke, or giving a girl looks across the room or something.'

'Trust me. Cock your head to the side a little, stare into her eyes, and talk about *the statutory national minimum wage, price capping, unbundling infrastructure.* She'll be thinking about you holding her down, ripping off her top, telling her what you want her to do. . .'

Natwest hovered over a profile. It was a middle-aged man wearing goofy wraparound sunglasses. His name was 'Daddy'.

Hey

Daddy replied immediately.

How old?

👀 for younger

Natwest lowered his age by a few months.

I'm just about to turn 23

'I think you're wrong there, Ed.' The smaller one removed Ed's arm from his shoulder. 'I'll keep it one hundred, speaking about regulatory economics is only going to turn an otherwise well-disposed girl off. You're right, it *does* make girls think about rules and control – but not in the way you think. It's less like kinky domination, and more like your dad telling you to wear a condom. And also. . . if you want to do this properly, surely the way to turn someone on is by talking about free-market capitalism?'

'Everyone talks about the free market. It's hella boring.' Ed countered.

Great. Wanna meet tonight? I can accom

Yeah, let's do it

The small guy pointed at Ed. 'Talk free-market economics, and they're thinking, *Fuck. There's no regulation in the bedroom, anything could happen.* She's like, *We could do some real kinky shit.*'

'You're saying that talking about the free market is a guaranteed turn-on because it plants a seed in their brain—'

'In their pussy,' the small guy corrected him.

'—in their pussy, that you're going to fuck them like the free market has fucked the country?'

'Without limits.'

Natwest swapped details with Daddy, and they arranged to meet at 9:30 p.m. He felt a stirring in his crotch

– then dropped his phone on the floor.

'Mind out, mate!' Ed dodged the falling phone with a deft step, and it cracked on the pavement. 'Oof. That sounded nasty. You should probably get a phone case or something.'

'Yeah, maybe.' Natwest picked up his cracked phone, cursing silently.

'Oh shit, you're from school,' Ed said.

'Uh-huh.'

'What was your name again? You had a weird one, right? Northern Rock, Nationwide. . .?'

'Natwest.'

'Right! You remember him?'

'Oh shit, yeah!' said the small guy, laughing hyenically. Natwest noticed that he had a tooth missing.

'How are you, mate?' said Ed. 'You still at uni?'

'Yeah, I'm at Bradford.'

'Safe. Safe,' said the small guy.

Ed yawned. 'I might do a master's too.'

The small guy nodded. 'We just finished our undergrad. Weird coming back, right? For the summer?'

'Yeah, it is.'

The small guy pointed at the street. 'And it's shit weather out. One minute of sun, and then this.'

'Always. . . I guess you guys forgot your umbrellas too?' said Natwest, trying to muster some camaraderie.

Ed shrugged. 'If it rains, it rains.'

The three of them stared out from under the awnings. Sheets of grey rain washed the cars and windows up and down the street, and beyond them the low clouds formed inkblot patterns against the sky. It was like a melancholic moment from a movie, *Rashomon* maybe, and it filled Natwest with nostalgia for his schooldays.

He checked his phone again and considered asking Daddy for a picture of his cock, but decided against it, having had enough disappointment for one day.

A black Bentley drove past them. Ed nodded in approval. He stretched out his hand past the threshold into the rain and sighed happily. 'It's like my hand is in a different country.'

A new profile popped up on the app. The name was,

141

'Looking for FTM trans', and at the bottom it said, *This person is 1 metre away.*

Natwest looked up with a start and noticed the small guy scrambling to hide his phone.

Before the embarrassment could get any worse, Natwest clapped his hands and said, 'I'm gonna brave it. See you gents later.'

The small guy mumbled a goodbye. 'Have a good one,' said Ed.

Natwest stepped into the downpour, and it was indeed like a different country.

Twelve

Why the Long Face?

For most of her life, Ruth Edelman, of the Edelman Revue, had travelled up and down the country performing comedy skits and music hall numbers with her twin brother Mark. This was many years ago – she was now almost seventy-one – but at night she still sometimes woke with the memory of Blackpool, the summer of 1974, clear as day in her mind. It was their most successful show together, the first night they performed what later became their signature bit. Mark pretended to die on stage (as Tommy Cooper would do for real a decade later, at which point it ceased to be funny) while Ruth acted oblivious, taking his silence for stubbornness and growing angrier and angrier until eventually she was ranting at the motionless body. The gag went on for several minutes, depending on the audience, and that night she kept it going for sixteen. By the end the audience was wound so tight that it felt like one more second would ruin the entire show, then Mark suddenly got up and said, 'Just kill me already!' It brought the house down.

After the performance, her brother spoke breathlessly about their future. 'Ruthie,' he said, 'this is our big break! From here we can only go up!' But what had appeared to be the start of something new was actually the last burst of energy for a style of comedy that became deeply unfashionable, replaced by observational and political humour that neither Mark nor Ruth could pull off. Over the following thirty years they performed their old routines in smaller towns, in dingier venues, maintaining a punishing touring schedule to make ends meet. Because of this, Mark never married, and Ruth, gay before it was trendy, never met a woman she wanted to know for longer than a night. Soon they were both too old to make friends, and when they finally retired to a small house in the Midlands together at the age of sixty, it was a relief.

Her brother was a difficult man. He considered his life a failure, recalled their career with bitterness, felt he'd been cheated out of comedy fame and often blamed Ruth for the decline of their double act. On those occasions, Ruth would leave the house and sit in the bus shelter outside, smoking as many cigarettes as possible until he called her back in. Mark wasn't one to apologise, so he cracked a joke instead. She was happy with that.

During Mark's long illness, she kept his spirits up by hiring a student to write a Wikipedia page for him. Mark took great pleasure in recounting all the details of his career to this angular twenty-something typing on a laptop. Ruth listened in with glee, and she often added details here and there if her brother forgot them. But when they finally sent it to the article wizards at Wikipedia, they refused to upload it and replied with a note explaining that he wasn't significant enough, and there weren't sufficient secondary sources to verify his existence.

Eventually, Mark could no longer care for himself. Ruth did the shopping, cooked his meals, cleaned up after him. She was happy to do it, feeling that he would do the same if their roles were reversed.

Then Mark died and was buried in the local cemetery, leaving Ruth alone to finish the show.

*

A seventy-year-old Jewish lesbian walks into a bar.
This was the thought which passed through Ruth's head whenever she entered a public building. It didn't matter if it was a bar or not – she hadn't actually been in one for years – and this afternoon it was a Starbucks. Today was the first anniversary of her brother's death, and she was on her way to visit the grave. In the sixties, there was no sweeter sound on the regional comedy circuit than chairs scraping backwards as the audience stood to applaud; now she was assaulted by the same noise as they were shifted and nudged by people packing into the café to shelter from the rain. Many of them were soaked, and their faces had the peculiar beauty of the newly drowned. Or at least this was what she would think if she still believed that a concept like beauty was anything more than chemical reactions which occur when the person you love still exists.

It was not Ruth's nature to grieve; when she found out her father had died, she made arrangements for the funeral within the hour, crying only once during the whole week. And yet Ruth was hollowed out by her brother's death. The conceptual sadness she had imagined as Mark's health was failing was replaced by a real and devastating absence. There was nothing moving, or beautiful, or cathartic about the feeling. It wasn't even the thing which Mark had hoped it might be – it wasn't funny. Ruth hadn't learnt anything from the experience, except that the opposite of funny isn't sadness, but emptiness.

In the queue, Ruth tried to imagine the café without any people in it, but all she could picture was a uniformly white room, shrunk down to miniature proportions.

A middle-aged woman standing behind Ruth tapped her on the shoulder.

'Excuse me, I don't mean to be intrusive, but are you Jewish?'

Ruth looked the woman up and down – who also appeared

to be Jewish – and more irritated because of that fact she replied, 'No. I'm afraid not.'

The woman nodded, disappointed. A few seconds later, Ruth felt another tap on her shoulder. 'Sorry to be a pain, but really. . . are you sure you're not Jewish?'

'I'm certain,' said Ruth.

But the woman wasn't convinced, and after a moment of silence she repeated the question. 'Are you completely certain?'

Ruth winced. 'Okay. You've found me out. I'm Jewish.'

'That's funny,' she said. 'You don't look Jewish.'

Ruth shook her head, annoyed. 'Are you okay? What are you hoping to achieve by doing what you're doing, acting out this old joke? You ever think it might be offensive, getting in my face like this? Did you think you were going to make me laugh, or. . .?'

But the woman looked confused, almost frightened by the line of questioning. She apologised quietly and retreated to the back of the queue.

Ruth turned back to face the till.

It was the kind of encounter she would have gleefully reported back to her brother, and together they would have laughed about it, maybe even fashioned it into a routine to perform for themselves. Now it wasn't funny. Unfortunately, her comedian's brain was automatic and she couldn't help but remember jokes when an appropriate situation arose. She hated it.

When she was out on the street with her coffee, she opened her umbrella and recalled another one.

Two wise men of Chelm are walking down a path when it starts to rain.

'Open your umbrella!' one of them says.

He does so, but they still get wet.

'Sorry, the umbrella is full of holes.'

'Then why did you bring it?'

146

'I didn't think it was going to rain!'

Every joke came back to her now with a violence that was almost unbearable. After remembering that one, Ruth had to stop in the street to catch her breath.

Nobody could wring more from a gag than her brother. He used to say that the audience is a problem that it's the comedian's job to fix. And he could fix them, in a fashion that Ruth never could. She was grateful to make a living from it, and if she was a second-rate comedian, she accepted that too, because Ruth was also a worker, and whatever she did she did with commitment. But for all his talent, Mark could never escape the shadow of the greats – Buster Keaton, Arthur Askey, Peter Sellers, the Marx Brothers – and Ruth sensed that beneath all his self-laceration was a boy who wished he could *be* those other comedians, not just tell jokes as effectively as they had. Something of this was present in Mark's final request: that she dance an Irish jig on his grave, as Groucho Marx was reported to have done on Hitler's. It was a last joke, the only joke of his she didn't get. It brought no joy to Groucho Marx, and as Ruth trudged towards the cemetery to dance the jig she'd promised, she doubted it would bring joy to her either.

As Ruth got older, all she wanted to hear from the doctor was that a problem was 'normal for her age'; it reassured her that she was on the right track to being a thriving senior. But now she'd reached the point where what was 'normal for her age' was a problem called dying, and there was nothing to reassure her in the doctor's words. So: things started aching, her brain had become fuzzy, in the mirror she had her grandmother's face, and the famous hazel-green eyes which used to win the affections of dykes across the country were now dimmed and hooded. Her feet hurt all the time. The pavement got harder every year.

Time wounds all heels, she thought.

Up ahead there was a young man walking towards her with his face buried in his mobile phone. Ruth noticed – with some fascination – her slight resentment towards the boy quietly bloom into hostility. She continued walking in his path, waiting for him to spot her. Nothing. When he was a metre away, Ruth felt a sudden, blinding rage and decided that, whatever happened, she would stand her ground

– and just then realised it was the most she'd felt since Mark died.

The boy crashed into Ruth, spilling her coffee over the pavement.

'Exactly! I knew this would happen!' she said, shaking off the liquid which had stained her cardigan sleeve.

'I'm so sorry. Oh, I'm really—'

She shoved a finger at the device in his hand. 'I was watching you the whole time and you didn't move an inch because you were looking at that damn thing!'

The boy stuffed the phone deep into his pocket. 'Why did you crash into me then?'

'What!'

'I mean, I'm sorry.'

The boy was wearing an old rucksack, and he was soaked from the rain. Ruth extended the umbrella over him. 'And you're walking around in wet weather like this? Of course you're out of your mind!'

'I'm really, really sorry.'

Ruth pointed at the puddle of coffee that was steadily washing off the pavement. 'And that's my coffee gone.' The boy stared at the liquid running into the drainpipe, and her heart softened a little. 'Come on, you're going to buy me another one. It's the least you can do.' The boy nodded. 'Get under the umbrella, or you'll catch your death of cold.'

They walked back to the café, and she learnt that he was twenty-three years old and about to leave for university. He was endearingly repentant, and insisted that he was only glued to his mobile phone because he had a very important exhibition to attend. Ruth recalled her dentist mentioning something about it, but the thought of entering the town hall – which sometimes doubled as a theatre and performance space – depressed her.

'And what about you,' the boy asked. 'What do you do?'

'I'm retired.'

'Right. But before that?'

She considered the question, and something in the boy's voice compelled her to tell the truth. 'I was a comedian.'

He nodded and looked disappointed. Presumably he'd decided that the woman before him could never make him laugh. 'So, like stand-up and stuff?'

'No, not really,' she replied. 'More like vaudeville.'

'Vaudeville?' A surprising look of approval appeared on the boy's face. All of a sudden he lit up. 'Chaplin or Keaton?'

'Well. . .' She thought of her brother, who so often aligned himself with Keaton and the other greats. Unlike him, Ruth possessed no innate ability to make people laugh. She'd had to work at it. 'I like Harold Lloyd,' she replied.

The boy was incredulous. He hopped about on the pavement, gesturing wildly. 'Lloyd? You can't be serious? Is that a joke?'

She held up a hand. 'Not at all. Maybe Lloyd wasn't born a genius like the other two, but he worked just as hard. I always found that more inspirational. Don't you think?'

He shook his head. 'Not really. . .'

The response irritated Ruth, and so she indulged in some baseless fogeyism. 'Hard work – that's what's missing from your

149

generation's sense of humour. Instead it's so frenetic and cheap. I don't get it. Makes me feel old.'

The boy's brow wrinkled. 'It's very simple. The point about our humour is that if you laugh at the joke, you've missed the point of the joke.'

She shook her head, not understanding. Ruth was finished with the problems of pop culture. She wasn't interested in learning about new things that were destined to be made obsolete by ever newer things.

When they reached the café, she sent him in to get her another coffee.

While waiting outside, Ruth noticed something deeply peculiar. It was another young man, and he was running all the way up the street, absolutely naked from the waist up. He flew past her in a matter of seconds, an expression of pure joy across his face. Oy!

No doubt Mark would have turned it into a memorable bit.

The rain began to peter out and she hesitantly closed the umbrella. A gentleman walked by, and she asked him for the time. He tipped his hat and said it was 6.30 in the afternoon – the best time on a clock, hands down. How was it already that late? Time flies when you throw away your watch, thought Ruth. Which was exactly what she'd done a week after Mark died, because the watch was a present he'd given her on her fortieth birthday, and she couldn't bear to look at it.

The clouds drifted apart, and the September sun returned. The boy emerged from the café carrying a plastic cup and offering her a half-hearted smile. Ruth suddenly thought he looked very Jewish – although when he got up close, she wasn't as sure.

'It's stopped raining,' he said, handing her the coffee.

'Are you Jewish by any chance?'

He looked terrified at the question, which made her grin. 'No, I'm not,' he said. She registered that she had smiled for the first time in months. 'Are you sure?' she asked.

'Yeah. I'm not Jewish.' He flicked his hair off his face and sighed. 'Why? Can you tell? It doesn't really count if it's the dad, right?'

'Don't worry about it,' Ruth said, patting him on the shoulder. 'You should get going to your exhibition soon, I think it's about to start. Thank you for the coffee.'

He smiled sweetly. 'It's nothing. Are you going to the exhibition?'

'I may do. But I may not. Depends on how I feel,' she said.

'Cool, well hopefully see you later.' And off he went, annoyingly youthful, back down the road he'd come from.

The sun was waning, and Ruth could barely make out her murky reflection in the headstone. It was a simple grave. Grey granite, polished and shiny from the rain, inscribed with gold lettering. Mark had wanted her to put: 'Mark Edelman – Are You Kidding Me!?' but for some stupid reason she had told them to write, 'Beloved Brother and Comedian'. Now the grave was indistinguishable from all the others in the cemetery. She'd tried to make up for it a few months ago by getting one of the benches in the park inscribed, but in hindsight it was an inadequate gesture, because Mark had hated the outdoors.

The day he was told that his rare cancer was terminal, Mark said, hopefully, 'Do you think I'm the most famous person to die of renal transitional cell carcinoma?' But unfortunately he was beaten by a junior ice hockey coach called Bert Templewood – who had his own Wikipedia page.

Ruth let her umbrella fall to the ground and performed some rudimentary stretches. The reflection in the gravestone copied her movements, like the mirror scene in *Duck Soup*. As she stepped onto the rectangle of earth which covered the remains of her brother, six feet below, she imagined him watching down on her from someplace in the sky.

She began to dance an Irish jig.

It was a struggle to bring her legs up high enough for it to look like anything other than a mad shuffle, but she persevered admirably for half a minute, until her ankles began to swell and a sharp pain punctured her back. She stopped dancing and leant against the headstone, depressed.

The imaginary Mark she'd pictured had been replaced by physical pain, and she was reminded that he no longer existed in the world, and that the whole exercise was a stupid joke. When Ruth looked up, she had an audience – a kid, no more than six years old, munching on a chocolate bar and staring at her. The chocolate was all around his mouth, and she had to fight the urge to wipe him clean. She looked around for his mother and spotted a woman at the other end of the cemetery crying on her knees in front of a grave.

'You okay, kid?'

He took another bite of his chocolate bar.

'Yeah. Me too.' She tried a smile, but the kid didn't respond. She glanced at the mother and thought what a bad parent she must be to leave her son to wander around a cemetery alone. 'Hey, kid. You shouldn't leave your mother, you know that?' Ruth considered calling out to the woman, but then understood that the kid had no desire to be around his mother when she was crying like that.

Ruth pointed at the headstone. 'This is my brother by the way, since you asked.'

The kid said nothing.

'Well, what do you think?' She ran a hand along the cool granite of the headstone. 'Good-lookin' guy, huh?' She patted it and stepped to the side. 'Yeah. . . we came a long way together, didn't we, Mark? Didn't we?. . . Oh, he's not responding.' Ruth dropped her voice to a whisper. 'He's been a bit reticent in his later years,' she indicated the headstone – 'as you can see.'

She searched the kid's face for some sort of reaction. He blinked a few times and took another bite of his chocolate bar. Ruth had never felt joy on stage, only a kind of intensity and concentration. Now, for the first time in years, she'd been taken over by the old feelings. 'So Mark. . . while you're lying there all quiet-like, tell me. . .' She performed the bit with just as much zeal as she'd once had – all those years ago in the summer of 1974 – pushing the gag as far as it could go. The whole while, the kid remained silent. The toughest crowd she'd ever had.

'Come on, Mark. . .' She gently kicked the headstone. 'What's up with you? We really need you to tell some jokes now. Let's go. Tell one of your famous one-liners.'

The kid sniffed. She continued.

'Mark?'

Her voice had become high and scratchy. 'Nothing? Can you believe this? Hello? Hello?' After several minutes of this, her desire for a reaction had taken over common sense, and she found herself shouting at the grave.

'Stop joking around, Mark! I'm getting really. . . irate! I am irate! You're really embarrassing me here!'

Her hands started shaking. 'Give me something to work with! Do the thing, Mark! I've gone as long as I can! I can't finish it alone!'

The kid blinked.

'If you don't say something this minute. . . Mark! Please! Say something! Mark!' She buried her face in her hands and screamed. 'Kill me already!'

Ruth burst into tears and collapsed at the side of the grave. They were easy tears, like the ones she used to cry as a little girl. She wiped them away gently with the sleeve of her cardigan, catching a whiff of coffee from the collision on the street. When she rested her cheek against the smooth headstone, the scent of earth rose up from the newly wet grass.

Ruth felt a tap on her shoulder. It was the kid, standing over her, his tiny hands holding out the remainder of his chocolate bar. She accepted the gift and popped the chocolate into her mouth. The kid waited until Ruth had swallowed, then nodded authoritatively and walked back to his mother. The woman rushed to him, kissed him on the forehead and on his cheeks, then carried him out of the cemetery.

There was a pleasant buzzing in Ruth's ears, and for a few minutes she sat at the bottom of the grave enjoying the feeling of being so close to the earth. The wrapper of the chocolate bar depicted a penguin, and with a little gasp of delight she remembered from her childhood that they printed a joke on the back of every packet.

She read it out loud, so that Mark might hear.

'What did the dentist see in Antarctica?'

She laughed softly.

'A molar bear.'

There's an old Jewish joke: why are there so few Jewish alcoholics?

It numbs the pain.

Well, for better or worse, Ruth felt like a drink. It would be the first in a long time. The events at the cemetery had stunned her, and she'd walked away feeling as though she'd turned over a new leaf. Yet as the sun set above the high street, and the colours of the town transformed into shadows, she returned to a state of emptiness. The tumult of emotion felt like an echo from the past rather than an intervention in the present. Everything was drab again.

She used her umbrella as a walking stick and made her way to the nearest bar.

Everyone seemed to have disappeared from the streets, as if it were much later in the day than it actually was. The air was still too, and the town had the atmosphere of a theatre when you walk in and there's nobody there. She wondered about all the audiences in all the bars and theatres and seaside resorts she'd performed in, a whole life spent in the eyes of other people, and she thought, *I remember you, but do any of you remember me? Has a single person remembered the work we did? Or were we a pointless diversion, something to forget about the moment the curtain closed?* The only witness to her life's performance was Mark, and just as she kept a version of him alive in her memory, they both would disappear when she died. This obvious, embarrassing fact had never seemed real until now. And yet the scene in the graveyard had offered her some hope that these brief intervals of joy and laughter might be more frequent, and these extended periods of emptiness less persistent – at least for as long as she had left, before she joined her twin brother in silence.

Outside the bar, Ruth caught a glimpse of her reflection in the tinted windows of a passing car – a Bentley – looking much the same as when she'd left the house this morning. She thought there was something sad in that, then she pushed open the door with the tip of her umbrella and stepped inside.

A seventy-year-old Jewish lesbian walks into a bar.

The bartender looked up. 'Is this some kind of joke?'

Thirteen

Natwest Recalls His Lost Youth

(then meets somebody younger than him)

It was a cinematic sunset: pinks, oranges and periwinkle blues, intensified by the chill in the air. Beneath it all was lonely Natwest, a single figure on the empty street, whose loneliness was the most obvious fact in the universe, if anyone bothered to examine the facts. Seen from above – as he often imagined himself – he resembled a Pokémon character, and the unreal sense of this place where he'd spent his whole life struck him as hilarious. This idiotic town, with its strange, ordinary inhabitants who may or may not have interior lives as interesting as his; the ants marching out of a crack in the paving slab beneath his feet; a dangling skeleton in the window of the fancy-dress shop, swaying unnervingly on its strings as if there were a breeze inside. Natwest gave a fanciful salute to the dead, whose ranks he would be joining soon enough.

Outside the shuttered grocers there was a rotten head of iceberg lettuce rolling across the pavement. He picked it up with one hand and held it at arm's length – 'A lettuce, poor

Yorick!' – then he dropped it onto his foot and kicked it over a wall – probably the first ball he'd ever kicked well. He was visited by the popular feeling of being trapped in a video game, which he swiftly rejected because why would this Midlands town ever feature in a video game?

Often, Natwest imagined a gigantic consciousness in the sky that was personally and only in touch with himself. When he was a child he'd thought it was God keeping tabs on him in case he was needed for messianic purposes somewhere down the line. Why else was he smarter than everyone, if not because he was chosen? After that, it was his father, Jacob – for that was what his mother told him as a baby – but he couldn't sustain the fantasy for long, as his lack of knowledge about the man made it impossible to give the consciousness life. By the time he was a teenager the great thing in the sky was a person he tried to impress, usually his favourite artist, author, musician, filmmaker – whoever obsessed him at the time. Natwest would modulate his actions.– his thoughts, even – so the Most Exalted would look on him with fondness. e.g. What would this formidable French exotropic think of me, a humble teen, contemplating his most irritating work of philosophy? Or the great humanist filmmaker, interested in catching those spontaneous moments of LIFE: hey look at this beautiful human-y thing I, Natwest, a young kid enjoying the wonder of youth am doing! But for the last couple of years the fantasy had slipped out from under him, and now when he thought of a huge consciousness in the sky it was a future version of himself looking down and wrinkling his nose with disapproval.

As he passed by, Natwest spotted a cracked CD case in the window of a charity shop: *NOW That's What I Call Music! 106.* A great melancholy swept over him. The *NOW!* CDs were his generation's principal contact with physical media – compilation albums of the season's bestselling singles. As a kid he'd dreamed of what his life would look like when *NOW! 100* arrived. Would he be married? Famous? Prematurely balding? Yet he'd missed it. He'd lost track of the series around number *77*, and the unknowable future was already marching towards *NOW! 200*. Time had moved on without him. It resembled the feeling he'd had when his friends deserted him for university: left behind. *À la recherche du* T-Pain *perdu*. No doubt a younger version of himself would feel betrayed.

Poor and sad Natwest.

It occurred to him that the town was strange and sad tonight because his five years of miserable waiting had come to an end. He felt the first pangs of a regret which he suspected would return whenever he remembered this odd town, several years hence when he was the senior art critic at *The Times*.

I want more, he thought. More of everything: books, films, lovers, albums, opinions – and most of all, time. As a kid he had imagined he could freeze it in its tracks with a simple utterance, 'pause', 'play', taking his cue from the only experience a child has with the passage of time, the DVD player. But the fantasy did nothing to halt the goose-stepping march of a fascist time. His was a desire to eat the world. Stretch his jaws wide like he was sucking a thick cock, and swallow until there was nothing left. Eventually he conceded that most things would be left unseen, unread, unfucked.

He was hungry. The corner shop up the road was still open, so he ducked in to buy a snack. The shopkeeper looked up from his phone and nodded. Natwest grabbed a packet of stoneless dates – the homosexual snack of choice (regular bowel movements) – and laid them on the counter. As he tapped his card, he noticed a stand displaying a variety of phone cases – but having already paid for his item, and not wishing to go back on himself – stepped out on to the street again. At the end of the road, the town hall was lit up from below, so from a distance it resembled something much larger and American. It was in fact a modest four floors of Victorian brick built atop an old mineral spa, famous in the town because some king or other was rumoured to have bathed there.

A little clock tower poked out of the roof.

Natwest checked the time on his phone – 6:58 p.m. – and briefly drew up a plan for the night.

1. Enter the town hall.
2. Locate Dr. Hung and exchange packages.
3. Make small talk, admire art, apologise to mother.
4. Leave early by indicating a strong desire to pack for university – but in actual fact hook up with a middle-aged stranger named Daddy.

– but right there was a girl crying by the bus stop. She looked about fifteen. East Asian, short, ash-blonde, and wearing an oversized hoodie that concealed an extremely thin body. As she buried her face in her phone, sobbing, her left hand drew out a jelly turtle from a pack of Rowntree's Randoms. She ate with her mouth open, and Natwest observed her masticating the unfortunate turtle into a fine mush.

He continued on his way, feeling some sympathy for her. She was the second person he'd seen weeping in public today, the first being his mother, and one could easily take that as a sign. He was reminded of his staunch nine-year refusal to shed a tear after disastrously calling Mr. Claggert 'Dad' in class at the age of fourteen – and suddenly he realised he'd kept his emotions under control for so long, and so effectively, he'd forgotten what it actually felt like to cry.

The sight of the girl eating sweets reminded him of another thing too: a strange ritual Natwest used to perform with his friends in primary school. It involved the excessive consumption of Toxic Waste – 'The Hazardously Sour Candy' – whose astonishing sourness was legendary and much feared among the children. Once a week, a single unlucky child would be selected and ordered to hold as many Toxic Wastes in their mouth as possible, then endure the stinging pain of the sweets until the frosted sour coating had dissolved – or else spit them back out, and face the scorn of the hateful children. Unfortunately, eight-year-old Natwest was particularly sensitive to sour things, and when called on to eat ten of the hideously sour sweets at once – two of every flavour – he refused. But this was not sufficient for the other children, so they pinned him down and stuffed the sweets into his mouth anyway, clamping his jaw shut and laughing as he thrashed around on the polypropylene carpet, gagging, cringing, tears streaming down his face.

It was horrible being a kid. He turned back to the bus stop and approached the crying girl, feeling a new kinship with her.

She glared at him as he took a seat, then returned to her phone and resumed sobbing. 'Hey.' Natwest reached out a tentative hand and rubbed her right shoulder in a way he thought was tender and reassuring – but ended up shaking her back and forth like a flight attendant waking a passenger for breakfast.

'What the hell?' she said, removing his hand. Natwest got a clear look at her face, which appeared spring-loaded to snarl at any provocation.

'I'm sorry,' said Natwest, ashamed that he'd got it wrong.

'You should be.'

The girl was dragging a twig slowly across her wrist, not with any force, just so it made a light whitish scratch.

'I just wanted to say,' Natwest continued, 'whatever you're going through, it's okay. It'll be alright.' After a moment's consideration, he raised his eyes from the floor and added, 'Seriously.'

'Work on your game, man.'

Natwest went hopelessly red in the face. He thought of all those older men he'd pursued, and who had pursued him when he was her age. Now he'd become one of them.

'I'm gay,' he said. Then, lying to put her at ease, he added faintly, 'Very gay.'

The girl scowled. 'Whoop-de-doo, Basil. Welcome to the majority.' She went back to her phone and muttered, 'You do you.' But a few seconds later cocked her head to the side, 'Okay man, what do you want?'

Natwest asked her name, which was Yeong-hui, but he should call her Lily. 'Why didn't you just say your name was Lily, then?' And she slung him an ironic look which made him feel stupid and returned to her phone. It was impossible to talk to her while she was looking at that device. It reminded him that his whole generation had been fucked. The internet had put little airbags between everyone, and they were slowly expanding.

'I don't want to sound like an old man, you know. I'm not. But that phone isn't going to make you happy if you're feeling sad. You need to practise some... media hygiene. See –' Natwest realised he was holding his own phone in his hand; Lily noticed it too, and so he tried to make a point of it. 'Just put it away, like this.' He stuffed it into his pocket – but missed and the phone hit the ground. 'Shit!'

She laughed then, a big pumpkin grin, hastily suppressed.

At least she's stopped crying, he thought, examining the fine cracks across his phone screen, which now resembled the craquelure of an ancient oil painting.

'Dude?' She offered him a jelly turtle. Natwest shook his head and raised his packet of dates.

'Dates. Based,' she said.

He smiled. 'Lily, what's up? Why were you crying?'

'I can't explain it to you.'

'Try.'

Lily shook her head. 'I'm in this situation. . .' She pointed her nose just slightly towards the sky. 'It's so shit. Literally the worst possible thing, like. . . It's just fucking. . . Ah!' Lily turned away and swallowed the tears before they could begin again. She exhaled violently and tried a second time. 'So it's bad. A few months ago I was in this relationship, and we took some pictures – you know, Not Safe For Work photos. Whatever. But there was this website that I joined—'

But there was this website that Lily joined around the same time, and she became a very active user there, 'because it was a fun place to hang out'. It was a message board with a bad reputation where people shared images, memes, porn and joked about random shit like politics, video games and Anime. Admittedly, it was mostly populated by men – yet that was part of the fun, she insisted – and because she's mixed-race Korean-Irish, if there's one thing the people on those sites *love*, it's people like her. It was all a joke of course, except someone had got hold of her nudes – not her ex-boyfriend, *definitely not her ex-boyfriend* – and was threatening to post them all over the website and then send the link to her parents.

'That's a lot,' Natwest said, gloomily shaking his head. 'But you know,' – he put on a more cheerful tone – 'I have nudes all over the internet from when I was your age. They never got back to me.'

Lily took out her phone and began tapping at the screen. 'Yeah, this is completely different.' In one motion she pulled up her hood and lowered her head.

It was a terrible situation, and Natwest wished he had something better to say except the next words which tumbled out his mouth: 'I'm sorry that I can't help you.' She peered out from under the hood and gave him a weak smile as if to say, 'It's alright that you failed. . . and the Effort Cup goes to Natwest.'

He tried to look meaningfully into her eyes, to express his

thanks for the imaginary Effort Cup. At first, she became embarrassed and looked away. But then, with an air of determination, Lily returned his gaze.

They stared at each other for a minute.

'You feel that?' asked Natwest.

'The breeze?'

'The look.'

The silence that descended was womblike and pure. A strange gulf opened up between them – that thing which happens when you really look at someone for a long time – and it seemed to Natwest like an abstraction and a purification all at once. Lily was converted into a body, but also that body disappeared and it was as if he was really seeing her, through *her* eyes, and because she was staring back he imagined she felt the same way.

'You know what we're trying to do?' he asked.

'Yes, go beyond our selves, know one another, have a connection, be more than one lonely consciousness, etcetera etcetera.' She looked away. 'Whatever gets you off, man. No judgement. You do you.'

'No! I want you to do *me*!'

She laughed, then realised he was serious. Natwest lowered his forehead a little and indicated for her to do the same. 'There has to be more to life than this separation between us,' he said, only half mockingly.

'You're so cringe,' she said, but nonetheless touched her forehead to his.

They stared at each other again, so close that they had to flick between each other's eyes. When they'd settled on an eye of choice they held the gaze for another minute. Natwest pushed harder into Lily's forehead, and she did the same back, as if they could reach the other's consciousness by sheer force.

But the spark was gone, and they each sat back exhausted. 'I've got a headache now.'

'Same,' Natwest sighed. The reality of the town returned, and it was like walking out of the cinema into the dusk and feeling you've woken up the following day. Lily rubbed his shoulder and said, 'Thanks anyway, I guess.'

Outside the town hall, there was a hideous red King Kong statue by Orlinski, made of flat planes of fibreglass, beating its pointless chest. What a stupid, stupid thing to make, thought Natwest as he passed by. Here was another thing to obfuscate Imam Mishaal's binaries about art and life – something that is so utterly vulgar as to need no classification whatsoever. What the artist failed to understand about Kong was that he wasn't some primal celebration of unbridled nature, but a glorious creature who wished he were human and not the unfortunate animal he really was. And no one empathised more with the beast than Natwest, for he felt something of its failure. There was nothing he could do to help Lily, and he appeared useless before the girl, flailing around like some ragged animal let loose in the human kingdom.

Natwest gave the statue a surreptitious middle finger and pictured John Berger looking down and nodding in approval. The entrance to the town hall was up ahead. He'd nearly reached his goal and could now proceed with the rest of his life.

Still, there's something sad in that, he thought. And his mind once again returned to Lily. She had the same problem as him – faced with the unbearable threat of being exposed to the world and the people you love – but her situation appeared far more wretched. Natwest could hardly bear thinking about it.

Poor girl.

A profound melancholy touched his sole. He raised his foot and saw the dog shit underneath.

Fourteen

Femanon

1

RealConfessions

I want my mum to die

Femanon

17 Sept, 09:24

15 y/o female here. i hate that my mentally ill younger sister makes my mum depressed. mum never gets off the sofa and she's just unnecessarily evil to absolutely everyone in her life. dad got fired and can't get another job because someone has to care for my sister, and now mum is always putting him down, and she always brings up the fact that he's korean and she's irish too, usually to say how useless he is. e.g. 'you're the only korean without a job!'. she's got a major attitude problem and can't see that dad's a literal SAINT for caring for my sister AND cleaning up AND cooking for us. sometimes i want her to die so bad so dad can remarry and be happy. also she randomly lashes out at me, like this morning when she said 'make sure you eat all your lunch at school' as if i'm 10 or something, when really she means, 'you're looking way too skinny and that upsets me because i'm not'. GET OUT OF BED THEN AND GO TO THE GYM AND CARE FOR YOUR CHILDREN. and then when she realises she's being mean, she starts saying how much she loves me and it sounds like she's trying too hard. actually i want her to die most of the time. (but not too painfully).

hola.

Wut

stuck in english. mrs
pandey's off so we've got
mr claggert. bored.

Courage is grace
under boredom

bro always starts his stories
with 'an old friend of mine,
lovely chap, dead now...'
everyone's on their phones.

Well I'm honoured that
you only text me, your
oldest and dearest pal,
when you're bored ;)

passive aggressive much.

The winky face was put in to reassure you otherwise

I know it is often tricky to deduct the true meaning from my premium quality nuances

spent the whole lesson reading confessions online and shitposting on 9bord.

That site is gross, ew

I'm in DT watching ur ex, beloved Daniel, getting very close to chopping off his main fingerbanging digit with the electric table saw

Will report back the results

excited.

Femanon (10:50)   Honest pic rate

hello fags, honest rate/10.

are my tits too small?

Anonymous (10:52)   Honest pic rate

3/10, pass. (Trap titties)

Anonymous (10:53)   Honest pic rate

6/10, smash. Rank your holes in order of
fuckability?

Zelig (10:53)   Honest pic rate

5/10, pass if sober. Smash if fucked

Pliny's Testicle (10:53)   Honest pic rate

Backsnatch pics or GTFO

Klingsor (10:54)   Honest pic rate

@PlinysTesticle a man of culture I see.

@femanon 8/10, very cute. You wanna private
message me?

Femanon (10:55)   Honest pic rate

no.

Klingsor (10:57)   Honest pic rate

Well I'm actually a really nice guy, so it's
your loss.

Fucking dyke.

Anonymous (10:58)   Honest pic rate

Are women insecure about their boobs tho?

Goncharov (10:59)   Honest pic rate

Deffo. Particularly in the last decade where we've
been conditioned to want thicc girls

Tho as far as I'm concerned, petite girl with small
tits > bitches shaped like Cee Lo Green

Anonymous (11:00)   Honest pic rate

Apparently they're horribly insecure about their
pussies as well.

Can anyone confirm this?

Vita Sackville Baggins (11:00)   Honest pic rate

100%. What are women not insecure about lol?

Zelig (11:01)   Honest pic rate

But men are way more likely to kill themselves
over their insecurities!

Billy Budd (11:02)   Honest pic rate

@femanon, those really your pics?

Femanon (11:02)   Honest pic rate

si, all mine.

Billy Budd (11:02)   Honest pic rate

Nice to see some legit original content for once

Femanon (11:03)   Honest pic rate

what would you rate?

Billy Budd (11:03)   Honest pic rate

Smash, obviously. Age?

Femanon (11:05)   Honest pic rate

just turned 18.

Billy Budd (11:05)   Honest pic rate

Perfect

MIA AT 12:45

Sadly no permanently
deforming injury occurred

LILY AT 12:48

booooooo he needs something
to make him feel bad. used to
always say i was too small.

lunch in 20?

MIA AT 12:49

You? Small? Never

LILY AT 12:49

suck a dick.

Femanon (12:51)   true thoughts/random opinions

i want to ram dog shit up Malala's greasy cunt.

Anonymous (12:52)   true thoughts/random opinions

Jeez, Becky. You're a real humanitarian.

Girth Vader (12:52)   true thoughts/random opinions

tbf she is fucking annoying

Mark Labbett & Da Big Steppers (12:52)   true thoughts/
                                                random opinions

Just your daily reminder that late-stage
capitalism is not a multiplayer game :—)

Anonymous (12:54)   true thoughts/random opinions

Grow the fuck up @femanon, Malala is a fucking
peerless beacon for the rights of women across
the world. Including YOUR RIGHTS.

Femanon (12:55)   true thoughts/random opinions

this post isn't about her peerless human rights
work, it's about wanting to ram dog shit up her
greasy cunt.

Billy Budd (12:58)   true thoughts/random opinions

Need a hand, @femanon?

Femanon (13:02)   true thoughts/random opinions

hello again. you supply Malala — and I'll supply
the dog shit?

Billy Budd (13:04)   true thoughts/random opinions

Deal

RealConfessions

help

Anonymous
17 Sept, 13:11

21 y/o male. just really desperately want to be happy. i wish something would fill me up because i feel like im completely empty and i dont exist at all. i want to hang myself or jump off a bridge or cut my wrists or smash my fucking head into a wall. nothing makes me happy any more. im actually really loved by my parents and have lots of friends and they all care for me and ive never been in poverty or anything like that. plus i have a good job and when I want to i can get women and stuff. but i still hate being alive and its not fucking fair. only thing is im too chicken to end it.

for example

last night around 3am i drove around until i found a stretch of highway that i liked then i pulled over and got out the car and walked into the middle of the road. when i lay down flat i kissed the tarmac for some reason and it was warm from the tires and maybe the heat of the day.

dunno why but that made me not want to do it, so i got up when I heard a car coming in my direction and went home.

fucking coward.

2

I think I hate women

Anonymous
17 Sept, 15:06

31 y/o male. I've come upon this feeling after years of genuinely liking and respecting the opposite sex. I have a job, a car, a mortgage on a flat, but I have been rejected on all dating platforms, by thousands of women, which suggests that they, in general, are shallow. They would rather date abusers, steroid addicts, and unemployed idiots, because I am not attractive enough, apparently.

It's always been my dream to fall in love with a woman who I could lavish attention on, but everyone my age rejects me, or ghosts me and then tells me I'm a misogynist for being annoyed about it. It's literally just emotional abuse and it's all one-sided against me. I can't say how I feel out loud, because I would become an outcast.

I'm not advocating for violence or any such thing—everyone deserves the right to be left alone in peace—this is just my opinion.

So, ladies,

Do you care about me?

I don't think you do.

But here's the thing: if I was in your position I WOULD CARE ABOUT ME—so who's the better person?

bored af.

My mum always says, 'Only boring people get bored, Mia'

So...

my mum always says, 'leave me alone and go make breakfast for your mental sister!'

so...

Ever thought about auditioning to be the damaged kid protagonist in a sad Irish novel?

LILY AT 15:34

don't say it.

MIA AT 15:34

Salily–

LILY AT 15:34

i'm HALF irish HALF
HALF HALF.

MIA AT 15:35

Tbf you're not white enough

LILY AT 15:35

more BAME rep in
irish novels please!

MIA AT 15:35

Haven't you read
Finnegan's Sheik?

LILY AT 15:35

sally rooney is CANCELLED.

PSA Daniel's friend
Tariq: DAT ASS

actually tariq is meant to
have a truly big dick.

Fr?

According to?

daniel obv.

WAIT IS THAT WHY
YOU TERMINATED
YOUR DALLIANCE

don't push it.

you know it had nothing to
do with me and everything to
do with his cheating prick.

Billy Budd (15:40)   Honest pic rate

@femanon, where you at?

Femanon (15:42)   Honest pic rate

hola. what up?

Billy Budd (15:43)   Honest pic rate

So I really dig your pics. Any face?

Femanon (15:43)   Honest pic rate

thankies. no face pic though soz.

Billy Budd (15:43)   Honest pic rate

Why not?

Femanon (15:44) ·   Honest pic rate

nope.

Billy Budd (15:44)   Honest pic rate

You sure? What about if I track you down and
find out who you are myself?

Femanon (15:45)   Honest pic rate

lol nice one. try harder newfag.

Billy Budd (15:45)   Honest pic rate

Ooooh. Don't believe me?

Femanon (15:45)   Honest pic rate

nope.

Billy Budd (15:53)   Honest pic rate

Initials: Y-H

Femanon (15:56)   Honest pic rate

not me.

Billy Budd (15:57)   Honest pic rate

Korean Bitch. likes to be called by a certain
flower (according to your insta)

Councillor Murray (15:57)   Honest pic rate

Oh shit. DROP THE NAME

---

21 Cabbage (15:58)   Honest pic rate

do it do it do it do it do it do it do it

Anonymous (15:58)   Honest pic rate

face pics NOW!

Billy Budd (15:59)   Honest pic rate

You're in high demand @femanon, so what should I do? Should I expose you?

LILY AT 15:59

mia some guy has stolen my nudes and is threatening to leak them on 9bord.

MIA AT 15:59

Serious?

LILY AT 16:00

serious. wtf should I do?

MIA AT 16:00

Daniel? I'm going to fucking murder him

LILY AT 16:00

it wasn't daniel.

MIA AT 16:01

Wait, who else you
send nudes???

LILY AT 16:02

it definitely wasn't daniel.
i've been hacked or
something. they got my
IP address i dunno?

MIA AT 16:03

Nudes got your face in?

LILY AT 16:03

he's found my insta online
and says he's gonna leak the
nudes with my name and face.

i'm freaking the fuck out.

MIA AT 16:04

You sure it wasn't Daniel?

LILY AT 16:04

fuck off no. and DONT mention it to him DO NOT.

i promise you he didn't.

MIA AT 16:07

Ok, I think wait it out? Worst thing that could happen is some incels see your beautiful rack and you'll be the best thing that happened to them this week

LILY AT 16:08

fucking cold comfort mia. i'm literally so scared and angry rn. i'm freaking the fuck out.

MIA AT 16:10

Shit shit shit sending you so much love

Femanon (16:12)   fuck trannies

fuck trannies. fuck fuck fuck them. the suicide rate ISNT HIGH ENOUGH.

Anonymous (16:13)   fuck trannies

Just ignore them anon. Transsexualism is a bourgeois disease invented by capitalism. If you hate trans people, fight capitalism first, then they'll go away.

Polythene Pam (16:13)   fuck trannies

@femanon Did you put your name in the goblet of fire!!!!

Jackson Bollock (16:13)   fuck trannies

why you so threatened by them @femanon? they're just living their life?

Anonymous (16:15)   fuck trannies

TRANS RIGHTS!

Her Majesty (16:16)   fuck trannies

Trans wrongs.

Anonymous (16:15)   fuck trannies

Yesterday I watched a bunch of biker dudes beat the living shit out of two traps on the street below me

Jackson Bollock (16:16)   fuck trannies

that's fucking horrible. i hope the cops arrested
and brutally raped those bikers.

Femanon (16:16)   fuck trannies

@JacksonBollock, blah blah they brought it on
themselves. EVERYONE SUFFERS. who cares.

Milton Berle's Schlong (16:16)   fuck trannies

@femanon. At the risk of 'lecturing you on
the worm', an addendum to your insightful
comment: I have all the respect in the world for
Trans folk, but it seems to me that the people
who suffer most are the ones who can't talk
about their suffering. It's too painful and so forth.

It seems to me that the ones who insist on
mouthing off about it shouldn't be taken as
seriously as they want to be – because if you
have the energy and motivation to shout
about your suffering, I reckon you're going to
be alright.

Milton Berle's Schlong (16:18)   fuck trannies

e.g. Holocaust survivors won't say a word about what they went through, unless pressured to. But the CHILDREN of Holocaust survivors, they won't shut up about it!

Former child / aspiring DILF (16:22)   fuck trannies

@MiltonBerlesSchlong. based, but you didn't have to bring the judenrat into it.

Femanon (16:22)   fuck trannies

@JacksonBollock name one tranny that passes. i'll wait.

Billy Budd (16:24)   fuck trannies

@femanon. Hey, Lily! What you doing on this side of 9bord?

Felt like getting this off my chest

Phil
17 Sept, 16:28

25 y/o male here. I used to have an aunt who'd take care of me. My mom was quite heavy on drugs in those days (it was opiates), and when she was deep into it my Auntie Claire would come and pick me up and I'd live at her place (sometimes up to 3 months at a time). It was okay, but the house always smelled of her very old dog that would shed its fur all the time, which was problematic because I'm allergic so I would often sneeze myself to sleep. Still, Auntie Claire tried her best. She wasn't a very good cook, and she wasn't very good at conversation either, so we mostly just kept out of each other's way and ate microwave meals. She was quite aloof in that regard, and I wonder if she wasn't on the spectrum a little bit.

She was single, and she used to have men come round every weekend to make her feel happy. It wasn't a problem and I was actually glad that she was "getting some". But the thing is, when she used to have sex with these men, she would purposely leave the door to her bedroom wide open so not only could I hear, but if I went to the toilet I'd be able to see into the bedroom. I don't know if she wanted to show off that she had a different man every weekend, or if it was something weirder, but many times I would peek around the corner and watch her going at it.

And honestly, she was really, really good. Her shyness was all gone, and it seemed like she was really having a great time (and by the sounds of the men, they were also having

192

a ball). She would mount and ride them in a way that was impressive for her age, or make them sit in a chair, then lower herself slowly onto them. For most of my teenage years I used to masturbate to these scenes, her incredible, deafening orgasms, and interesting, slightly unreal sex positions. And when I finally did the deed myself with a sweet girl called Lucy (the daughter of a preacher in town), I kept picturing Auntie Claire riding joyful atop these men. I remember feeling proud of her for some reason.

I'm so glad that I got to live with her and have those experiences. You don't realise it at the time, but it made everything bearable, and I might not have made it out the other side in one piece.

I haven't seen her for 5 years and since then I got a job working in I.T. for a big furniture company, paid a deposit on an apartment, and met a girl I really like.

But I just heard my aunt died of a stroke this morning and I can't stop thinking about her. I went on this website because I needed to tell the world about the strange, amazing woman who took care of me. I just wanted to say, sincerely, thank you for everything Auntie Claire.

—Rest in Power.

3

RealConfessions

My grandad was a pedo

Sam
17 Sept, 18:26

18 y/o female here. My grandpa died last year, which was really sad for me because I used to spend a lot of time at my grandparents' house, and especially with him because my grandma was often running errands. He was like any old grandad, a bit fusty with some backward opinions, but generally he respected everyone and always made sure to say hello to people he recognised in the street.

Right after he died, I was staying with my grandma and I was poking around upstairs in my grandpa's old study. I found an envelope stashed under a drawer in a desk, and inside were dozens of gross sex images of kids. I got so frightened that I stuffed them back and I've literally never said a word to anyone.

Well I saw my grandma this morning, and she seemed like she'd finally moved on from his death because she had arranged a date with another man. But every time I go over to visit, I can't help thinking: does she know? Surely she had to. I live in a small town in the midlands and everyone is connected to everyone else by some way or another, which means that you know people's business. Surely my grandma knew about this, because how can you hide that from your wife your whole life? I can't stop thinking about it now. The question is driving me insane. Because if she knew or even suspected, how could she leave me alone with him for all those years?

MIA AT 18:28

Any news?

LILY AT 18:30

he literally knows my name.

MIA AT 18:33

Are you sure it's not someone you know? It would require some serious KGB-grade skill to hack your computer and steal your nudes, THEN find out who you are on 9bord

I know you're seriously technosecure when it comes to passwords and stuff

LILY AT 18:35

it's not someone i fucking know.

and the worst part is that i DON'T EVEN GET TO SEE THEIR FACE and they get to RUIN MY LIFE.

MIA AT 18:36

Honestly if that's the case and this guy is serious, I think you should go to the police

LILY AT 18:36

no. that won't help and i don't want my parents involved.

wtf is my dad gonna think?

MIA AT 18:37

Yeah but at least you'll stop it being spread around the internet and stuff, that shit sticks to you FOR LIFE

Go to the police Lily

LILY AT 18:40

i can't go to the police.

i haven't (UGH) been 100% truthful with u i'm sorry.

i posted the pics myself on 9bord.

i just wanted some feedback.

don't judge.

Um

Okay, not sure what to say

say that you empathise and it doesn't matter WHERE they got the nudes from, only that they are going to do something awful and malicious that is going to destroy my life.

Like, I empathise of course I do, but I want to say I told you so?

Isn't the expression, you play
with fire you get burnt, a thing?

when i kill myself you're
going to look back on that
text you just sent and feel
so fucking guilty it's unreal.
that is some crazy evil
thing you just said to me.

Billy Budd (18:48)   Honest pic rate

@femanon. Hello

Billy Budd (18:50)   Honest pic rate

I know you're online

Margaret Atwood's Final Resting Place (18:51)   Honest pic rate

@BillyBudd just post the pics bud

Lev Yashin (18:51)   Honest pic rate

Yeah hurry tf up, my cock is fucking sore

Anonymous (18:52)   Honest pic rate

@BillyBudd have you even got the name?

Billy Budd (18:52)   Honest pic rate

@femanon alright I'm posting

Femanon (18:52)   Honest pic rate

wait please don't.

Billy Budd (18:53)   Honest pic rate

After I'm done here I might even send these pics
to your parents and friends to show them exactly
the kind of slut they're dealing with

Billy Budd (18:54)   Honest pic rate

Daddy's phone number ends in 242 right? Or
should I email your school instead?

---

666 (18:54)   Honest pic rate

Bro, you're going a bit far.

Femanon (18:55)   Honest pic rate

@BillyBudd what do you want from me?

Billy Budd (18:56)   Honest pic rate

Post a pic of your pussy and I won't expose
your name here

Schrödinger's Foreskin (18:56)   Honest pic rate

Can you do close up of asshole?

Femanon (18:57)   Honest pic rate

@BillyBudd you're not going to stop if I do.

Billy Budd (18:57)   Honest pic rate

Okay. Here we go. First line of Address is House
number 151

Femanon (18:57)   Honest pic rate

wait.

Femanon (19:01)   Honest pic rate

@BillyBudd please. i'm writing this sincerely and
truthfully. please, please, please don't post my
face and name and address. please don't send
them to my family or anybody close to me. i
know it gets people off to feel like they know
someone when they see nudes online, they
know their name and a little bit about them so
it makes fapping better, but it really is going to
ruin my life. please don't. please, just this one
time, i would be so grateful if you didn't do it to
me. please.

I'm so sorry for what I said Lily, I didn't mean it like that and I'm a stupid idiot, I want to help you, I really really want to be here for you

LILY AT 19:03

i'm literally crying right now.

MIA AT 19:03

I'm so sorry

LILY AT 19:04

fml i'm such a mess.

i literally had to leave the house cause mum was being so passive aggressive w me. dad's away for the night and i couldn't stand it with all this shit so i went and bought fucking loads of sweets.

but then i just burst into tears on the high street and had to sit down and now i look like such a dick, crying in public.

MIA AT 19:06

You could come over to mine? I'll ask my mum

LILY AT 19:06

yeah maybe.

omg some dude just walked past then doubled back and sat on the bench with me.

MIA AT 19:07

Ew

LILY AT 19:09

he's literally started talking to me.

MIA AT 19:09

Who is he?

lmao he's lecturing me on my phone, and then just dropped his.

MIA AT 19:11

Does he know who you are? He could be the guy online?

LILY AT 19:13

said he's gay.

MIA AT 19:13

Don't trust him

HE COULD BE THE GUY

MIA AT 19:16

Hello?

Are you safe

MIA AT 19:20

Where are you? Are you alive?

I'm really worried,
please answer

LILY AT 19:22

yeah yeah all good. he's
just left. was actually
kinda goofy and sweet.

stopped crying.

Laszlo Jamf (19:22)   Books on how to sleep with many women

Hey anons, looking for any literary suggestions
that will help me fornicate with more women.

Slutty Hipster (19:23)   Books on how to sleep with many women

Beckett's Molloy

206

Susan Boyle's Diary (19:23)　　　　Books on how to sleep with
　　　　　　　　　　　　　　　　　　　　　　many women

My diary

Sigma Fail (19:24)　　　Books on how to sleep with many women

anything by Martin Amis. I read Lucky Jim every
night, motuweth frisas.

Sontag's Bone Marrow (19:25)　　　　Books on how to sleep with
　　　　　　　　　　　　　　　　　　　　　　many women

basically all of Marx, he's the GOAT — Capital is
the best for normies methinks

Alyosha (19:26)　　　Books on how to sleep with many women

Don't read. Just sell drugs and hit the gym.

Volcel Of Suburbia (19:26)　　　　Books on how to sleep with
　　　　　　　　　　　　　　　　　　　　　　many women

. . .the detail of the pattern is amusement. . .

And/Or (19:26)   Books on how to sleep with many women

Try Buster Keaton's biography. Dude was a serial womanizer. Ironic cus the character he always plays is basically an incel by today's standards. We Stan Chaplin too.

Kynesgrove (19:26)   Books on how to sleep with many women

Read Walter Bae-jamin — OR ANY OTHER BOOK WRITTEN BY A JEW

Hyperlink Novel (19:27)   Books on how to sleep with many women

Jews are responsible for every tragedy in the world. Prove me wrong.

Femanon (19:29)   Books on how to sleep with many women

cool it with the antisemitic remarks.

Hyperlink Novel (19:30)   Books on how to sleep with many women

Jews invented climate change to distract everyone from their lack of foreskin

Hyperlink Novel (19:31)   Books on how to sleep with many women

Look at their main stooge. greta thunBERG

Hyperlink Novel (19:31)   Books on how to sleep with many women

Huh, @femanon? what you say to THAT?

Femanon (19:32)   Books on how to sleep with many women

grow up.

RealConfessions

Call of Duty

Dwayne
17 Sept, 19:34

24 y/o male here from Texas. I used to play Black Ops online with another kid from the UK. He was so British and always called me 'mate' or 'bloke', and I'd say 'hold your horses' or 'howdy' in a stereotypical southern drawl. We spent thousands of hours on BO and MW3 and BO2. And they were the best times of my life, meeting all these different people across the world, cracking jokes and growing up together. He was a year younger, and one day I mentioned I was going to my school prom the next day: 'Finally done it. University next.' And he was like, in a fake southern accent: 'Yeehaw! Next year I'll be doing the same thing. Congratulations pardner!' And I replied, in British: "cheers mate!"

Well I went to college, it's a whole new decade, and I'm working towards a Masters. On his Xbox profile it says 'last online 6 years ago'. Crazy how time flies. Wherever you are, and if by some crazy coincidence you're reading this: I hope you're living your best life – you bloody lovely bloke!

4

relapse   Anonymous
17 Sept, 20:08

i just cut myself over a KFC bargain bucket

LILY AT 20:09

i begged the guy on
9bord not do it.

MIA AT 20:12

What he say?

LILY AT 20:13

no reply yet. maybe it worked.

MIA AT 20:13

What a nice guy

LILY AT 20:13

or he's having dinner.

I've got an idea - if he comes back, pretend you're the FBI and say that if he posts the photos he's going to jail cause you're underage

already said i was 18. these people are smart and they can smell weakness from a mile off. you can never go back on what you say. don't want to risk pissing him off any more.

they punish you if you don't tell the truth.

Billy Budd (20:16)   Honest pic rate

@femanon, after considering your plea, LILY, I've decided that you're still a slut and I'm sending off the pics to your family and friends

Anonymous (20:16)   Honest pic rate

About time...

Nationwide (20:17)   Honest pic rate

He's not gonna do it or he would have done
it by now.

Tom Wanks (20:17)   Honest pic rate

I'm so ready.

Beiherspielen (20:18)   Honest pic rate

Post the dad's reaction

Two Endings (20:19)   Honest pic rate

Let's goooooo

Billy Budd (20:20)   Honest pic rate

But first, dropping name and face pic here in
approximately 10 seconds

9

Billy Budd (20:20)   Honest pic rate

8

7

Billy Budd (20:20)   Honest pic rate

5

4

Femanon (20:20)   Honest pic rate

i'm underage stop this is the Fbi.

Billy Budd (20:22)   Honest pic rate

?????

Femanon (20:23)   Honest pic rate

i'm underage. if you post the FBI will get you. i
will send the police.

Billy Budd (20:25)   Honest pic rate

Seriously?

Femanon (20:26)   Honest pic rate

to repeat: i'm a child.

Billy Budd (20:26)   Honest pic rate

?

McFly (20:29)   Honest pic rate

Busted!

Symparanekromenoi (20:30)   Honest pic rate

MODS!

Femanon (20:32) Honest pic rate

@BillyBudd you there?

Femanon (20:34) Honest pic rate

@BillyBudd anything?

Femanon (20:44) Honest pic rate

helloooo @BillyBudd.

Femanon (20:48) Honest pic rate

thought so.

Femanon (20:50) Honest pic rate

I THOUGHT SO.

Femanon (20:51) Honest pic rate

@BillyBudd so there we are.

Femanon (20:51)   Honest pic rate

@BillyBudd motherfucker.

Femanon (20:52)   Honest pic rate

fuck off back where you came from you scum.

Femanon (20:52)   Honest pic rate

fucking lowlife prick.

Femanon (20:53   Honest pic rate

absolute cunt pedo prick.

Femanon (20:53)   Honest pic rate

fuck you nonce.

Femanon (20:53)   Honest pic rate

absolute fucking CUNT.

Femanon (20:53)   Honest pic rate

CUNT CUNT CUNT.

Femanon (20:53)   Honest pic rate

I HOPE YOU FUCKING DIE CUNT.

LILY AT 21:08

i did it. he's not responding.

MIA AT 21:10

You sure

LILY AT 21:10

yeah.

MIA AT 21:11

What did you do

LILY AT 21:11

fbi.

FBI?

F-B-I !!!

Fucking Brilliant Idea.

Fucking Bossed It

Fighting Braindead Incels.

Fuckers Be Irrelevant

Friends Before Idiots.

Fabulous Beautiful ICON

tysm for everything btw.

It's what oldest and dearest pals are for

;)

gracias.

Ok now let's breathe a collective sigh of relief, seriously

yeah, fuck me.

Phew

so how was your day? lol.

MIA AT 21:20

> Could have been worse

> You still wanna come
> over to mine?

LILY AT 21:20

> gonna ask mum now.

MIA AT 21:20

> It's pretty late, you sure

> ?

LILY AT 21:21

> Yeah. I really want to.

MIA AT 21:21

> Amazing. Love you.

Femanon (21:27)   more true thoughts/random opinions

ok. Blue Lives Matter. prove me wrong.

Anonymous (21:28)   more true thoughts/random opinions

Cops kill more people than the army.

Not Michael Fish (21:29)   more true thoughts/random opinions

Army > cops

---

24 (21:29)   more true thoughts/random opinions

Army lives matter

Anonymous (21:29)   more true thoughts/random opinions

All lives matter

Schopenhauer (21:30)   more true thoughts/random opinions

No lives matter.

Femanon (21:34)   more true thoughts/random opinions

@Schopenhauer, don't be a faggot.

Not to be cringe or anything

Femanon
17 Sept, 23:55

but it's nearly midnight and i couldn't sleep, so i got up and woke up my friend and together we went out to the park. she's right this minute trying to do cartwheels. it's a full moon so i can see her quite clearly, even though there's barely any light in the field.

she's not very good and keeps falling down onto the grass. now she's complaining that her hands are all damp.

i'm sat against the trunk of a big tree, and the roots are poking out and it's not the most comfortable sitting position. but it's actually really peaceful being outside at this time.

an ant is crawling up my leg i think.

i don't mind, for some reason, even though i usually hate insects.

well good luck.

goodnight.

crawl on, soldier!

Fifteen

Natwest Sheds a Tear

E ven the minor ambitions of our hero – and this was how
Natwest thought of himself after the events of the day –
were at the mercy of a malign fate intent on his humiliation. He
stood before the large double doors of the town hall, embittered
by the frustrating sense of an ending a few metres away, while
the sounds of merriment floated gently out onto the street. He
was unable to enter until he'd found a twig of suitable size to
wipe away the shit from underneath his shoe. Life was endless
misfortune. Natwest was the lone poker chip on a smoky table
getting shoved around for sport, and the table in his mind was
Coolidge's *Dogs Playing Poker* – adding considerable insult to
considerable injury, for the excrement on his shoe was indisput-
ably canine in origin.

He searched the pavement for a stick like the mangy dog
he had become, as if he were the one who'd laid the steaming
turd he'd unwittingly stepped in. Who was the architect of this
comic reversal? There were many people he could blame, but
presently the honourable thing was to blame himself. Despair
was upon him, the despair of a comedian – someone like
Keaton, probably. Or was this a Chaplin situation? He couldn't
make his mind up.

Finding nothing of use in the immediate vicinity, he limped

towards the nearby park – the most obvious place to look for a stick.

T he evening air was cold, and the newly risen moon was trying its best to be full. It was too early for the streetlights to illuminate the edge of the park, so instead Natwest used his phone torch to search the pavement. Up ahead, mounted on the kerb, was an ominous black Bentley – the same vehicle Natwest had noticed cruising around town the whole day – now parked. One of its doors was open, and a middle-aged man stumbled into view. He carried a heavy object and deposited it in the boot of his car. What exactly was he doing? Natwest noticed that someone had dumped a load of shit on one of the nearby park benches, mainly spare building materials and household junk, and the man was diligently clearing it away, storing the rubbish in his boot. Was he from the council? Driving a Bentley? They'd obviously had a huge boost in funding. The man glanced in the direction of Natwest's phone torch. 'Alright, mate?'

'Uh-huh.' Natwest switched off his torch and prepared to walk the other way, but the man called after him.

'Can you believe this?' He indicated the junk on the bench. 'Special place in hell reserved for fly tippers.' He leant down and grabbed a large cinder block from the ground. As he carried it to his car, he tripped up and dropped the object.

'Bollocks!' He jumped out the way, and the block narrowly avoided crushing his foot. 'Can you, er...' The man swayed slightly. 'Can you give me a hand?'

'Uh... sure.' Natwest crouched down and lifted the cinder block. He smelt alcohol on the man's breath.

'Thanks...' The man grabbed the other side of the block. 'You live here, mate?'

'Uh, yeah. Well, I'm going to university tomorrow.'

The man grunted. 'I used to live here too. Twenty years ago now. . .' They lowered the cinder block into the boot of his car. 'Came back yesterday for a. . . an anniversary.' He blinked twice. 'Memorial, really.'

'Sorry to hear that,' said Natwest, somewhat automatically. The man appeared to be one of these people who believed that oversharing was the same thing as being honest. He wouldn't stop talking.

'Now that I'm back, I've just been driving around town all day. Checking out my old haunts, how much everything has changed. Memory lane and all that. To be honest, I was probably about your age when I left town—'

'You've been *driving* around?' The man was obviously drunk, and Natwest admonished him for driving.

'Fuck. Relax.' The man waved it off with a gesture that was so reminiscent of Natwest's own famously dismissive wave, that he briefly imagined that this middle-aged man was himself – in twenty years' time. It was a depressing sight.

'Where are you living now?' asked Natwest, carrying another block to the car.

'London.'

'How is it?'

'It's always the same conversations,' the man said. 'New Builds and Tube Strikes.' He threw a few more bricks into the boot.

'Right.' Natwest shook the cinder dust from his hands and prepared to say his goodbyes, wary of both the exhibition, and the dog shit on the bottom of his shoe. But the next thing the man said made a swift exit impossible.

'My mum passed some years ago.' The man nodded at the bench. 'We got this installed for her.' He picked up a long piece of plywood, snapped it in half over his knee and chucked it in the boot. 'She was sixty-five.'

Natwest leant over and read the inscription on the bench.

The Best Mum In The World
Gone Too Soon
Irene Wilson
1953–2018

A quiet sadness took hold of him as he realised it was the same bench he and Georgie had once had sex on – when they'd ditched prom together on the last night of school. That was years ago now. Georgie had lit a fag after they'd both come, and on this very bench he'd cradled Natwest like a baby. Georgie, who always smoked like the cigarette was giving him life, and not the opposite. Natwest used to write little poetic notes, or tiny pieces of art criticism, or occasionally love letters on the rolling papers, and that night he'd watched his boyfriend imbibe his precious words with an extraordinary feeling of hope. How dispiriting to think back on that memory now; the two of them, watching the smoke curling upwards into the night sky, wondering what the future would hold.

He checked the time – 7:36 p.m. He was late for the exhibition. He glanced at the man, who was taking a photo of the bench. 'So I think I'm going to head—'

'Fuck-sake!' The man dropped his phone. It made a hateful sound as it bounced off the pavement and landed in the road.

Natwest retrieved it for him. 'It happens.' The screen was a mess, so many cracks that they were all joined to one another, like a glass Jackson Pollock. It was in an even worse condition than his own phone. 'Here,' he handed it back.

'Thanks, mate,' the man said, shaking his head, and then burping loudly. 'Pardon me.' The last thing on the bench was an IKEA bag filled with old household rubbish. Broken mirrors, plant pots, an old stereo, a doll's house. The man reached into the bag and pulled out a cheap plastic clock. 'Look at this junk.'

Natwest glanced at the clock. It was broken, the hour hand

bent back on itself. 'Is it bad luck or good luck to throw away a stopped clock? I can't remember,' he said.

The man shrugged drunkenly and turned the clock sideways, then mimed throwing it as if it were a Frisbee. 'Go long?'

Natwest laughed. 'No thanks. I'm not really that sporty—' But the man had already thrown the clock, and he found himself running to catch it. He leapt into the air – and lifting his arm as high as it could go – miraculously grabbed hold of the object.

'Let's go! What a catch, mate!'

He stared at the clock, amazed at his hitherto undiscovered frisbeeing abilities. He threw it back to the man, slightly concerned by his erratic behaviour.

'Clock Frisbee. Should be an Olympic sport,' the man said, flinging it once more in Natwest's direction.

For a second time, Natwest jumped dramatically into the air and caught hold of the clock. 'Got it!' He even performed an elaborate spin as he landed back on the pavement.

'Not sporty, my arse.'

He laughed and tossed it back to the man, who took aim once again and launched the clock into the sky with a mighty arm. Natwest leapt to catch it, but this time it slipped through his open hand and smashed into two pieces against a tree behind him.

'Ah, fuck...' He retrieved the two halves of the clock and held them up. 'You want it?'

The man indicated the watch on his wrist. 'A man with a watch knows the time. A man with two is never sure.' He snorted violently. 'I should write that down.'

Natwest nodded and dumped the two pieces of clock in a nearby bin.

When he returned to the bench, the man was staring at the inscription.

'Mate... I wish I'd spent more time with her... Honest to God.'

'Why didn't you?' Natwest only realised how rude the question sounded after he'd asked it.

The drunk man didn't seem to mind. 'The usual story, mate. I left her behind. Left her and did other things, spent a lot of time finding out who I was. I've basically perfected the art of describing myself.' He laughed bitterly, and the enormous regret on his face was wretched. Natwest had to look away. 'If you want to know who you really are, mate – I mean really – the cost is like... never knowing anyone else, you know?'

Natwest felt he ought to respond with something profound, but unsure what he could add, replied with a general philosophical point:

'Damn.'

'Exactly.' The man lifted up his phone for a second time and took a photo of the bench. 'Got it.' He swayed in place, and there was a moment of silence between the two of them. 'I'd forgotten about that sound,' he said.

'What sound?'

He paused and lifted a finger to the sky. The sound of cars on the motorway, a mile east, carried into the park. The motorway, which took the people of this town towards bigger towns; it sounded like the wind, and you wouldn't notice the sound was constant unless an outsider pointed it out. 'It's like I'm hearing it for the first time. I bet you'll forget all about it too,' he said. The man's brown eyes were big and sad. 'How did I get so old?'

'Time?' responded Natwest, unhelpfully. He'd intended it as a joke, but the man just sighed.

'Yeah.' He turned to Natwest and shook his hand. 'Good luck, mate,' and got into his car.

'I don't think you should drive like—' But the man waved off Natwest's moralising.

'I'm fine.' As he put the car into gear, he wrinkled his nose. 'It does smell a bit funky here, doesn't it?'

Natwest watched him depart into the night, mortified that the shit on the bottom of his shoe had been emitting a noxious odour the whole time.

His phone vibrated in his pocket.

Wherer you!!!! You are an hour late!!

It was a message from his mother.

Doctor hung very disappointed you're not here

He was irritated by the tone of her text, and it reminded him again of his miserable circumstances. He typed out an angry reply.

OK! I'M ALMOST THERE! 10 MINS!

He pressed 'send' furiously – but pushed the screen so hard that the phone catapulted out of his own hand, bounced off the memorial bench, and landed viciously on the pavement.

'Fuck-sake!' He kicked the bench in anger. The fall had added more disastrous cracks to the phone screen. It might be funny, how many times he'd dropped his phone, if it weren't so concerning. It was foolish at this point to blame simple clumsiness. Something was trying its best to destroy Natwest, perhaps his own subconscious; or maybe in the space of twenty-four hours he'd developed a life-threatening neurological disorder. If either of these things were true, what calamity awaited him next? His thoughts spiralled dangerously, and he was seized by an insane feeling of panic. Suddenly he felt dizzy, had to lean against a lamp post for support. His heart rate had apparently quadrupled, and in the corner of his vision terrifying dark spots appeared. He attempted to calm himself down by performing several yogically sound breathing exercises – but nothing worked. His corkscrew brain was winding closer and closer to a blind fear whose inevitable conclusion was nothing less than the end of the world.

Seeking a distraction, he grabbed the packet of stoneless dates from his rucksack and desperately bit into one of the dried fruits. It was delicious. Smooth. He chewed the date methodically, concentrating on the sweetness of the flesh – but it didn't fully divert his attention. He pulled out a second date, eager to continue – but as he took a bite, he cracked his teeth on a huge stone lodged in its centre.

He yelped. A fierce pain burnt at the crown of one of his molars. He spat out the fruit and kicked the tiny thing into a bush. One date in his packet of stoneless dates had plotted against him. The packaging had promised a 100 per cent stone-free experience, but it hadn't delivered. Like Royal Mail this morning, thought Natwest bitterly. He held his jaw, astonished at the pain now dispersing throughout his mouth.

So he had another reason to go to the exhibition – he needed a dentist.

Yet unexpectedly, Natwest realised that the dates had done their job, for instead of contributing to his growing hysteria the immense pain of the unexpected stone had forced him back into the real world. And oddly enough, the real world seemed different. He was experiencing a comedown from the panic attack, and rather than being stuck in his head, Natwest was stuck outside himself. In this new setting he felt decentred, small beside the totalitarian oaks in the park behind him, and tiny before the enormous washing machines in the window of the laundromat opposite. Beside it, the nail salon. *Nail Again. Nail Better.* He thought of Mrs. Pandey, who'd always tried her best – but like everyone else had failed to change him. He sighed, calmly swallowed his bloody saliva and concentrated on the gentle evening breeze sweeping the hair from his face.

He was alone. Dreadfully alone in this world. Summer was over. Everything was ending. The future he was dragged inevitably towards was unknowable, and he was frightened of it. He finally admitted to himself that he didn't want to leave town. He wished he could return to his mother's house, leap into bed and stay hidden beneath the covers for another year. But the world insisted he move. For the first time in years he felt his eyes shaking with the possibility of tears. He ran his tongue over his cracked tooth – which wobbled dangerously in his mouth – and was seized by an unfamiliar sadness.

'Think I'm going to cry?' he said aloud, to the night – and the night responded with the quiet rustling of a nearby tree.

Natwest looked at the bench commemorating the dead mother, and thought of all the unhappiness in that drunk man's face. He gently traced the inscription with his finger, and, pulled along by his own melancholy, walked along the edge of the park, reading the memorial plates that were fastened to the other benches.

Dedicated to:
Mark Edelman
'ARE YOU KIDDING ME!?'

He smiled a little at that, and moved on to the next one.

In memory of
Gene Shapiro
A loving father, grandfather, and husband

Natwest recognised the name on the bench. It was his neighbour Joan's late husband, who had died the year before. A kindly pensioner who'd given Natwest a lift to the station – five years ago when he travelled up to Oxford University for an open day. Funny that he should find the old man's name on this evening, of all evenings.

Joan.

His interaction with her this morning felt like years ago. He'd met so many people during the course of the day – and yet he'd done so little with his time. Instead, he'd floundered about looking for the rotten package while they went on with their lives, his whole day merely a series of brief distractions. He pictured all these people, standing on a large West End stage, like the cast of some '80s musical. What was their relation to our hero? Like everyone else, Natwest had always imagined himself to be the main character. Of course he knew that everyone contained their own wonderful interior lives, etc. etc., and that this main-character syndrome was a universal human delusion. But deep down, in his bones, in the core of his being, and regardless of what he knew to be true about other people, he'd refused to believe he was a bit player. Until this present moment, nothing could have shaken that feeling.

But something had shifted.

It was all the people he had met today. He'd always thought he was leaving them behind, but it dawned on him now that it was more likely *they* were leaving *him* behind. He was but a minor character in the drama of their lives. Present for a season, for a storyline, to add some texture to their narratives, but written out of the script before the start of next season because it was convenient for the writers. In truth, he barely existed at all.

On a normal day, this realisation would have taken him to the edge of despair; this evening, it took him beyond it. He turned to petty nihilism. Why did any of these thoughts matter if, at the end of our lives, all that was left was an inscription on a bench, in a park, in a nowhere town like this one? He was reminded of Imam Mishaal, who wanted to pivot the world on a binary. Chaplin or Keaton, McCartney or Lennon, Hegel or Kierkegaard – and thinking of all the disparate people he'd spoken to today, Natwest added more pairs to the list: old or young, Muslim or Jew, male or female, teacher or student – and he wondered whether all these binaries about art and life were just two punchlines to the same joke.

All these human bodies: he pictured them now dead and buried; or more likely, their ashes scattered in various back gardens and/or seaside resorts. Did their absence make him feel anything? He stared down the long line of benches and continued walking sadly along the edge of the park. As he passed by each bench – all commemorating someone or other – he closed his eyes and imagined their inscriptions.

Richard Hung
Dentist and Painter
Dearly missed

In loving memory of
Mrs. Pandey
Teacher
Thanks for trying

Dedicated to Imam Mishaal
Man of Wisdom
'Nobody's perfect.'

For Georgie
Lover and Friend
Never forgotten

235

For Lily
So young

Against all his expectations, it was a heartbreaking exercise. Lily's name in particular had brought him to the brink of tears. *Now* you cry, he thought. *Now* you cry. As he passed another bench, the image of his father appeared unexpectedly before him.

For my dad
Who I never knew

And then there was another person. The one whose death he feared most of all.

In loving memory of my mum,
Penny
Who was always there for me
Whether I wanted her or not

He wiped his eyes and smiled at the single tear he'd managed to produce. It was a start. He wandered over to the last bench at the end of the row and thought of one final inscription.

We remember:
Natwest
A hero in this town

He took a seat on his own memorial bench, falling smoothly onto the wood as a log slips over a waterfall. Then he looked down between his legs. There was a stick on the ground. He laughed loudly then, as if someone had told a great joke.

He picked up the short, bifurcated stick. It looked like this:

His phone vibrated. It was his mother again:

?

Natwest stood up and began to scrape away the shit on the bottom of his shoe. But there was an issue with the angle. He could not look sufficiently far enough over his shoulder to see if his vague jabbing motions were dislodging the shit, so he stabbed blindly at his foot, removing nothing and occasionally scratching his ankle.

Suddenly, every streetlight in town decided to ignite, for the automatic timers had colluded for the exact moment of his humiliation.

His bench was lit up and his face brilliantly illuminated.

'Natwest?'

It was Mrs. Pandey, teacher of English, carrying two drooping plastic bags and watching with bemusement as he struggled to remove the shit.

'I stepped in poo,' he said, as apologetic as a child, and the second the words fell from his mouth he was consumed by a deep shame. He hung his head like a dog.

Mrs. Pandey heaved her huge glasses further up her nose. 'I can see.' But she smiled then and pointed at a black mark on the toe of her leather boot. 'Happens to the best of us.' She offered Natwest a tender hand, and he was reminded of poor Lily at the bus stop. Overcome with feeling after his profound revelations, he passionately grabbed his old teacher's hand.

She pulled it away. 'No, Natwest. Give me the stick. Let me try.'

Whatever dignity he had left departed then, like a missed train. He handed over the stick. 'Sorry, Miss.'

Yet she was apparently unfazed. 'Put your hands on the bench and lift up your foot.'

He did just that, and with some tenderness Mrs. Pandey scraped the dog shit from his shoe. There was a moment of quiet, only the sounds of a stick lightly brushing the rubber of his sole, and the end-of-summer breeze whistling down the street.

She dropped the stick in the gutter. 'There.' Her voice carried the same authority it had when Natwest was at school, so when she ordered him to dip his shoe in a puddle to wash off the remainder of the poo, he obeyed as if he were still a student. When the shoe was finally clean, Mrs. Pandey pointed in the direction of the town hall.

'Exhibition?'

Natwest nodded and they began the short walk back to the building. There followed five minutes of peaceful footsteps – some sort of calm before the storm, he thought. When the two of them reached the double doors of the town hall, they each pushed one half of the door open at the exact same moment – in such a way that a casual onlooker might have thought it planned – and together stepped into the exhibition.

Sixteen

Chiasmus without End

Anita Pandey – woman, English teacher, second-generation immigrant, thirty-five-year-old cancer survivor – woke up with her arm dangling off the side of the bed. Unfortunately, this early in the morning her left–right coordination was somewhat misaligned, and so instead of turning over onto the other side of the mattress she rolled the wrong way – following her arm off the bed and plummeting to the carpet, frantically dragging the duvet with her to cushion the fall. She lay there for some time, her breasts pressed lazily against the floor, a gentle heat rising from her crotch. What would her students think if they saw her like this?

Well, Pandey does as Pandey pleases.

Anita tugged the charger cord, and her phone tumbled off the nightstand and landed by her face. After a number of unsuccessful attempts she entered the passcode, and using the carpet as her pillow, called in sick, coughing unconvincingly into the ear of the nice secretary whose name escaped her. Then, sprawled beside the bed – and before she'd even fallen asleep – Miss Pandey began to snore.

*

Out on the street, Anita spotted her old student, Natwest. He was sitting on a bench and fiddling with a package. He looked up at her, and they made regrettable eye contact.

'This is a nice surprise,' she said, approaching him – but it was a lie. Anita disliked seeing her former students around town in this fashion. It reminded her that she was a teacher and they her pupils, and that this dreadful equation contained a question she wanted nothing to do with: what had they done with the knowledge she had imparted? Her brain couldn't help but ask it, and the answer was usually that they became successful in other fields, and so forgot all about their English Literature teacher. On those rare occasions that they pursued the arts, they soon gave up and went into recruitment, sending Anita into a spiral of doubt about her capabilities as an educator.

She and Natwest made small talk, and she asked after his university plans.

'I'm leaving tomorrow,' he said.

It was about time, thought Anita – and immediately felt ashamed of herself. The thing she disliked most about her interactions with Natwest was that she knew he felt condemned in her presence. It was obvious in the way he avoided her eyes, fiddled with his phone. The way his cheeks so often flushed. It was the opposite of what a teacher wanted a student to feel. And she also hated that Natwest was correct. Some part of her *was* disappointed in his false start.

But then an odd thing happened. Natwest pointed at the nail salon across the street. 'Look at that. Such a stupid image.'

Anita looked at the sign, a tongue-in-cheek reproduction of *The Creation of Adam*, but with the nails on the thumbs painted pink. 'It's not that bad. Quite clever, really.'

'Clever? I have to disagree with you there, Miss.' And he did, calling the picture 'a debasement', 'a meaningless joke'. It was irritating, and for no reason other than the sport of it, Anita felt compelled to defend the image.

'Natwest, you're looking at it wrong. I think you've made a judgement about the work of art without fully considering the image before you. . .' She continued this way, and surprised herself by launching into a breathless monologue praising the picture, some part of her hoping to sway her former student in the process. It worked, for Natwest soon joined her in applauding the nail salon – and in turn she got far too carried away with her point.

'. . .there's no such thing as simple faith anymore. People have to be lured in by the promise of beauty, by the grandeur of cathedrals and ceremonies and basilicas. The nail salon comments on the essential vapidity of the church. Even God has to wear nail polish. The contemporary individual is forced—'

She felt a sharp pain where one of her kidneys used to be, and cried out. She'd overexerted herself. Anita waved away Natwest's concern – now embarrassed before her old student.

There followed an awkward pause. What was the point in teaching him anything anymore, when nothing useful had come of it? she asked herself – and then reproached herself for the thought.

Her old student helpfully filled the silence by dropping his phone. 'Fuck-sake.'

She returned it to him.

'So uh. . . when does school go back?' asked Natwest.

It was the question she'd hoped he wouldn't ask. 'We went back two weeks ago,' she replied.

'Oh so aren't you—'

'I called in sick.' There was some judgement in Natwest's look. Yes, Pandey had skipped school, like an errant pupil.

It was a quarter to two, and the afternoon sun generated interesting shadows across Natwest's face, so from certain angles he looked like a noir detective, and perhaps she the interrogated woman. He'd grown into quite a handsome young man.

That's your former student, Pandey.

Anita glanced around the empty park and raised a finger to her lips as if to say, 'Don't breathe a word of this to anyone.' She was unconvincing. In response, Natwest ran an oddly seductive hand through his fine, dark hair. The situation was in need of defusing. Anita spoke about something inconsequential – gossip about the new head of department and his draconian laws on the pedagogy of iambic pentameter – but Natwest looked bored. She changed the subject and asked him what he was looking forward to doing at university.

'Yeah, yeah,' he replied, evidently missing the content of the question.

In the ensuing silence, Anita considered the young man on the bench. Natwest had been very important in the first years of her career, when he was only fourteen, and she – impossibly – was but a few years older than he was now. Most people assume that teachers hold an outsized sway on their students' lives, but in Anita's case certain students could take up an immeasurable space in *her* brain. For instance, once upon a time she imagined herself as Natwest's mentor, thought her fate was closely tied to this most brilliant and curious of students. She'd had guilty visions of his great success. Pictured her name printed in the back of all his books. There would follow the inevitable Oscar acceptance speech – 'for all the teachers who taught me, especially Miss Pandey...' – but now he'd grown up, and those things had not come to pass. Even worse, she thought, he'd grown up into a *less* interesting person than he used to be.

Or was it she who had changed?

'Good luck with university, Natwest. I think you'll really like it.' She offered him a kind look, but it came off sterner than intended.

242

'Thanks Miss.'

Anita waved goodbye and left Natwest to open the package he'd been fondling before she had rudely interrupted him. She wondered how long it would be before she would see him again – and if he would return from university a changed man.

M iss Pandey had failed as a teacher. There wasn't a single student who'd passed through her class who had done anything worthwhile with the knowledge she'd given them. The self-righteous idealism she'd experienced as a twenty three year old arriving at the school gates, doe-eyed – clutching her bag of important books on pedagogy – had been ground down, one allusion to alliteration at a time. The whole project of teaching literature was a lie designed to line the pockets of the RSC. So she thought at least, on her gloomiest mornings when, permanently exhausted from her surgery for renal transitional cell carcinoma, she limped into a classroom to teach ungrateful kids Shakespeare – or worse, an Ode on a tediously Grecian Urn.

She would like to be in Greece right now. Some rocky island somewhere, with a tall Jamaican poet reading her sonnets in a lilting patois. Yet unfortunately the reality was much different: she was not in Greece, but rather turning into her mother's road, to pay a brief visit to the woman who forced her out of her vagina and then spent the next thirty years complaining about it.

The distinguishing feature of the house she'd grown up in was a bright red door. Everything else was what you'd expect a semi-detached house in this town to be. As she approached, there was some movement behind the curtains, and the door opened before Anita knocked. 'Come in, come in! I made you pasta,' her mother said. She was a cataclysmic woman; her continuous consumption of pasta had ballooned her weight and soured her mood.

'I've eaten.'

'But I've made it for you!'

Anita took a seat in the kitchen. She was surrounded on all sides by packets of unopened vermicelli. They were lined up along the counter, stuffed in cupboards and piled up in boxes in the corner. There was more vermicelli in this room than in all the supermarkets in a twenty-mile radius. Anita's father, a pleasant Punjabi man and a traitor, had dreamed up the idea of importing luxury pasta from Italy to sell at high prices in boutique food shops in London. Wasn't that the immigrant dream, he'd once said, to sell Italian Vermicelli to Rich Russians in England? But her father had run off with one of his Italian suppliers, been promptly dumped, and was now living in poverty in Naples.

Which served him right. The business was a failure because, like Balzac's Goriot, the Pandeys only specialised in vermicelli, and Russians don't eat vermicelli. Her mother had been abandoned with thousands of bags of unsold stock, each with a three-year expiration date. During this time, she'd hopelessly attempted to sell it all to her Indian friends, but they could only purchase so much vermicelli out of kindness, and the experience left her permanently nervy and miserable. Now her mother's time had finally run out, for in two months everything expired.

So it was pasta for lunch.

'I've eaten,' Anita repeated, irritation creeping into her voice. Her mother ignored her daughter and laid a plate of steaming vermicelli on the table.

'How long have I got you for?' she said, turning towards the cutlery drawer. Anita glimpsed her mother's scalp beneath the thinning hair, and the sight of it made her nauseous. 'Anita?' She handed her a battered fork with a sad red handle she recognised from her childhood.

'Not long. Sorry, Mum.' Her mother crossed her huge arms, seeking an explanation. 'I've got a date later,' said Anita.

It was true. Faced with the extraordinary expanse of a free day without school work, and in a surprising bout of confidence, Anita had organised to meet a man from a dating app. It would be the first date since her kidney surgery last year. She'd arranged it for thirty minutes from now so she wouldn't have to stay in her mother's house very long.

Her mother heaved herself into a chair and let out a long sigh. 'You're very ungrateful to me. I'm always doing things for you.' She pointed at the vermicelli. 'So?'

Anita looked around the kitchen to avoid her mother's eyes. There was a crack in the windowpane. The fridge had been pulled out from the wall and hadn't been pushed back into place. Things hadn't been fixed. Her mother's mental health was deteriorating – that was clear – but the idea that it was Anita's responsibility to solve the problem sent her into a panic. She had enough on her plate already. 'It's good,' she said, eating a few mouthfuls of pasta to appease the woman.

Her mother sat back and watched, satisfied. 'One thing you can always rely on is me. I'm always here for you.' She coughed, making an awful sound. 'I was just thinking the other day about the time I took you to the zoo to see the animals. How old were you? Thirteen? Your father wasn't there. Whenever I'm upset I try and remember that day.'

'That was the pond, Mum.'

'There were animals.'

'The ducks had migrated.'

Her mother stuck a pinkie in her mouth and cleared out some old food from her gums. 'But I took you, didn't I?' For a moment she was lost in thought, then she added wistfully, 'You're so skinny now...'

Anita lay down her fork and pushed the plate away.

They hugged at the door. 'Tell me about your date,' her mother said.

'I don't know. His name's Benjamin.'

'Well, make sure he's a gentleman, Anita. I don't want my daughter to end up like me, all alone in this house. Life's so hard... Here.' She handed over two Asda bags filled with pasta. 'Give Benjamin a present.'

'No, Mum. It's weird.' Anita pushed the bags away, seeing in the pathetic gesture her mother's entire, failed life.

'It'll give you something to talk about,' her mother said pushing them back.

Anita turned away, but her mother grabbed her hand and forced her fingers around the bags. 'Who doesn't like vermicelli? He's not gluten intolerant, is he?'

'Mum! I haven't met him yet!'

'Anita!' She seized hold of her daughter and began sniffing the air violently – which was the cue that there'd be tears if her daughter refused the pasta.

There was a scar across her abdomen where they had removed her kidney. The tumour was so big they'd had to take out the whole thing, so Anita was left with an unfortunate keloid scar that she hated more than the organ they'd ripped out of her. They had caught the cancer late, and for a few weeks it was more likely that she would die than live. She remembered walking around the corridors of the hospital, seeing various other terminal cases and thinking, despite

246

herself: you don't know what it's like to be me. My suffering is unique.

In the days before the operation she read books about cancer; but in all the good ones – Sontag, Hitchens, Diski – the author died in the end. When you have cancer, you don't want wisdom about death, you want not to die. The obvious, boring question she repeated to herself: why me? Why am I the one with cancer? I'm so *young*. Why am I the sob story you hear about on TV? But the operation had been a success, and after a year of waiting to see if it would return she had been removed from the priority list and pushed out into the world.

And the world was no longer pleasurable. Most days she preferred sleep. A cancer therapist told her that when you have a life-threatening illness, you come up against the limits of your own empathy; sacrifice is impossible. 'It's okay to prioritise self-preservation. Ignore the world.' It seemed unthinkable until she was back in it. These days she found herself contemplating the tattoo on her ankle with bitterness, for it said: *Anne Sexton 24/7* – a reference to that haunted American poet who killed herself at the age of forty-five. Yet Anita had never been happier than when the tattoo had been inked on her as an eighteen year old. Only now did the tattoo ring true; she was always depressed. Once upon a time she had believed the truth of the human condition could fit between the pages of a work of fiction or poetry – and at the age of twenty she decided to devote her life to this fact. But she'd lost the desire to teach literature – despised it, in fact – because a book was a lie you hold in your hands, a bourgeois pastime designed to distract us from the truth that people who never read books are living and dying without ever considering them.

'A shift in world view is normal,' explained the facilitator of the cancer club she attended once a week. 'You just have to embrace the change.' She had trouble doing that, especially when the club was hijacked by the stage-one BCBs, the Breast Cancer Bitches who hogged the entire meeting by recounting in detail the trauma of finding a cancerous lump, and the torment of having a thirty-minute lumpectomy to have it removed. On those days, Anita would look at the young man with brain cancer, sitting silent in the corner while the BCBs babbled on, and concluded that the world was designed for the wrong people.

Anita turned into the bustling high street – past a row of ancient men smoking cigarillos and a young Turkish boy handing her a flyer for Mormonism. 'I'm dying,' she said irritably, and continued on towards the estate agent where Benjamin, 31, was due to meet her at half past two. From each of her hands hung a plastic bag filled with luxury vermicelli.

Pandey was concerned.

She wanted nothing less than vigorous sexual intercourse. And yet, she was afraid of it. It'd been eighteen months since the last time she'd had sex – a regrettable turn with Mr. Claggert, thirty years her senior, after an apocalyptic staff party at the local bowling alley. That was before her cancer. Now with the awful scar across her abdomen, she was frightened of her own body. Something had to change. Her frustration had reached boiling point. Every week she wasted dozens of hours watching porn, her favourite category being Gay Male – largely because it allowed her to imagine herself as someone else – specifically, the meek blondie getting pounded by the enormous abdominally privileged Swiss actor (her legs akimbo over his shoulders, his large hand at her neck, gently stroking her Adam's apple). This excessive desire of hers had become problematic. Occasionally at work she would excuse herself during lunch hour and masturbate in the staff bathroom. Or on particularly dark days, the same during Cancer Club. Last night it had got out of control after a particularly disturbing dream involving Martin Amis, a nine-inch dildo, and the ghost of Melvyn Bragg.

The point is, today her desire had won out over the fear of her body, and now she marched bravely towards her date, motivated by the horrible feeling that if she didn't get some soon, she'd expire like the vermicelli in her bags.

Anita glanced down just in time to avoid stepping in dog shit. She had lightly grazed the steaming pile with the toe of her boot, but otherwise disaster had been avoided. It was just her luck, she thought, to have a date ruined by an unsightly smear across her shoe. Quickly, methodically, Anita grabbed a packet of vermicelli and used it to brush off the shit. She promptly binned the packet and carried on as if nothing had happened.

Outside the estate agent, she opened up the dating app. Benjamin looked a lot like Wayne Bridges, the most popular boy in her year when she was fifteen – he'd once described her as minging. It was depressing that her basically unhappy time at school still held an excessive influence over her adult life. At least Wayne Bridges now worked as a PR guy for a car rental company, which was immensely gratifying because he used to brag about becoming an investment banker. Funny. But then Anita remembered that she was still in the town she was raised in, teaching at the school she had once attended, and was on diligent course to have sex with a man who looked suspiciously similar to a fifteen year old she used to hate.

Hopefully her shoe didn't smell.

Something flew past her – a boy – and she dropped one of her bags. It was Natwest, looking back over his shoulder and pretending not to recognise his teacher. The young man continued on in the direction of the post office and Anita shook her head with bemusement.

Unlike Natwest, she could no longer run. Anita was fatigued all the time, for her illness had aged her body and radically reduced her life expectancy. Her therapist had informed her that 50 per cent of people with a renal transitional cell carcinoma of her severity die within ten years of their first diagnosis, either of recurrence or some other illness. But, he'd added cheerfully, she was young, so what was she going to do with the last twenty years of her life?

It was a quarter past three and Anita had waited around for forty minutes. She was worthless – an obvious fact – but it still crushed her.

She thought she'd spotted Benjamin half an hour ago, but the figure walked past as if she didn't exist. When Anita caught a glimpse of herself in a shop window, she decided she would have done the same: her reflection was stooped, her arms pulled low by the two plastic bags on either side of her, and – she realised with horror – the corner of her mouth was stained with pasta sauce. She had been sabotaged by her mother.

A black Bentley drove swiftly past her, swerving dangerously around a corner. She sighed and opened the dating app. The last of her energy was spent wording a text to Benjamin.

Hey. I'm here.

After several minutes, she sent another.

I think I saw you earlier?

A quarter of an hour later, she sent a follow-up message.

?

Thirty minutes passed.

Please answer. I'm not angry. I just want to know.

A few minutes later, Anita received a reply.

I'm sorry my train was delayed, there's no wifi here.
Don't think I can make it!

She blocked him, wandered around the high street for half an hour debating if the weather would change, then sat down on a bench and wept.

A sharp voice penetrated her consciousness. 'Anita!' She winced at the woman who took a seat alongside her. It was one of the BCBs – Olivia Foreman, mid-fifties. Anita had been on this bench for some time now, swiping furiously through profiles on the dating app. She nodded at her. 'Olivia?'

'That's me!' The BCB was immensely satisfied at the sound of her own name.

Wearily, Anita exchanged pleasantries. Olivia was a person who was interested in anything, which was a way of saying she had no interests. Every topic was addressed with the enthusiasm of a child. Anita countered by making impassioned comments about the weather, or about some new shop on the high street – the usual inanities – but Olivia never noticed she was being ridiculed, only accepted the conversation with a generous smile. She was completely without irony.

'What did you get up to today?' Anita asked.

'Well, it's funny you should say that. . .' – Olivia had an irritating habit of responding to any query by first suggesting it was funny – 'It's funny you should say that, I've just been to see my consultant about some scan results.'

'Uh-huh,' said Anita. 'All clear?'

'Nope.' She rested her arm across the back of the bench. 'Looks like I'm going to need another round of nuking.'

'Oh, I'm sorry.' All of Anita's scans since the operation had been clear, and hearing the opposite from someone else, so plainly, produced an alienating effect, as if she no longer existed.

Empathy, Pandey.

'Yeah, I'm really sorry.'

Olivia raised her fists in reply. 'Keep fighting, right?' Then she laughed and pointed at a German shepherd staring out the back of a passing car. 'So cute!'

In just a few moments Anita's opinion of the woman had shifted. There was something shocking, almost violent in her positivity. It was more like denial than bravery, for how could anyone say something like that knowing that death was – as Eliot says – holding your coat and snickering?

The first drops of cold rain splashed down on their heads. In a single, fluid motion, Olivia lifted an umbrella from her hand-bag, pressed a button, and the thing slid open and unfolded itself. She held it above them, and for the next fifteen minutes they talked about their respective experiences with cancer; it was just like Cancer Club, except Anita listened to Olivia's story for the first time. She'd wanted to be a pilot as a teenager, but because of an eye problem she went into law. She'd never married. When she was diagnosed she quit her job and started an online embroidery business selling bespoke designs on Etsy, which, she added coyly, had taken off quite well. Anita was moved by the ordinary fabric of this woman's life and the can-dour of its telling, a life made extraordinary by the plain fact of being. In comparison, Anita's similarly ordinary life felt stripped of feeling. Why couldn't she be moved by her own banal life story as she was by Olivia's?

Just then the town shook from the sound of engines over-head. Four aeroplanes flew past, emerging from the clouds for a few seconds, the wings glistening in the rain, before disap-pearing again.

Olivia jumped to her feet. 'Spitfires! Look! Isn't that something?'

Anita nodded and cleaned the rain from her glasses. 'I wonder what they're celebrating.'

'There's always reason to celebrate,' Olivia said, which made Anita laugh, even though Olivia was serious.

Soon the conversation regressed to pleasantries, and eventually Olivia had to run. 'Sorry to leave you in the rain, Anita. But I'm sure I'll see you at the group?'

'Yeah. See you soon.' She gave her a wave and Olivia started up the street, her umbrella bobbing lightly up and down as if she were conducting a tiny orchestra. Suddenly inspired, Anita called after her.

'Wait!'

Olivia turned around.

Anita pointed at the Asda bags at her feet. 'Want some pasta?'

'It's funny you should say that.' Olivia patted her stomach. 'I'm gluten intolerant.'

A nita was on a bus heading for the town hall. She'd spent the evening dining at the fish and chip place, thinking of all the ways she could get out of attending her dentist's exhibition. Coming up short, she'd tried to cheer herself up by eating an entire four-pack of Cheesestrings, but then pictured her mother doing the same and felt depressed.

So she was keeping her promise to Dr. Hung.

The hideous thing about cancer is that it wouldn't end until she did. And taking into consideration her brand-new life expectancy, that could come at any point. Endings were all she thought about now. If her life was a novel, it was destined to have a bathetic climax. There was no dramatic payoff with this illness. The rest of her life was now one long ending. Whether she spent the next ten-to-twenty years in utter bliss or despair, it would finish the same way: with her premature death. There could be no consistency to her life because of this random life-altering disease; it wasn't like in a good book, when your favourite character appears to have agency and is generously gifted the dramatic choice to do something spiritually uplifting or sacrificial. Anita was never given those choices. Instead she waited patiently for the premature ending to the inconsistent novel that she called her life. She only hoped that when it was over, at least the sentences were good. That there was at least an occasional moment of brilliance, wit or joy, among all those incoherent pages.

But it was so hard to appreciate those moments when your defeated body was permanently exhausted. The only thing that energised her now was the promise of an early bedtime after the exhibition.

On the other side of the bus, a red-headed twenty-something of indeterminate gender was reading from a battered paperback. Anita strained her neck to see the title – *Olly Murs: Collected Essays*. The reader noticed her staring and hid the cover. Anita glanced at the floor. She was not a pervert, but she did have a proclivity for trying to see what people were reading in public, and this sometimes made her look like a pervert. Still, her curiosity about the work of literature surprised her, and she wondered if it was Olivia's influence. It was a brief conversation, but the woman's joy for the world, despite her dreadful situation, was inspiring – even if it seemed impossible to attain.

An elderly gentleman boarded and sat directly opposite her, which was odd because the bus was mostly empty. She looked conspicuously at the spare seats to indicate her annoyance, but the man ignored her, and so she spent the rest of the journey staring out the window. When the bus pulled up outside the town hall, Anita stood up to leave. As she did her eyes flicked briefly towards the elderly gentleman's crotch: he was wearing dark tights with a perfect circle cut out of the fabric around the groin. His large, flaccid penis flopped out of the hole – in fact had been resting out in the open for the whole journey – and Anita, shaken, grabbed her two plastic bags and hurried away.

She'd been flashed. Once her shock had subsided, Anita rested against the bus shelter and shook with laughter. Flashing was so... *retro*. Like she'd stepped out of a bus from the 1960s and had been abruptly dumped back in the much-less-innocent present. How perfectly antiquated! Like someone wearing a top hat or riding a penny-farthing. She thought of Jameson's definition of 'pastiche' and wondered whether flashing as a *cultural form* could ever be salvaged from the black hole of postmodernism. The answer, of course, was no. Still, it was the first penis she'd seen in the flesh since... and Anita recalled the image of Mr. Claggert diligently wiping the cum off her chest with a baby wipe, and shuddered.

The street was dark; then all of a sudden it lit up as the street-lights around town ignited in unison. A lone figure appeared at the edge of the park, beneath a lamp. Natwest again, huddled over and attempting to remove dog shit from his shoe.

'Natwest?' Anita said it instinctively. She hadn't wanted to embarrass him, but the name had already been said, and noticing his ex-teacher staring at him the boy mumbled the most pathetic reply: 'I stepped in poo.'

'I can see.' She pointed at the shit-stain on her own boot in a show of solidarity. 'Happens to the best of us.' Her pedagogical impulse was to take the stick and clean the shoe for him, but when she reached out for it, Natwest passionately seized her hand with his own. Anita pulled her hand away immediately, and her former student blushed and looked embarrassed. She'd humiliated him further, and immediately wished she could go back in time and accept the gesture of communion.

Impossible, Pandey.

'No, Natwest. Give me the stick. Let me try.' She affected a businesslike manner as befitted the relationship of a teacher and her former student. She ordered him to face the wall and lift his foot so she could get at the excrement, and for a quiet minute Anita worked at the shoe, using both prongs of the Y-shaped stick to clean the sole. Perhaps it was the exhaustion of the long day, her cancer-fatigued body, her romantic failures, and maybe she wasn't thinking straight; but it seemed there was something other-worldly in the air. The stick resembled a divining rod – the ends branching off in two directions – and like the mystics of old who searched for water or jewels or oil with the stick, it was as if she was presently engaged in an act of divining. What did she want to find? If she allowed herself a rare flight of fancy, and imagined that this muck removal was a supernatural or spiritual practice, it could indicate that tonight was something more important than she thought. As perverse as it was, she was struck by the idea that this shit-covered stick pointed the way to her future.

When the shoe was clean, Anita threw the stick away and told the boy to dip his sole in a puddle. The usual weariness descended as she watched him shake the water from his foot like a fool – and she thought, bitterly, that she had given so much of her life for so little reward.

She glanced at the clock tower in the distance – quarter past eight – and gestured in the direction of the town hall. 'Exhibition?'

He nodded in agreement, and they walked towards the exhibition in silence.

I t was more impressive than expected. Throughout the main room hung paintings of various sizes, all depicting – amusingly, she thought – open mouths. Some were propped up on easels, others framed and attached to the walls. The most significant piece was at the end of the room: a huge work, taller than a human being and wider than a car, portraying a woman's mouth. It was all very striking, and even though Anita felt the idea pointless, the unity of the subjects gave the amateur exhibition the illusion of significant art. The exhibition was attended by dozens of people moving back and forth between the paintings trying to find their own mouths. But they moved fearfully, she thought, uncertain if their painted and framed mouths were a compliment or a perversion. She noticed one woman standing in front of a small canvas, frantically comparing the mouth in front of her to the mouth in her make-up mirror. On the other side of the room an old man lined up in front of one particularly grotesque mouth and bared his teeth while his partner snapped a photo.

The moment they entered Natwest peeled off and made for Dr. Hung. The dentist was clearly revelling in his local celebrity, fielding questions from all manner of people and patients. Anita drifted around the room, her amusement at the subject wearing off. She yawned, once again aware of her exhaustion.

Wait –

She doubled back to one of the smaller paintings. Was that her? Anita stared at the large mouth and recognised something familiar in the tone of the skin and the blemish above the lip. She glanced at Dr. Hung, who gave her a cheerful thumbs up. It was her. The dentist's happiness irritated her. It might have been an accurate painting, but it was horrifying seeing such an intimate part of herself blown up and displayed in that way. It wasn't just the ugliness of it; she felt as if a part of her had been stolen – *appropriated*, some might say. Who was Dr. Hung to paint *her* without permission? She immediately resented the dentist's easy existence and his wilful misuse of her property. Yet the longer she looked at the image, the more it dissolved into what it was: simple brush strokes. In truth, this likeness had nothing to do with Anita Pandey. It might be her mouth in the image, but the painting wasn't her. Only she had that misfortune.

'You look thirsty,' said a voice from behind. The speaker was in his thirties, wearing a white suit jacket fastened by a single gold button. European, for sure. He produced two glasses of Prosecco from behind his back. 'It's complimentary.'

'Thanks.' She accepted a glass. 'I'm Anita.'

'My name is Dario,' he said. Italian! He somewhat resembled a less-attractive version of the protagonist of *La Dolce Vita* – although she thought that of all Italian men.

She was acutely aware of the plastic bags of pasta in her left hand.

Dario indicated the painting. 'It looks just like you!'

'Yeah.'

He turned to Anita and stared intently at her mouth. She took a long, self-conscious sip of Prosecco. 'No, really. That looks just like your mouth.'

'And what do you do, Dario?' She wanted the subject to move as far away from her mouth as possible; mercifully, Dario consented. He worked for a luxury car rental company in Rome, for celebrity tourists, and he travelled around the world negotiating marketing contracts with car manufacturers. Tomorrow he would meet a client at the Aston Martin factory, and then in the evening he'd be on a flight back to Italy. He was staying in town overnight and thought he'd check out the local culture.

'What do you think?' asked Anita, amused that a term like 'culture' could have anything to do with her town.

'How do you say. . . it's not Michelangelo.' The way he pronounced the name, his mouth – she wanted to kiss him. 'And what are you, Anita?'

It was the question she always dreaded, and when she said,

'teacher', she hated it because the word did not describe who she was. She wanted to add, 'I'm a cancer survivor, a child of immigrants, a woman, a prodigious masturbator, an ex-cat owner; I've had two boyfriends and seventeen sexual partners. I enjoy Latin jazz and hate the poetry of Emma Lazarus. There is a tattoo on my ankle that says *Anne Sexton 24/7*. Sometimes I like to sleep in the daytime...' But even this list failed to describe who she was. All she could do was look at the painting of her mouth, which also failed to describe her, and say, 'I teach English Literature to sixteen year olds.'

Dario nodded politely. 'So... Keats, etcetera?'

'Yeah,' said Anita. 'Endless chiasmus.'

He smiled, not understanding. 'What's in the bags?'

There was nothing to do but tell him the truth. 'Pasta,' she said.

'Oh!' Dario leant in close to her, and he could feel his European breath on her shoulder – but he was just peering into the bag. 'Spaghetti!' He threw up his hands in adulation.

'Vermicelli, actually.' She corrected him with a pang of disappointment, for the Italian had lost some of his authenticity.

'Of course, of course,' he said, unfazed. 'But... why have you got so much vermicelli?'

She hesitated a moment. Why did she have these bags of pasta? Accepting the gift from her mother wasn't an act of kindness, exactly; it was because she was weak.

'My mum—'

Dario held up a hand. 'Say no more! There is no question on this earth that cannot be answered satisfactorily by "My mother".'

Marcello! Love! His smile was infectious, and buoyed with feeling, she boldly reached out and straightened a lapel on his jacket.

This is it, Pandey.

263

Dario whisked away her empty glass and returned with another. 'Grazie,' she said.

Careful. One kidney, Pandey.

After a monstrous swig of Prosecco, a little liquid dribbled down her chin, and she hid her mouth behind her hand. 'Excuse me.' And just then, Anita recognised a man entering the exhibition.

It was the elderly gentleman who had flashed her on the bus, now dressed up in a suit and tie, wandering around the room.

'Oh my God!'

'What? What is it?' Dario looked about in mock panic, and she grinned. She explained the incident on the bus, then pointed at the man. 'Over there.'

'He's coming this way!' cried Dario, and dragged Anita behind his back to block her from view. She squealed with delight, grabbing his waist and giggling as the elderly gentleman passed by, oblivious. 'I think we managed to fool him, no?'

Anita took a long sip of Prosecco in agreement.

She wanted to suck Dario's dick. She decided it right then, in the most resolute terms: His European Dick – Her English Mouth.

As if he could read her mind, Dario said, 'I think I'm going to leave in a bit. But if you want to come back to mine for a drink. . .?'

'Yeah, I'd love that.' It was true. It was all true! She was exhausted, her body impossible, but she was deliriously happy for the first time in twelve months.

Dario lightly touched her wrist. 'Great. I'll go get—'

But there was a great cry and the sound of glass smashing on the ground. Those nearest turned to gawp at the commotion. It was Natwest, of all people, and his face was wet with tears. Anita had never seen him cry, and as he pushed through the crowd towards the exit, she looked on with sadness.

'Mrs. Pandey, please...'

Natwest's mother, who was also crying, had noticed her son's former teacher and was clawing at her hand and begging, 'Please talk to him. He always listened to you...'

'Come on, come on.' She was led away by a bald man, and soon everyone returned to their conversations – now with something to talk about. Dario raised his eyebrows and chuckled. 'You know, in Rome we say... '

Anita Pandey considered the commotion. Something inside her, that part of her consciousness that could never leave the classroom, emerged from its sleep. She recalled the divining rod she'd cleaned Natwest's shoe with and wondered if this was the fateful decision she'd fantasised about. Now, she was pulled in many directions: between her aching cancer scar and the beautiful Italian standing opposite; her sweet bed and the bed of a sweet stranger; Natwest out on the street, and Dario in the exhibition.

She looked at the gorgeous man before her and sighed. 'Some other time, sorry. I've got to go.'

She walked towards the exit, and Dario's sweet Roman face dropped – but then Anita stopped in her tracks. What was she doing with this?

She turned around to face her would-be lover. 'Dario...' His face suddenly hopeful. 'I hope you have a safe flight. Here.' Anita handed over the bags of pasta.

'Anita!' But she'd already turned back to the exit and left the town hall, now exhausted, now purposeful; purposefully exhausted. Her body ached, her head was spinning from the alcohol; but despite it all, she stepped out into the night to find her former student.

Seventeen

Natwest and

H ow many ways could this go? thought Natwest, stepping
into the exhibition. He spotted the dentist immediately.
Dr. Hung was the centre of attention, and he pontificated with
broad gestures at an important-looking man with a sharp black
goatee. When the renowned dentist noticed Natwest, his wine-
ruddy face lit up and he threw his arms wide and embraced
him. 'There you are!'

Natwest was speechless. Certain unthinkable boundaries had
been crossed. His dentist had hugged him. 'Uh... hi...'

The dentist in question was drunk – which wasn't as funny
as it sounds – and there was something off-putting about the
fumes of success which hovered about him. 'Natwest,' he said.
'This is Xavier. Xavier, Natwest. He's an art dealer.'

'Nice to meet you.' Natwest shook the art dealer's hand.
Xavier was the one with the goatee, and that was all there was
to say about him. 'Doctor, I think we mixed up our packages
at the post office today?'

'Yes we did! It's been a funny day, hasn't it? To think we were
talking in the post office only' – he checked his smart watch –
'eight hours ago!'

Natwest couldn't decide how long eight hours was meant to
feel, so he equivocated on the matter – 'Mhm' – and removed

the dentist's parcel from his rucksack. 'So I think you've got mine?'

'Yes, yes, I just gave it to your mum a minute ago. She should be around here somewhere.'

'My mum. . . ?'

'Yes, your mum.'

Natwest suppressed a sudden urge to scream. Everything he'd feared had come to pass. Dr. Hung had sided with his mother, and our hero had been betrayed.

'And I believe you have mine.' When the dentist asked for his own parcel Natwest almost refused out of spite, but after considering the situation he decided there was still time to avoid humiliation. His mother had only received the package a minute ago, and she wouldn't open it in the middle of the exhibition, would she? Then again, anything was possible with a mother like his.

'The parcel, Natwest?' Hung's drunken grin was pitiful enough for Natwest to hand it over, and the dentist passed it to a woman beside him. 'Thanks. Sorry about the mix-up.'

'You're fine,' replied Natwest, showing, he felt, admirable restraint.

Dr. Hung reached for a glass of wine that was passing by. 'And what do you think of the exhibition? I've been waiting on your academic opinion. . .' But Natwest's back was turned in search of his mother, and by the time he realised the question was aimed at him, the dentist had shrugged and resumed a discussion with the art dealer.

It was at this point that Natwest registered that he was surrounded by mouths. He approached the nearest painting – an old woman's wrinkled lips and yellowing teeth – and grasped the subject of the exhibition. Every painting was a mouth. The whole event was suddenly ridiculous. He began to laugh – big, breathy guffaws – and recalled his discussion with Hung earlier that day. Well, Doctor, this most certainly is *not* art. At most it was a lesson in anatomy, or a fetish. Beside him an elderly couple tutted at his laughter. It was Joan, from next door, holding hands with a bespectacled old man. Natwest, thinking of the bench that contained what was left of her late husband, nodded politely at the couple and moved on.

He couldn't find his mother in the crowd, so he texted her – but as he removed the phone from his pocket he collided with a woman.

'You!' Natwest stared in horror at the speaker – Ruth, the lady he'd bought a coffee for a few hours ago. 'Look where you're going!'

He apologised, but she chuckled and shook the Prosecco off her sleeve.

'I'm just kidding,' she said, slurring her words. 'Thank you for reminding me about this thing. I never would have remembered if you hadn't bumped into me. It's nice to get out...' She looked at her empty Prosecco glass. 'And at least it's free!'

Natwest returned the old lady's smile.

'What a nice boy you are. Anyway... exit Ruth.' And she disappeared into the crowd in search of another drink. It was an odd but pleasant encounter.

He texted his mother.

I'm at the exhibition now. Where are you?

Her reply:

I'm by the big mouth.

He looked at all the big mouths in the room. He texted her back.

Which one?

A hand appeared on his shoulder. Natwest spun around to find – yes, that really was him – his ex-boyfriend on the other end of the arm. 'Natwest! I've been looking literally everywhere for you!'

'Georgie?'

He'd run all the way here from the restaurant, and for some reason he was happy about it. But Natwest wasn't. He was backed into a corner. All these acquaintances were stacking up on top of each other, like the world was converging on him. Even the pleasant encounter with Ruth moments before felt cursed now, a symptom of this small town and the congested past he was drawn back to, but which he knew he had to leave behind.

'Where did you get the hoodie?' asked Natwest, indicating the top Georgie was wearing. On the front it said: *What's a chicken's favourite composer?*

Bach Bach Bach.

'Dr. Hung's girlfriend lent it to me.'

'What about the—'

Georgie stuck out a hand. Balled up in his fist was the Hawaiian shirt. 'I wanted to give it back.'

'Oh... Cheers.' Taken by surprise, Natwest softened a little. Georgie was finally putting his master's in Conflict Resolution and Peace Studies to good use.

'I'm sorry about everything that happened today,' Georgie said, then stumbled over his next words. 'And... and listen, I need to tell you something I should have said earlier...' Surprisingly, he proceeded to spend several minutes expressing his gratitude for their relationship.

'You don't have to—'

'No, you taught me loads about myself, things that would

have taken me years to discover, and that's like... the best gift. Honestly.' When Georgie was finished, he pulled up the hood of his sweatshirt. 'Thanks for listening to my TED Talk.'

Natwest didn't need to think about it, he just hugged him. 'You too, brother,' he said, and it felt as if something had been resolved.

'Okay cool,' said Georgie. 'I'm heading off. This isn't really my scene anymore.'

'Yeah. See you, man.' And Natwest watched him leave. At the exit Georgie threw up an East Coast gang sign, which Natwest returned, sensing that from now on they would be seeing less of each other.

'What took you so long? I've been waiting here for ages! Now it's almost...' He accepted the beating from his mother with admirable patience. Clive, the stranger from the café, watched the exchange from the sidelines. Every now and then he nodded in agreement.

Eventually Natwest's patience ran out. 'Where's the package, Mum?'

'Oh my God, stop with the package! You know when I was your age I had to—'

'That's great, Mum. I didn't come here to see you. Where is it?' He hadn't meant to sound so brash, and when his mother looked hurt, he added, 'I mean, we're here for this.' He gestured generously at the mouths surrounding them.

'Don't be rude to your mum,' Clive broke in.

Natwest waved dismissively in his direction. 'I'm just asking where the package is.'

'Okay, okay. I'll get it for you.' His mother handed him her wine glass and searched through her handbag. 'Oh, I put it in your bag, Clive.' Natwest registered this new intimacy with annoyance.

'Clive, you got it?' he asked.

'Alright, relax son. No need to be rude.'

'He's not normally like this,' she added. 'Natwest—'

'I'm not being rude.' He was angry at her for siding with the stranger. Plus, he believed he had every right to be rude – nobody knew what he'd been through today. 'I just want the package, Mum. . .'

Then Clive did something extraordinary.

He stepped in between Natwest and his mother, as if Natwest were a threat. 'Work on your attitude, son.'

'Sorry?' He moved Clive out of the way. 'Who's being rude now, *son*?' It came out by accident, but Natwest was nothing if not committed, and so the two of them went back and forth for a minute debating who was really being rude.

'I'm just saying, you're acting like a spoilt child.'

'*Me*? Are you joking?'

'No, I'm not. You need to grow up.'

Natwest was hurt by the comment, and so he replied in the most dismissive tone he could manage, 'Who do you think you are, my dad?'

Which shut him up, because Clive reached into the duffle bag at his feet and removed the package. But he muttered something under his breath. 'At least I'm here. Your dad isn't, so. . .'

'What the fuck does that mean?'

His mother intervened. 'Clive, please—'

Natwest turned on her. 'Let him say what he wants.' Then to Clive, 'Repeat what you just said to me.' Evidently something unforgivable had passed between his mother and this man. Natwest couldn't let it go.

'It was a joke,' Clive said.

'Really?' The desire to hurt both of them was suddenly overwhelming. 'A joke? Mum, what the fuck are you doing with this guy!'

She tried calming him down, but Natwest was taken with the theme. 'Who even are you, Clive? Why the fuck are you here?'

'Alright, alright… Calm down…' Clive offered him the package. 'Here it is.' But when Natwest reached out, Clive pulled it away. 'Let's see what all the fuss is about.'

'No—'

'Clive…'

'—don't open it!'

Yet Clive had already ripped off the tape and the package fell open. 'I've gotta give it to him personally, haven't I?' Then he glanced at the object in his hands – 'Oh shit!' – and dropped the nine-inch dildo on the floor.

There was nothing to think about. The only sensation in Natwest's entire body was localised in the movement of his right hand, as if his whole life had been concentrated in a single action. One moment he felt the wine glass in his palm, and the next he threw it at Clive's head.

And then there was no more feeling.

His mother cried out. Clive ducked and it flew over his shoulder. The glass shattered on the floor behind him, and he yelped pathetically. Then everyone turned to watch the scene – that is, everyone except Natwest, who must have been crying because his face was wet and he was running for the door.

He walked around town for an hour, quietly sobbing and occasionally tripping over the edges of pavements. His cheeks were still burning from the shame of it. He'd burst out of the town hall, gasping, lightheaded, nauseous – for a moment, almost suicidal. It was the worst possible ending to his day. His eyes were raw and red by the time he finally calmed down. Then there was silence, and it was as if he were the last person in the whole world. It was only when he felt the vibration in his pocket that he registered he wasn't alone.

Where are you? I'm waiting!

A message from Daddy. He dimly remembered arranging the hookup for 9:30 p.m. this evening; it was almost 10:00 p.m. Natwest was no longer in the mood to be penetrated by a middle-aged stranger, but he felt a strong sense of guilt at his lateness and therefore beholden to him. Why did he only feel this profound guilt towards randoms from the internet, and not the people he loved? What exactly was he searching for in all these older men with unnaturally large knobs? There was an easy answer, one his old school counsellor Faith Fletcher might suggest: his father. But it was just that, a cliché. He was above such conclusions. It was more likely a way of getting revenge on his mother for her involvement with Clive. Just imagine her face if she knew how he was debasing himself with these men. . .

When he looked up Daddy's address, he discovered he'd already walked most of the way there by accident. There was no excuse then. He cursed the enhanced geographical capabilities of his id, much better than his own sense of direction, and within ten minutes found himself knocking on the door of a fifty-year-old man's house.

'Hey.'

'Hi,' said Natwest.

Daddy – there were no names exchanged – was a greying queen with surprisingly supple cheeks, freshly shaved. He invited him in, and after a small bout of coughing the older man pointed at the worn couch in the living room and asked if he'd like to listen to music. A moment later the room was filled with violins.

'Obama's dick,' said Daddy approvingly, handing him a glass of water.

273

'Obama's dick?'

'No, *Erbarme dich*. . . the aria.'

Natwest felt a strong urge to kill himself. But Daddy laughed, and instead of lingering on his intellectual gaffe he surprised himself by laughing too.

'Are you a serious Christian or something?' asked Natwest.

Daddy sipped his water and pondered the question. 'Yes. But it's complicated. I'd say my brain's Protestant. My mouth's Baptist. My arse is Catholic. My cock's Gnostic.' He smiled to himself. 'What about you?'

'No, I'm just. . .' He considered the Jewish Question, but thought it pointless because his penis would make it clear. 'I'm nothing,' he concluded. 'Just queer.'

Daddy nodded. 'What denomination?'

'Uh. . . Bi. Bisexual.' He said it quickly, to get it out the way.

'Oh! Listen to this,' and Daddy traced invisible notes in the air. 'He's singing, "Have mercy, God. Have mercy, Father. . ." It's sublime.' He lowered the tone of his voice, 'So. . . you want me to have mercy on you?'

'Uh. . .'

'You into that stuff? Daddy play?'

'Um. . . sometimes, I guess. . .'

Daddy took a swig of water and crunched the ice between his teeth. 'You little mutt.'

'Excuse me?

'I said you're a little slut.'

'Uh. . .' Natwest stared at a single loose thread in the carpet at his feet.

'That's what you are, right?' asked Daddy again.

'Maybe. . . I don't like talking so much.'

Daddy coughed into his hand. 'That's alright, no worries. Oh! Listen to this bit. . .'

When the *Erbarme dich* aria came to an end, they moved to

the bedroom and took off their clothes. The dream of a huge dick was the dream of obliteration, thought Natwest, staring at the nine-inch cock before him. He would like to be obliterated, to no longer exist as the bundle of mistakes, gaffes and humiliations that the world had decided he had to be. Maybe a big schlong was the answer. Maybe all the embarrassing parts of himself would be destroyed when he received Daddy's apocalyptic member.

With this thought, he pressed his face into the pillow and allowed the older man to enter him from behind.

For twenty-five minutes, he ceased to exist.

Post-coital Natwest collapsed onto Daddy's chest. He had been voided. The calm after the storm settled around him, and there was quiet. Gradually this new absence inside him filled with the many images of the great artists he'd studied – and he became a gallery. The figures in these great works were transformed into images of real people, with real faces, many of whom he couldn't recall meeting, as if his memory had been replaced with someone else's. But there were faces among them he recognised – especially prominent were those of the people he'd met today. Turns out his love for the world was boundless. He cared for every individual who existed, with and without him. His only wish was that he could leave this useless body and become one of them, even for a minute. Become an old woman. An Imam. A dentist. His own mother. Wouldn't that be something? There were odd pulses of light in Natwest's vision now, and his body was open to every sensation. Daddy was mumbling something about the pleasures of his ass, a dog was barking outside, maybe a kettle was boiling in the flat below. His consciousness had dispersed into the world.

The greying chest hairs against his cheek, the large nipple

a few centimetres from his nose – he imagined Daddy's chest as the surface of the Earth, and every person in the world was down there. He was lying among them; Citizen Natwest, he thought. And of all the other citizens down there, who would he most like to meet? To his surprise, the answer was not a celebrated artist or philosopher. The answer was his missing father.

So he pictured it. Squeezed the man lying beside him and imagined he was lying with his dad. There may not be such a thing as peace, but right this moment, he felt as if there was. He luxuriated in this sensation for some time, even as Daddy's cum dried on his stomach – he was exactly where his dad wanted him to be. The sound of the *Erbarme dich* aria played in his head. 'Dreams... from... my father,' he mumbled, and descended back into the world.

He buried his face in the older man's torso. 'That was great.'

'Amen,' said the voice above his head.

When he left the house he watched his phone tick over to 12:00 a.m. with some satisfaction, looked around and realised he was lost. According to Google he was on the outskirts of town. It was a long walk home.

Natwest's phone took him on a shortcut through an unknown park. After banging his head on several low-hanging branches, he slowed down and switched on his phone torch to illuminate the path. He got some way into the trees when he heard voices.

'...I said she's going to Hull, not going to hell.' It was a woman's voice – no, a girl, thought Natwest. For some reason he ducked down, as if he had something to hide, but deciding there was nothing left that hadn't been exposed, he stood up and carried on. When he looked into the clearing, he saw a dark-haired teenager cartwheeling on the grass. Standing by a tree beside her: Lily, the fifteen year old from the bus stop. He wasn't in the least bit surprised to see her. There was a lightness in him after the encounter with Daddy, and everything was harmless.

He discreetly avoided the teenagers, skirting around the clearing and leaving them to their innocent fun. But then he glanced over and noticed Lily carving something into a tree with a penknife:

He was disturbed by the swastika, even if it was a bit wonky. It was a vulgar image, totally lacking in significant form, or artistic merit – but worse than that, his undesired Jewish identity was deeply insulted. He considered this to be a great weakness on his part, and yet he was still upset by the symbol and realised that no amount of intellectualising would do away with the emotion. He felt no malice towards the girl, for he too had a fondness for drawing offensive images when he was Lily's age. Adult Natwest knew better, and was now impelled by good taste to intervene.

He tapped her on the shoulder. 'You think that's funny?'

'What the fuck! You following me?' But she wasn't angry, and she grinned at him. 'Not on my phone, see?' Lily pointed at the tree. 'I'm getting in touch with nature.'

'You okay, Lily?' said a voice behind them.

'All good.' She introduced Natwest to her cartwheeling friend Mia.

'This swastika, you've got to get rid of it.'

'It's just a joke,' she complained, but didactic Natwest – attempting his best Mrs. Pandey impression – berated her with surprising severity. 'Lily, some things are actually serious, you know?' He was so successful that she actually looked ashamed of herself.

'Okay. But how am I meant to get rid of it? It's not like I can cut down the tree.'

Natwest considered the options. Then Mia joined the discussion: 'Well, I'm stumped.'

The three of them debated the best course of action, and in the end they decided to change the symbol to something else. It was Natwest who had the idea. 'Make of hate a house,' he said – 'What does that even mean?' asked Lily – but he'd already grabbed the knife and began carving:

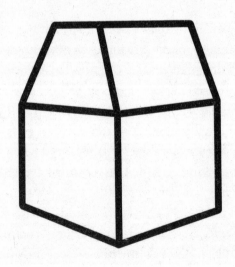

It was hard work, and when he finished he ceded control to the girls, who each took turns chiselling in the detail. When the picture was completed they stood back and marvelled at their work of art:

'It may not be a masterpiece, but. . .'

'I love it,' said Lily, and she ordered the three of them to line up in front of the tree for a selfie.

They chatted for a while, then Natwest said his goodbyes. 'Lastly, uh. . . what happened with your online problem?'

'All good. Nothing leaked,' said Lily.

'Great. Well don't. . . you know, stay out too late.'

'Thanks, Dad.'

The night had turned out much better than expected. He'd performed a vital service for the younger people of his generation – and now a precious phrase began rattling around his mind: *put your money on me*. What exactly was his brain telling him? Everything was collapsing. Everyone was fucked. Nobody had the answers. And yet maybe he was the one who could lead his generation safely to the opposite shore. If you have to put your money on something – and you always have to put your money on *something*, he thought – put it on Natwest.

He was seized by the urge to urinate, and so straddling up to a convenient bush, whipped out his penis and pissed happily into the shrubbery. After a pause he looked down at his circumcised cock. So okay, maybe he was Jewish. What then? Despite his best efforts, he felt something like pride for his heritage – he'd even erased one more swastika from the world. When he finished pissing, he blew a kiss at his circumcised cock and put it safely back into his pants.

Generosity! Forgiveness! In a flurry of emotion he started dialling his mother to apologise (and also, to ask for a lift). The phone began to ring.

And he dropped it on the ground.

Of course he did.

When he picked up the phone the screen was black. He held down the power button – nothing. He tried again. Nothing. And again. Nothing. And then, as if he could go back in time, he dropped the phone on purpose and picked it up again. Nothing. It had finally died. But there was no insane panic attack that followed. Only a curious feeling of relief.

H e didn't know where he was, he didn't know how to get home, and he didn't know the time. Natwest sat on a tree stump and tried in vain to remember the map he'd seen on his phone. Above him, there was a nearly full moon of extraordinary brightness.

After some time, he heard a sound.

'Natwest!'

Had he heard that right?

'Natwest!'

He followed the voice through the trees until he was out of the park, and as in a miracle, there was an angel on the road – his teacher, Mrs. Pandey.

He was used to these kinds of encounters by now, so he strolled casually into her eyeline and said hello.

'Oh!' Mrs. Pandey clapped her hands in delight, a remarkably youthful gesture. 'Where have you been, Natwest?'

Natwest considered lying, as he was so used to doing when it came to his sexual preferences, but instead told the truth about his trip to Daddy's house.

Mrs. Pandey looked embarrassed. 'Well… thank you for your candour. Sounds like you had a more exciting night than I did.'

'Yeah… It's amazing that you found me,' he replied, leaning against her car.

'Natwest, I've been looking for hours. We're not in a very big town, you know.' She lowered her voice. 'And I promised your mum I'd find you.'

There was something amazing about this teacher who still cared about him, despite all the reasons he wasn't worth the effort. 'Thanks, Miss.'

'You're okay.' Then Mrs. Pandey did something unexpected. She grabbed Natwest and hugged him. Natwest was immediately uncomfortable.

'Feeling weird yet?' she said.

He nodded.

'Give it a minute.' She kept on hugging him, and he relaxed. He thanked her and said, without exaggeration, that she was the most unselfish person he knew.

She shrugged and let him go. 'I get something out of it too, don't forget that. You know about art as well as anyone else, it's always the same answers in the end: service, sacrifice, other people. It all makes you feel good, right? It's not a complicated medicine.'

'I know,' he agreed. The moonlight passing through the trees made beautiful patterns on the windshield and he pointed them out. 'Look.'

She followed his finger to the car, then shook her head. 'Now don't go getting all sentimental on me, Natwest.'

He laughed. 'Sorry, Miss.' Then, discovering there wasn't much else to say, they stared at the road in silence.

S he dropped Natwest off outside his house. Something in the texture of the night and the sight of the building before him charmed our hero. He scanned through the library of images in his mind until he found a suitable reference – the *Bladelin Altarpiece*, a work by Early Netherlandish painter Rogier van der Weyden. It's a daylight nativity scene, and the Virgin kneels with the Christ child, while angels and benefactors crowd the image in various devotional poses. It's comforting and idealised, as with many van der Weyden works; but what makes the image unique is the dilapidated building that frames the scene. It's not a thatched inn – as is usually the case for the subject – but a stone house. The emotional quality of the painting comes from the house, which is falling apart and yet, through the presence of the Virgin and child, appears simultaneously in a state of restoration. To some this might indicate Jesus' healing of the world, but for Natwest it was an image of his own life. In the most literal sense, he was walking into his mother's house, and his only desire was to heal and be healed.

His mother was at the kitchen table, sipping a cup of tea. Before she could say anything, he apologised.

'It's okay. You don't need to say sorry.'

'But Mum, I want to.'

'A child should never have to apologise to their parent.'

'With all due respect, I'm not sure about that, Mum.'

'But Natwest, I don't want you to apologise.'

'Well, I want to.'

'Please, Natwest. . .'

'Mum—' And he stopped himself. 'I'm sorry. . . about the apology thing.' She smiled then, and Natwest took a seat. He cautiously touched her hand. 'Listen. . . I'm sorry about what happened with Clive too. Like. . . I don't know what happened, but when he mentioned Dad, and then opened the package, I—'

'Don't worry about him. He's gone.' Natwest was delighted to hear it, but he kept quiet for his mother's sake. She stood up and washed her mug in the sink. 'I've got a lot of stuff to tell you, Natwest. About your father and me. I haven't been completely honest about things.'

'It's okay, Mum. We'll speak tomorrow.'

They exchanged a tender look, and before the scene became excessively sentimental Natwest turned away and started up the stairs. His mother shouted something from below.

'I packed your bags for you!'

Filled with gratitude, he stepped into his room and unzipped the suitcase to see what clothes she'd packed. As the lid fell open, he noticed something nestled in the corner of the bag: his dildo.

The early morning sun made everything appear colder than it really was. People were leaving their houses, dogs were being walked, and at the bottom of the lane the postman was doing his rounds. There was life everywhere. Natwest carried the suitcase to his car, reflecting on the story his mother had told him. There were many revelations about his parents, and it was a lot to process. Fortunately, he had a long car journey in which to do it. He had drawn up a plan of all the things he needed to do when he arrived at university, and chief among them was buying a cheap phone so he could stay in contact with her.

After a good night's sleep, the day before seemed less significant. He'd probably had a hundred days just like it – everyone had, if they bothered to remember any of them – and he supposed that this one would fade too, which was okay because in the end he was only interested in the future.

And this red Hyundai was going to take him there.

When he started the engine he suddenly had an urge to sneeze – which he did, loudly, and with much ceremony. Then he took a final melancholy look in the mirror at the house he grew up in and gave it a salute. The tears in his eyes were from sneezing, Natwest assured himself, and he put the car into gear and started up the road. As he drove, the widescreen frame of the windshield played an optical illusion on our hero. It was as if the car were stationary and it was everything else that was moving towards it, and not the other way around. He just had to sit there, and the world came to him. It was like that for miles; every time he put his foot down he dragged the image closer: the motorway, the country, the city, everything in front. It was a pleasant view.

Seventeen

Natwest or

There was only one outcome he wanted, and yet the moment Natwest entered Dr. Hung's exhibition he expected the opposite. The dentist was waving his arms enthusiastically at a goateed figure, conspicuous among the gaggle of middle-aged patrons that surrounded him. Natwest left Mrs. Pandey at the entrance and marched towards the group.

'Natwest! It's good to see you again. This is. . .' He introduced him to Xavier, an art dealer. The dentist was drunk, and Natwest impatient. He ignored the pleasantries and asked where the package was.

To his surprise, he got what he wanted.

'Yes! We've got it right here. Ariyah?' The woman beside him removed a long package from her handbag. 'I've been carrying this around all day, haven't I?' she said, and the two of them shared a troubling smile. She offered it to Natwest, and there was something unusually sympathetic in her face as they exchanged packages. It suggested mutual understanding, which in this case was the exact opposite of what Natwest wanted. But the package was in his hands at last. He experienced an overwhelming surge of joy and hugged the dentist. 'Thanks, Doctor!'

Hung was happy for him. 'So Natwest, what do you think of

the exhibition? I've been looking forward to your opinion.' He gestured around the room.

It was the funniest thing Natwest had seen all year. Every single painting depicted a person's mouth.

When he saw the look of hurt across the dentist's face he stopped laughing. 'No, I mean—'

'I understand,' said Dr. Hung. 'It's not to your taste.'

Natwest chuckled again, and the goateed art dealer joined him. Dr. Hung apparently hadn't realised the joke he'd made because he continued to berate himself.

'No, no, it's easy art. I understand that. Just. . . mouths, and I'm a dentist, and I understand that. It's not a deep subject or. . .' He looked desperately at Ariyah for help.

'It's okay, Doctor,' said Natwest, controlling himself. He took pity on the dentist and promised to take a proper look at the paintings and report back. When he left the group, Ariyah had taken over from Hung and was explaining, quite ineffectually, the strength of the works to the art dealer.

The burden was lifted. He wandered around the exhibition with joy in his heart and a lightness in his step. Across the room, he spotted Georgie. How odd. He wasn't wearing the Hawaiian shirt, but rather a hoodie with a joke printed on the back: *Knock Knock, who's there? Philip Glass. Philip Glass who? Knock Knock, who's there? Philip Glass. Philip Glass who? Knock Knock, who's there? Philip Glass. . .*

His ex-boyfriend probably wanted to cause more of a disruption, and Natwest, having had enough of disruptions, successfully avoided him. They'd had their time together – sometimes good, sometimes bad – but it was over now. He could happily live his whole life without resolving that conflict.

There was only one worthy canvas in the room: a small image of an ugly mouth. The front tooth was chipped, the tongue coated white, and there was a sore on the lip. The piece was of interest because of its terrible clarity and the candour of its depiction. Best of all, nobody was looking at it, so Natwest thought his discernment superior to everyone in the room – including the dentist who painted it.

After spending several minutes reflecting on his singular judgement, he overheard two elderly ladies talking. Under normal circumstances he would ignore them, but he'd recognised a familiar name among the babble.

'It's just awful! I didn't think something like that could happen here. And to Joan!'

'She's usually so careful.'

'I told her not to play around with the internet. I said to her, "You never know who you might be talking to." And now look!'

'Terrible, terrible, terrible.'

'You can imagine the scene, can't you? She opens the door expecting a distinguished gentleman – as if they still exist – and then it's a Middle Eastern boy who's come to rob you!'

'Is that what they said? Middle Eastern?'

'Oh come on, Sally!'

'We should visit her in the hospital.'

'Yes, yes. It's awful! Do you want another glass?'

Natwest processed the information. Was that the same Joan, the same old woman he'd spoken to at the beginning of the day? The poor thing. He imagined her beaten bloody by a villainous intruder, her body left dripping on the ground – and for some reason it brought to mind Warhol's *Campbell's Soup Cans*. Perhaps she too would soon have her name inscribed on a memorial bench in the park.

'Natwest.' A hand grabbed his shoulder. It was his mother's friend, Clive.

'Uh... hi, how are you doing?'

Clive grinned and pointed at the centre of the room. 'Go say hello to your mum. She's been looking for you for an hour.'

His immediate instinct was to resist. Clive seemed too pleased with himself, as if Natwest were a prize fish to be delivered back to his mother in exchange for credit. 'I'll see Mum when I get home,' he countered.

'No,' said Clive. 'Go now.'

His tone of voice had triggered something in our hero, and Natwest replied aggressively, almost by accident. 'No. I'm not a dog, Clive.'

'Christ. You are like your father, aren't you?'

'Sorry?' The remark caught him off guard. The idea that Clive had anything to do with the man in his mother's bedside cabinet was impossible. 'How would you possibly know?' he asked.

'We grew up together, didn't we? Me, him, your mum... I still see him around Liverpool now and then.'

Natwest had nothing to say in response. What he'd long suspected had turned out to be true. But how dreadful to hear it said aloud – and from the mouth of this awful man.

'You didn't know that?' Clive continued, a cruel look in his eyes.

'Yeah, your mum had an affair with him. He's married with kids and everything.'

Natwest blinked, struck dumb by the sentence. *Affair?* The hundreds of possible meanings contained within this revelation assembled to form one devastating interpretation in his mind: he was his father's dirty secret.

'Natwest!' His mother appeared. 'Have you heard about Joan? I just found out she got broken into—'

'Mum, he says Dad's still alive?'

'Did he?' She glanced at Clive and went pale.

All Natwest wanted to do was leave the town hall without incident, but he'd been defeated by his curiosity – and his anger towards the woman standing before him. 'He said he still sees him. You said he was dead, Mum?'

'Natwest, please. . .'

'What the fuck?' He doubled down, scolding her, speaking faster than he could think. 'Why didn't you tell me the truth? Why not? Why lie?'

'It's complicated.'

'And you had an affair?' He couldn't believe he'd said the word aloud, and his mother looked appropriately horrified at the revelation. From her expression he knew the devastating comment was true.

'Let me explain—'

'Mum!' Melodrama was the form Natwest was engaged in, whether he liked it or not – the only way he knew how to act in a conflict.

'It was so long ago—'

'You raised me in a house of lies!'

'It doesn't matter,' she was saying. 'It doesn't matter—'

'It's my dad, of course it matters!' The line had brought tears to his eyes, partially because it resembled similar scenes in movies – and several of them flashed through his mind when he said it – and partially because it was the truth. His whole life he'd thought this business about his father a minor inconvenience, a small part of his childhood he'd missed out on. Of course it would be nice if he'd known the man, but he'd done perfectly well without him. Yet standing in the middle of this exhibition, surrounded by these gaping mouths, it turned out his dad actually mattered to him. This was the meaning of the tears – not the fact of the lie, or his father's absence, but the realisation that he had successfully deluded himself for so long.

She tried to hug him and he pushed her away. This inspired Clive to enter the conversation with a philosophical comment: 'Oi! Be nice to your mum.'

'I can do what I want,' said Natwest.

'Spare me the bloody ivory-castle waterworks.'

289

'Piss off!' He'd become hysterical, and had lost control of the volume of his voice. It was the permission Clive had been waiting for.

'I'm just saying don't be a sissy, yeah? Your mum's been through a hell of a lot more than you—'

'Clive, stop it,' she broke in.

'—and we've already got enough sissies in the world.'

Natwest was shaken by the comment. It made him feel small and weak, because it was exactly what he thought of himself. His mind travelled to the dildo in his rucksack and he imagined Clive's words embossed along the rubber shaft, and that same shaft being shoved inside him.

'Who the fuck are *you*? Why the fuck you even here?' He turned to his mother, seeking an explanation. 'Mum?'

'He's my friend,' said his mother, hopelessly.

'Friend?' Natwest pursued a course of ruthless action. He made a show of looking Clive up and down as if he were a piece of second-hand clothing, paused for dramatic emphasis, and spat out his words with as much vehemence as he could. 'This guy's your friend, Mum? You can do better than this scum.'

Suddenly an object was flying at Natwest's head. He only registered what it was after it had passed over his shoulder and smashed on the floor – it was a tiny glass model of a house.

The veins that were bulging out of Clive's neck quickly deflated and he stammered an apology. 'Sorry. I didn't. . .' But Natwest barely heard, because he was already running for the exit. He glanced back and saw Clive punching himself in the side of the head and shouting, 'Fuck! Clive! Idiot fuck!' His mother was also crying, which served them both right.

N atwest slunk past shuttered shop fronts, quietly mumbling to himself. He was trying to recall the particular details of his father's face, based on the few photos of the man he'd seen – but he couldn't produce a convincing picture in his mind. The most distressing revelation from the exhibition was that our hero was the accidental child of his mother's affair with a married man. It was another rude confirmation that Natwest had never been the main character. He wasn't even important *to his father* – at best he was an inconvenience; at worst, a mistake his father wished he could erase. At some point the man must have been shown his illegitimate son and given the choice to live with or without him. He'd chosen without.

And what about his mother?

As Natwest passed a bin, he kicked it in frustration, denting the metal and disturbing the contents inside. It was the same bin he'd visited earlier in the day, because one half of the broken clock slid from the top of the rubbish and fell to the ground. He didn't return it to the bin like a good citizen, instead deliberately stomped on the clock and left it smashed on the pavement. His mother's illicit sexual appetite had begotten our hero – was it any wonder that Natwest so often followed in her footsteps? That was his principal thought as he marched towards Daddy's house, filled with self-loathing, wishing to debase himself. The degenerate cycle continued; he was determined to uphold his mother's wicked legacy.

It was 8:55 p.m.

On the other hand, he'd achieved what he'd set out to do, for the package was safely in his rucksack, and that ultimate humiliation had been avoided. Nothing else had happened which couldn't be fixed by a long chat and a hug. Already his consciousness was reconfiguring around this new set of facts about his parents, and he began to find positives in the situation, namely that he had gained a subject and now had one more thing to write about. Was there a more compelling narrative than the Trauma Plot? Probably not. If 'daddy issues' were a little predictable, so be it. The most predictable story, Christ's Passion, is one of the deepest stories – and that's the most famous example of daddy issues in history. As long as he explored his with depth and candour, there would be no problem.

In this new spirit, he set off at a smart clip towards Daddy's house.

The journey was unremarkable. The only notable incident was an argument he overheard on the path behind Imam Mishaal's house. First, there was a volley of insults, and then Mishaal's wife kicked open the back door and hurled a film projector into the garden. The sound of glass smashing against a paving slab was followed by a howl of pain from Mishaal, somewhere inside. After a few minutes, he watched the Imam step into the back garden and take a weary seat on a fold-up chair, clutching his head in his hands.

Natwest peeked over the garden fence and considered saying something comforting, but hearing the Imam muttering violent curses to himself – so unlike the leader of prayer he'd always known – he thought it best to avoid the scene entirely.

He arrived at Daddy's house on time. It was a small terraced building on the outskirts of town, and there were flyers for at least three different takeaway pizza joints trapped in his letterbox. Natwest considered this an ominous sign. It took two doorbell rings before the man appeared.

'Hey.' Daddy was greyer than in the photo he'd supplied, and he hadn't shaved. 'You're twenty-two, right?'

'Uh-huh,' lied Natwest.

'Great.'

Once they were inside, Daddy led him up the stairs and then, rather maddeningly, spent several minutes trying to convince Natwest to listen to classical music.

'It gets me in the mood—'

'I've got to get up early tomorrow. Can we not?'

'But it's Bach!' the man exclaimed. 'Bach Bach Bach!'

Natwest refused a second time, and Daddy conceded. 'Okay, fine. Bedroom's just through there.' He directed our hero to a filthy double bed. 'Here's where the magic happens.'

The bed sheets weren't washed, the man was perspiring, and there was a noticeable scent of barbecue Pringles about the room. This is the bed I've made, thought Natwest, now I have to lie in it.

He undressed as fast as he could, then Daddy smacked Natwest's bum and abruptly picked him up and threw him onto the bed. After some unnecessary foreskin-centric foreplay involving the furious slapping of cock against Natwest's forehead – an unholy anointing of sweat and smegma that for the first time made him grateful for his own cock – the older man entered our hero's arse.

He managed about six of the nine inches before the numbness set in.

During the long intercourse, images of his father, and his mother, and Clive, cycled through his head. Despite his best efforts, he could think of nothing else, and eventually he gave in and allowed the fantasy to play out on its own terms. He imagined that by fucking this older man – his father – the two of them were united against his mother and the villain Clive. While it improved the sex considerably, the victorious sensation only lasted a moment because the older man flipped him over and Natwest was assaulted by bad breath. Following a brief struggle, he managed to turn himself on his front again, but Daddy soon pulled out and – spreading our hero's cheeks – came on his asshole.

293

Natwest leapt into action, going straight for the older man's cock and submerging it in his mouth to clean the evidence of his insides from the shaft. Daddy, oblivious, groaned with pleasure. Natwest choked a few times and removed the thing from his mouth. Dirty, and saturated with a general loathing.

H e was back on the street over two hours later. Daddy had insisted on listening to the entirety of the *St. Matthew Passion* after the sex, and Natwest, refusing at first, finally acquiesced when he began receiving phone calls from his mother. While the older man pontificated on the music of Bach, he watched the missed calls rack up, delighted at the distress he was causing the woman, wishing to punish her for her lies. When his phone hit 12:00 a.m., he left the man's house, having accumulated twenty-four missed calls and seventeen texts.

He pocketed the phone, impressed by his own ability to be loved

– but he missed the pocket, and there was an awful crunch as the phone hit the concrete.

Natwest winced. It was over, he thought. Why hadn't he purchased a stupid phone case?

Yet when he stooped to pick it up, the device vibrated in his hand. The thing still worked! Natwest performed a little jig in the middle of the road, then checked the source of the vibration: it was an email sent to his old school address, which was odd because it had been years since he'd received anything there. It was a mass email, delivered to everyone who was currently at, or who had ever possessed an email address with the school. The subject said, *Now we know you're the school slut.* Attached to the email were photos of Lily, the girl he'd met at the bus stop, taking naked selfies in her bedroom.

He was devastated.

The poor girl. He tried to picture her, but the image of Lily in his mind was already being replaced by the nude figures on his phone. Natwest had averted being exposed, while Lily had suffered a humiliation infinitely worse. He thought of Joan too, lying in a hospital bed somewhere. Horrible. Life wasn't fair. He wished he had Lily's phone number, because all he wanted to do now was call and tell her, *it's going to be okay*, even if it wasn't, because everyone who thought they knew her were wrong. He'd say: *If you ever need a friend, just ask for Natwest, and I'll be there.*

He actually attempted it. He closed his eyes and imagined he was transmitting the message with his consciousness, imagined he could find Lily's own personal mind outside of his own – as if her consciousness were a phone number that could be contacted without language. But as hard as he tried, the search engine that was his brain returned nothing. Nothing except for a few nudes of himself which he'd sent out when he was the same age as her, now floating about somewhere on the internet. Would *they* ever come back to haunt him? What would become of all the internet debris of *his* life once he was dead and buried? Natwest reproached his brain for thinking only about himself, then realised he was a fool for attempting to think about anything else.

Poor Lily.

He deleted the email and followed Google Maps towards his mother's house.

It was a quiet journey, and for most of the way nobody passed by him. He was filled with sadness for the young girl, and seeing so much of his own life mirrored in hers, felt the same for himself. As he walked, thick with feeling, through this town that he both loved and hated, was drawn towards and desperately struggled to break free from, the urge to urinate crept up on our hero. He looked both ways down the street – nobody was coming – and began to piss against the base of a nearby tree. He couldn't bear to look down at his own prick, circumcised as it was, and so stared at the branches above him. This was the Jews' lot: endless misfortune.

In the distance he heard the sound of an engine – it was a car, hurtling down the road towards him. Mid-piss, he ducked out of sight, sending a volley of urine into night sky. As the car passed, he thought he saw Mrs. Pandey in the driver's seat. But a few seconds later concluded it couldn't be her, because why would she be driving around town at a time like this?

There was a van outside his house, and on its side it said RE:HEAT in ugly red lettering. The owner of the vehicle was at the front door, speaking in hushed tones to his mother. It was 12:30 a.m.

From afar, Natwest thought the scene resembled *The House of Ill Fame*, a work by Early Netherlandish painter Hieronymus Bosch. The painting depicts the titular brothel as a house falling apart; exposed beams and window shutters hang from their hinges, animals feed just outside and crows fly in the sky. In the doorway, a man kisses a prostitute farewell. It was this last detail that stuck in Natwest's mind as he watched Clive embrace his mother. If Clive was the stranger, then his mother was the whore. Something about that rang true.

After a few minutes Clive drove away in his van and his mother returned inside.

When Natwest entered, she was in the kitchen. Her puffy, swollen eyes followed him as he sat down at the table, and he felt like a stranger in his own house. 'Cup of tea?' she asked, and after a torturous minute involving the boiling of a kettle and the spooning of tea bags, she placed a mug before him and asked, 'What do you want to know, Natwest?'

It was a while before he answered. The whole issue had escalated into something more dramatic than he wanted, so in the end the words he assembled were simple: 'Just tell me about my father.'

She nodded and began to explain her past, the long relationship with Clive, her affair with Natwest's father, Jacob – a married man.

'Was I an accident?' asked Natwest cautiously, although he knew the dreaded answer.

'Yes. . . But it wasn't like I didn't want you,' she said helplessly, grabbing his hand. 'You're everything I ever wanted.'

'But Dad felt differently?'

His mother didn't respond. There was never going to be an easy synthesis between the positions of his parents, no matter how much Natwest wished it were true. Something was always lost. He felt like the disappointing outlier on a Venn diagram, forgotten, eliminated when the data was collected and the average calculated. He didn't exist.

When his mother reached the end of her story, he couldn't escape the thought that she was benefiting more from her monologue than he was. The sobbing that began shortly thereafter was to be expected, and, in an irritating reversal, Natwest found himself comforting her. 'It's alright,' he whispered. 'It's alright.'

But for Natwest nothing had been resolved – and where he wanted to feel full, he felt a vast absence.

'What about Clive?' he asked. 'Are you going to see him again?'

His mother stiffened at the question. 'I would like to. But if you don't. . .'

'It's fine. I'll be gone soon,' said Natwest, and there was some bitterness in his voice when he added, 'You do you.'

His mother nodded and they shared a hug.

'Have you packed your bags, Natwest?'

He trudged upstairs and threw some clothes in a suitcase. He'd expected her to do all the hard work. It was nearly 2:00 a.m. when he finished packing and finally collapsed onto the bed. Time passed. Then, moments before he drifted off into sleep, he felt a strong urge to sneeze. He sat up, took a deep breath – but the sneeze never came.

Something was missing.

First, he stubbed his toe getting out of bed. Second, he removed the package from his rucksack and buried it deep in the suitcase.

T he early morning sun had woken everyone up again. People were leaving their houses. Dogs were being walked. And Natwest had been sitting in his car for the past ten minutes, waiting to leave. He was unwilling to go.

He would have stayed like this for even longer had it not been for the Royal Mail van which pulled up outside his house. The postman didn't notice Natwest watching from the car as he sauntered to the front door, whistling an unknown tune and stuffing a few letters through the letterbox. For a moment, Natwest thought he was back where he had started the previous morning, and the postman was delivering the package like he was supposed to.

Then the postman waved at him – had in fact known he was watching the whole time.

Natwest waved back.

After the Royal Mail van had moved on, he was ready to leave. There was no use looking at the house – he'd be back in a few months anyway – so he put the keys in the ignition as if it were any day of the year and turned. It took him two attempts to start the engine. Finally, he put the car into gear and drove away. As he did, the world opened up through his windshield. The image was so big, and the car so small. There was no other way to look at it.

When he put his foot down the car dragged him in the direction of the image. He was pulled towards the motorway, and then towards the country, and then towards the city. Every metre, a little closer to the world. He wondered if he'd ever get there.

References to Other Works

p. 37: 'A man's work is nothing but the slow trek to rediscover, through the detours of art, those two or three great and simple images in whose presence his heart first opened' is from *The Wrong Side and the Right Side* by Albert Camus.

p. 38: 'Everyone is born with a subject but it is fully expressed only through a commitment to form, and Yiadom-Boakye is as committed to her kaleidoscope of browns as Lucian Freud was to veiny blues and the bruised, sickly yellows that it was his life's work to reveal' is from *Feel Free* by Zadie Smith.

p. 44: 'The agenda of the consciousness' is from an interview with David Foster Wallace in *Harper's* magazine.

p. 161: 'Whoop-de-doo, Basil' is from *Austin Powers: The Spy Who Shagged Me*, written by Mike Myers and Michael McCullers.

p. 174: 'You're a real humanitarian' is from the film *American Psycho*, written by Bret Easton Ellis, Mary Harron and Guinevere Turner, as is the line on p. 208: 'Cool it with the anti-Semitic remarks'.

p. 190: 'Did you put your name in the Goblet of Fire' is from *Harry Potter and the Goblet of Fire* by J.K. Rowling.

p. 207: 'Motuweth frisas' is from *Pnin* by Vladimir Nabokov.

p. 279: 'Put Your Money on Me' is the title of a song by Arcade Fire.

Acknowledgements

Massive thanks to my early readers and friends, without whom I'd never have finished the book: Abi Smith, Ali Fletcher, Alpana Sajip, Arnold T. Rice; and the ones who don't begin with A: Judith Papenkort, Lindsay Reeve, Zadie Smith. For 'head and board', thanks to my reluctant patron, Rob White. For an amazing early cover, Cameron O'Loan. For excellent, patient editing: Anna Kelly and Patrick Nolan. For everything else: my exceptionally lit agent, Charlie Brotherstone – apparently the only one in the country silly enough to respond to my query letters, and the one who changed my life.

Even massiver thanks: Mum and Dad.